this ~~isn't~~

OVER,
baby

Elijah,

Do nice guys finish
last? I wouldn't know.

K WEBSTER

This Isn't Over, Baby
Copyright © 2016 K. Webster

ISBN-13:978-1536962192
ISBN-10:1536962198

Cover Design: All By Design
Photo: Dollar Photo Club
Editor: Premier Romance Editing
Formatting: Champagne Formats

Books by Author K Webster

THE BREAKING THE RULES SERIES:
Broken (Book 1)
Wrong (Book 2)
Scarred (Book 3)
Mistake (Book 4)
Crushed (Book 5 – a novella)

THE VEGAS ACES SERIES:
Rock Country (Book 1)
Rock Heart (Book 2)
Rock Bottom (Book 3)

THE BECOMING HER SERIES:
Becoming Lady Thomas (Book 1)
Becoming Countess Dumont (Book 2)
Becoming Mrs. Benedict (Book 3)

Alpha & Omega
Omega & Love

WAR & PEACE SERIES
This is War, Baby
This is Love, Baby

Thanks to my hubby for always sticking by my side...even when I'm being a CRAZY bitch.

Warning:

This Isn't Over, Baby is a dark romance. Strong sexual themes and violence, which could trigger emotional distress are found in this story. This story is NOT for everyone.

This IS a love story.
This IS a dark story.
This IS a story about the villain.

Villains need love too…

No cucumbers were injured in the making of this book.

"Rules are for children. This is war, and in war the only crime is to lose."

~ *Joe Abercrombie, Last Argument of Kings*

I | Gabe

The Past

"**N**EXT."

My father's bored, gruff tone grates on my nerves and I itch to tug at the knot of my tie. But his shrewd nearly black eyes are on me—always on me—waiting for me to show one tiny sliver of weakness. Weakness is what he feeds on. What he has for breakfast, lunch, and fucking dinner. And he's been feeding on me since I was ten years old. So instead, I fist my hands and I keep my features re- laxed as I wait for his stupid little show to fucking end. He may be hungry, but I won't be the one feeding his crazy-ass monster tonight. No, one of the shivering, bound, and crying girls standing in front of our fireplace will. As the next girl stumbles into the room, I close my eyes and let my mind flit to the past. Almost eight years ago, my life changed with the whap of a belt against my flesh.

"Your whore mother left us." That was his only explanation of why Donna Sharpe wasn't in the living room slurping down one of her signature dirty martinis after school one day. I'd been confused because, quite frankly, at ten, I had no idea what a whore was. When I cried for the loss of the calmer parent in my home, my father changed. His annoyed expression turned into one of rage, and that day he took out every ounce of his fury of her leaving on me. His expensive leather belt on my bare ass tore the skin to shreds.

But that's not what broke me.

He crushed me later that night. When the house grew silent, and I'd cried myself dry, he stepped into my room and promised to make it all better. That night, he kissed away the pain on my backside, and in the process, twisted my head into a tangled mess of strings that he would go on to pull whenever he wanted.

My father devoured my innocence, and now that he can no longer feed on me, he's transforming into a starved animal. His need to prey on the weak disgusts me. It only shows he isn't as strong as he thinks he is. He may traipse around in five thousand dollar suits and drive an expensive sports car, but my dad is a pussy.

It took this past summer for me to come to this conclusion. When he'd come into my room after I'd spent a week at summer camp, something in me snapped. I'd watched other guys my age sneak off with girls at night. Kids all around me were happy. Naïve. Untouched. And I realized that I owed him nothing.

But he owed me everything.

The moment he slurred out my name and dragged the covers off my half-naked body, the fear and revulsion that

2

always made me immobile was no longer present. Instead, rage—a glorious fucking feeling—lit a fire inside of me and I exploded. The fucker put up a good fight for a drunk asshole, but I bashed my fists against my father's face until he was unmoving. My knuckles were bruised and achy, but my pride was restored.

My father never touched me again.

Instead, he treated me like an annoyance. A burden. A fucking bother. Like nothing ever happened.

But *everything* happened.

That night, I transformed.

I became someone better.

I became my own monster. A monster dead set on not letting him feed off me ever again. I became invincible as far as he was concerned.

Next month I'll be graduating from high school, and I'll go on to college. Away from my father. Away from my hellish past. I'll make a life and become someone. For once, I'm not the scrawny, lanky kid with the messy hair and quiet disposition. After that night, I began working out—fueled on by the desire to always be stronger than that beast. Eight months later and I had filled out everywhere. My shoulders were broad, I had abs, and I was no longer someone he could intimidate. Girls started to notice me and guys wanted to be my friend.

I was no longer weak.

"They're all so terrified," Grant Sharpe's gravelly voice growls, interrupting my thoughts when the last girl comes to stand beside the three others.

Four girls.

All of them young.

Some my age, some considerably younger.

But one stands out among the others.

A girl with bright blue eyes and messy blonde hair eyes the group in the living room with disgust. Where the other girls are crying and huddling together, this one looks as though she wants to slaughter every one of us.

My father, his best friend, Lance, his accountant, Gordon, his attorney, Jack, and me. Four girls, four men, and me. These "pussy parties" as good 'ol Dad called them, were nothing more than a sick form of human trafficking of under-aged girls. Lance, Gordon, and Jack are all married, and their wives think they participate in monthly poker night with my father. Something innocent and legal. None of them know.

I've always known.

At fifteen, I walked in on one of their parties by mistake when I was supposed to be sleeping. It was then that I became the official mascot. The kid they poked fun at while they smoked their cigars and bid on girls. I hated every second of it. You see, father, in his spare time, recruited girls for a human trafficking ring. And their monthly "poker night" was where they test drove the merchandise before they sold them to the distributors.

Despite hating what happened during them, I began to look forward to those nights. Those were the nights when I would watch girls who were weak and breakable. I was stronger than them. Not the weakest in the bunch. For one night a month, I was a man.

Of course, he never let me do anything but sit and watch from afar, a hard-on straining in my slacks and heat burning my cheeks. I'd craved to lose my virginity to one of them. I even fantasized about falling in love with one of them—had thoughts of rescuing them from the biggest villain I know and running far, far away. But each time, my hopes and dreams were snuffed out as every one of my father's friends took their pick and disappeared to the other rooms of the house. By the next morning, they were always gone.

Tonight wouldn't be any different except when girl number four's eyes meet mine, I see a flash of something that stirs my heart. She's caged and wild. Everything in her screams to be set free. The girl is different. Not weak at all.

My gaze skims over her naked flesh and lingers over her perfect tits. Small and perky. I can almost feel my mouth watering with the need to suck on her nipple. A small groan escapes me the moment my dick thickens. I continue skimming over her flesh. Unlike the other girls, she's dirtier. Bony. Hardened. She has a small tattoo of a black heart on her hipbone. I become fixated on the ink that mars her flesh and wonder how old she really is. The other three girls are sixteen or seventeen, but number four looks like she might be eighteen or nineteen. Our eyes meet again, and something passes between us.

Not a plea.

Not fear or terror.

A threat.

I will kill all of you. Just untie me and watch.

The smile on my lips is immediate, and I wink at her, flashing her a message of my own in one simple glance. *I'd cut you loose and help, if I could.*

"What's the matter, boy?" Gordon says with a sneer from beside me. "You got a thing for one of the pieces? Which one? Let me guess…" He trails off and saunters over to them. They shriek—all of them but number four, of course. She bares her teeth at him, and I wish he'd get close enough for her to take a bite. "Not this one. Her tits are too big for a little boy like you, and this one looks like a fucking boy with her stupid haircut. This other girl has some fucked-up acne and you're way too pretty for that, Gabey," he mocks. Then he continues down the line until he stands in front of the last girl. "But this one. She's something special, isn't she? Is this the one you like?"

A growl rumbles in my chest, but I swallow it down, knowing *he's* watching me. When I don't answer, Dad tosses a piece of ice from his glass at me. "Answer him, Gabriel."

I swallow down the fury and swat the ice out of my lap onto the floor. "Four. I like four."

"My name is Krista. I am *not* a number," she hisses, spittle spraying him.

He wipes at his cheek with the back of his hand. "Krista," he says with a dark chuckle. "You'd eat that boy for lunch. He's kind of a wimp. You need a man like me or his daddy over there. A man who'll fuck you until you bleed. Gabriel wouldn't even know where to stick it in."

All the men laugh at my expense, and my cheeks blaze with embarrassment.

"I know where to put it," I snap and cross my arms over my chest. I may be a virgin, but I'm not stupid.

Gordon laughs again and grabs a handful of her tit. She yelps out in pain, and I'm already at my feet before I even realize I've blown my cool facade.

"Let go of her," I bark out. My jaw clenches and one of my newly defined muscles ticks in my neck. "I want to buy her." The words are spoken before I even register what they mean. But as soon as I say them, I stand behind them.

She'll be the girl.

I'll save Krista and show them I'm not weak.

Her determined eyes meet mine and they flash with appreciation. She sees me as an accomplice. A stepping stone to get her the hell out of here.

"Absolutely not." Father's voice causes prickles of rage to wash over my flesh.

"Ten thousand," I blurt out.

I know how these things work. These guys pay a certain amount for the girl they want, and Dad collects the money. Once a year they go to Vegas with the money in the pot, somewhere I'm not invited—mascot or not—and they have a boys' weekend where God only knows what takes place. The most any of them have ever paid was six thousand and that was for a pretty Hispanic girl who shockingly had her clit pierced. She certainly wasn't a virgin, but they all wanted her.

"You don't have ten thousand." Dad laughs and slaps the leather of the arm on his recliner. "You don't have shit, Gabriel. It's all mine, remember?"

I swallow down my hate for the man and jerk my gaze to meet his glare. "I have a trust fund," I seethe. "Mom started it for me, remember?"

He doesn't like his words thrown back at him and the reminder of my mother has him quaking with unmasked rage.

"Oh, come on," Lance says, poking fun at me, "let the wimp get his dick wet. The kid's not as scrawny as he used to be. Maybe it's about time he fucks for the first time."

I let Lance's comment roll off me as I keep my hardened stare on my father. Dad's lips pull into a sneer. "You're not eighteen yet, mama's boy. So don't go getting all high and mighty."

"I'll lend it to him, Grant," Jack says, and I jerk my gaze over to where he sits with his fingers steepled in front of him, hiding his wolfish grin. "Plus sixty-nine percent interest."

His friends all laugh, each one bolder than usual as they fly high on their high dollar cocaine, but I snap my glare back to my father who regards me coldly, a humorless expression marring the face so similar to the one I see in the mirror each morning. Several seconds pass while he remains motionless. I know he's contemplating ways to hurt me, but I don't care. In a couple of months, I'll be out of here anyway so it doesn't matter.

"Five thousand. Lend him five grand. I'll pay the other half because we're going to share her." His words dig a knife deep into my gut, but I don't argue. Instead, I give him a clipped nod.

"Fine."

The men holler with obnoxious cheers, but I tune them out as my eyes find Krista's. She now seems shaken, and I momentarily wonder if it's by the idea of two men having her instead of one. I implore her with my gaze to be strong. Her lip trembles, but a certain understanding passes between us.

I will save you, beautiful. Just give me a chance.

The rest of the evening is a blur as the men negotiate what—scratch that, *who*—they want. Apparently, the one with the boy's haircut was their choice piece of meat because they engage in a bidding war over her. Once the money passes hands and the men drag away their prizes, I turn to Dad.

"Take her to your room. I'm giving you an hour with her before I come up. Don't try anything stupid," he barks out as he stands and strides over to the bar to refill his tumbler.

I nod, adrenaline surging through me, and make my way over to Krista. As soon as I reach for her, she shies away and turns her back. I grab on to her bicep and pull her to me. My lips find the shell of her ear and I whisper into it. "Trust me, sweet girl."

Then, I guide her out of the living room and toward the stairs without sending a glance my father's way. She stumbles up the steps, but I'm there to keep her from falling. Soon, we're in my room and I'm shutting the door. Once I've locked it, I smile at her.

"You're so beautiful," I praise. I know I sound like a fucking fool. I'm not exactly Casanova with the girls, but it's the truth. Underneath all the dirt and bravery, she's really pretty. Her lips are full and pink. I love how slender and pale her neck is—I crave to mark it up with my teeth. My dick reacts to the mental image, causing the heat of embarrassment to singe my skin.

"Untie me," she orders.

I frown, disappointed in her not acknowledging my compliment, and motion for her to turn around. "Don't try and run away. Dad'll end this as quickly as it started if you do. Play along with me and when the time is right, I'll get you out of here. But you have to trust me, Krista."

"If that's your way of asking me to go steady, I'm going to have to pass. Your *family* is a touch too dysfunctional for my taste," she snaps and wiggles her purple fingers at me.

I sigh because there isn't any response to what I already know. With a grunt, I drop to my knees behind her and start to work at the knots at her wrists. Her ass is perfect, and I'm overcome with the strong urge to kiss it.

"How old are you?"

She huffs. "Almost nineteen."

My eyebrows knit together as I wonder what made them pick up a girl who wasn't young like the others. "Don't tell my dad that. You're seventeen like me if he asks."

She doesn't respond. The moment I've loosened her wrists, she slips out of my grasp and runs to the other side of my bed. Her hand is free from the bindings in an instant and she snatches my bedside lamp up.

"Stay away from me!" she hisses and casts a wary glance at my bedroom window.

I shake my head at her as I stand. "Put the lamp down. And you'll eat pavement if you jump from that window. Let me handle this, beautiful."

"Stop calling me that!"

Another pang of disappointment washes through me. "Please just put it down. If he comes in here and sees you like this, he won't be as nice as me. Let me figure out a way to get you out of here."

Ignoring me, she throws the lamp in my direction but it doesn't go very far, since it's still plugged in, and lands on the bed. She's fiddling with the window by the time I reach her. My arms wrap around her and I pin her naked back to my chest.

"Stop," I order. Having her bare flesh pressed against my suit has my dick hardening. She's dirty, but a faint scent of lotion—something unfamiliar to me—floods my senses. It smells fresh and clean. It's a direct contrast of the girl wiggling in my arms.

"Let go of me!" she shrieks. "Are you hard right now?!"

Her words have me clenching my eyes closed. *Fuck. Fuck. Fuck.* "No," I lie and wrangle her over to the bed. "I told you to stop moving."

She cries out when I tackle her onto the bed. Her body is beneath mine, and I have to look away from her wild eyes, so

I don't go crazy with the need to thrust into her. Her thrashing is only serving to make me more excited.

"If he thinks I can be a man, he'll leave me be. So just go along with this and he'll leave us alone. I'll get you out of here. Trust me, you want me fucking you and not him. He's a cruel bastard."

Her body trembles, but resignation courses through her. "Don't hurt me."

Grinning, I slowly pull one hand from beneath her and stroke a blonde strand from her eyes. "I would never hurt you."

I lean forward and press a soft kiss to her lips. I'd kissed a girl named Julia at summer camp because the other kids dared us. After what was the most dizzying and exhilarating moment in my life, she laughed at me and told everyone I tasted like cucumbers. Something tells me this kiss will be better. Krista won't belittle me because she needs me to be her hero.

I'll be her fucking hero.

"He's probably listening on the other side," I whisper to her. "Get it together for me, sweet girl."

Her eyes well with tears and she nods. "Okay."

I reluctantly release her and right the lamp back on the table while keeping my eyes on hers. Her perky tits bounce with each nervous breath she takes. When I shed my jacket, her eyes widen with fear.

"I. Won't. Hurt. You."

She nods again and tears her gaze from me as I undress. My dick is nothing to be ashamed of and I want her to see it. I want her to see I'm all man—not a wimp like my dad and his friends say. Her curiosity wins out because she once again flits her eyes over to me. I watch with pleasure as she skims over my body with a look of interest.

Once I'm fully naked, I crawl onto the bed beside her. I'm not sure what to do with her, but I know what my dad expects. He is going to want me to take her. Hard. The way he and his repulsive friends do. And once he takes his turn, I'll make him sorry. I'll save her from this hellhole, and we'll go somewhere. Together.

"I have a confession," I say with a smile as I tenderly stroke her flat stomach.

She shudders at my touch but regards me with pinched brows.

I can't look at her when I say it. "I'm…a, um," I struggle, my father's taunts echoing in my head. "I'm a virgin. I know how sex works, though, so you don't have to worry about me putting it in your ass by accident…like they said," I rush out and then snap my mouth shut. *So much for not making a stupid ass out of myself.*

Her eyes flicker to mine. "We don't have to do this," she murmurs. "We can pretend."

Groaning in frustration, I run a shaky hand through my hair. I hadn't thought of that and now I feel foolish that I'm three seconds from losing my load against her naked thigh. I need to fix this. "What I mean is, I have had sex." My eyes clamp closed and I hate the way my cheeks burn with shame. "It's just been—"

Her eyes widen. "It's just been what?"

A heavy sigh rushes out of me. *God, why do I have to be such a fuck up?* I push myself up and turn my back on her, sitting on the side of the bed, my head hanging between my legs.

I hear the bed shift, and after a second, she's sitting next to me.

"Hey, are you okay?"

I shake my head and let out a bitter laugh—a laugh that's far from funny. "My dad...he used to force me," I mutter. Our eyes meet and her concerned, furrowed eyebrows motivate me to continue. "He used to force me to do things a dad shouldn't do with his kid." There. I said it. I drop my gaze to the floor and fixate on the carpet to avoid her gaze. I've confessed, and now it's hanging in the air between us—dirty and dark but no longer hidden. And, although I can't stand the thought of looking over at her, at seeing the pity probably in her eyes, it feels good to get it out. To share it with someone. I've held it in for all these years. His filthy secret.

"I'm so—"

I jolt and glare at her. "I don't need your pity."

"Did I say I felt fucking sorry *for* you?" she snaps, but then flashes me a small smile. "What I was going to say was that I'm sorry your dad's an asshole. People like us deserve better than the lot that's given to us."

People like us.

Abused. Beaten. Molested. Hated.

My chest aches from her words and I lie back down on the bed. "Uh..."

A pound on the door saves me from the mortifying moment.

"Yeah?" I bellow.

Krista scrambles to sprawl out next to me on the bed and flashes a quick smile at me as she tenderly runs her fingers along my chest. "We don't deserve this," she whispers. "We'll get out of here. There's a whole wide world out there for people like us—a world where *we* get to decide our fate."

Such a concept is mind-blowing. A world without a greedy, sick, manipulative father sounds pretty good to me.

"Did you fuck her yet?" he demands, interrupting my thoughts.

I grit my teeth and say the words I hate myself for saying. "Yes, Dad."

His laugh is demented on the other side of the door. I can hear the key turning in the lock and soon his giant frame fills the doorway. My entire body quakes at seeing him in my room after so long. His eyes lazily skim over us and he shakes his head.

"Nice try, Gabriel. Fuck her. I'm going to watch."

She whines, but I run my fingers over her stomach in a way I hope soothes her.

"I can't do it with you in here," I growl and my jaw clenches.

He smirks as he sits in my desk chair. "Wouldn't be the first time I've watched you come."

The room spins as flames of embarrassment engulf me. I force out the things he's done to me—the things my body did that were out of my control—and I quiver with hate.

"Fuck you," I snap.

He laughs but thankfully doesn't respond. "Just fuck the girl and we're all good, son."

I roll myself on top of her and my lips graze along her ear. "I'll be so gentle. I swear. Please let me so I can get you out of here." My words are soft and nearly inaudible.

Her slight nod is enough, and I waste no time. Our lips meet again and this time, she lets me kiss her like I kissed Julia from summer camp. Krista tastes sweet, like gummy bears, and I want to suck on her tongue all night. My kiss must turn her on because she untucks her legs from beneath me and wraps them around my hips. The heat of her pussy pressed against my aching dick is too much. I want inside of her so bad, but I don't want to rush this.

"Just hurry," she begs.

I groan with disappointment and sit up slightly. Using my hand, I stroke myself for a second. Blindly, I poke at her opening and am met with tight resistance.

"Wrong hole," she bites out.

Dad laughs from behind me, and I nearly lose my hard-on. "I'm sorry," I grit out, overcome with shame. I move the tip of my cock up a couple of inches.

She squirms and spreads her legs further as if to help me find the right place. Her pussy feels dry, not at all like what I'd imagined it would feel like, and I'm still having trouble pushing it into her. My dick is practically weeping with need and it causes it once again to slide between her ass cheeks.

"Jesus," she whimpers and grips me. I nearly go blind with bliss. Letting go of the embarrassment of her having to put me inside her, I allow her to guide me to the right place. As soon as the thick head of my dick makes it past the dry opening, I easily slide the rest of the way in. My dick throbs with the need to come. I hold still for a moment, so I don't lose my load right away.

I fall back against her and try to kiss her, but she keeps her lips pressed together. I'm humiliated that she's treating me like I'm the villain. With gritted teeth, I thrust into her as hard as I can. She yelps, and it dizzies me. I do it again and again, her small moans driving my need. I'm about to explode at any second.

"Stop."

Dad's harsh command has me halting and jerking my angry gaze over my shoulder. "The fuck, why?"

He rises from his seat and stalks over to the side of the bed. "Hurt her."

My cock begins to soften as I shake my head. "No."

Fuck my life. His salacious glare confirms that he knows he's got me. "Fucking hurt her or I will."

She whimpers again, and I gape at him in horror. "No."

He pulls his 9 mm from his slacks and points it at her. "Now."

The need to rescue her from his bullet wins over and I do the only thing that feels right. I slide my hand to her throat and grip it. She immediately clutches my wrist and claws at me, her eyes wide with an unspoken plea. Instead of releasing her, I hold her tighter. I'm saving her. If I don't do this, he'll kill her. I won't suffocate her—just hurt her a little, like he says.

"Perfect," he says with a growl.

Ignoring him, I thrust deep into her. My cock is hard again and I like the way her body grows limp beneath mine. I like the way her pretty pink lips are slightly purple.

"Will you kiss me now?"

She tries to nod, and I release her neck slightly so I can press my lips to hers. God, she tastes so fucking good. I'm pounding into her like a madman when my dad once again stops me.

"Did you even give her an orgasm?"

I jerk my head to him and once again my cheeks burn. "I, uh…"

"Let her ride you. You can access her clit better that way."

She gasps for air the second I release her throat to roll onto my back, our bodies still connected. Tears roll down her cheeks, but she doesn't try to evade me. Her sad eyes meet mine and she places her palms on my chest.

I don't even know where her clit is. Clumsily, I fumble between her legs until I touch something that makes her clench around my dick. The little nub stands out between her pussy lips and I massage it slowly. She continues to work her hips in a way that sends tingles down my spine while I rub her back in return. It's fucking sensational.

"Oh, God," she whimpers, and I realize I'm actually about to make her come. I intensify my efforts and seconds later, she's shuddering above me and shrieking. Her pussy clamps down around my cock and I explode inside of her.

My eyes slam shut as her body milks me for all I've got. It's the best feeling I've ever experienced. I'm still basking in the orgasmic glow when she's unceremoniously ripped from me.

"My turn."

I gape, too stunned to move, when he pushes her over the end of the bed. His dick is out, and he spreads her cheeks apart before slamming into her. She screams in pain, her eyes finding mine in panic.

"Stop!" I roar and rise to my knees ready to attack him.

He grunts and waves his gun at me before shoving it against the back of her skull. "I'm not finished fucking her tight ass yet."

She once again begs me with her eyes and I see red. Krista is mine to make love to. Not fucking his! I've made a promise to myself I'll save her. I won't let him ruin one more person. When I launch myself at him with a hate-filled scream, a bang echoes around the room. Something warm splatters my thigh and I nearly pass out.

No!

In a moment of uncontrolled fury, I tackle him off of her and wrestle him to the ground. The gun is still in his hand, but when I stomp on his throat with the heel of my foot, he groans and releases it. Once I snatch it from his uncoordinated drunk grip, I stand and tower over him.

My gaze travels over to the unmoving body of Krista, and I swallow down the bile in my throat. Leaving him choking on the floor, I rush over to her to check her pulse. I quickly ascertain that she won't be coming back from the deathly gunshot to her head. There is no pulse. She's dead. Fucking dead. I promised her I'd saved her and I didn't deliver. I *am* a goddamned pussy.

"Awww," he rasps out from behind me. "What're you going to do, boy?"

I growl and aim the gun at his cock. This man has done nothing but take and take from me. Well, now I'm the one taking whatever the hell I want. And right now, I want his pain. Another bang and he's howling for a God he's never worshipped to save him. *Yeah fucking right.*

"Fuck you."

I don't know if his life flashes before his eyes, but mine certainly flashes before mine.

Bitter images of a shattered childhood. A mother who once loved me—who used to take me to the zoo or the children's museum while Dad was away on business trips to offer a tiny bit of normalcy for her son. But my father's fists eventually ruined all that was good in her life, so she drank away the pain. Until the day she gathered the courage to save herself.

She left me behind though. With a monster. A father who never hugged me. Never took me to Little League practice. Never loved me.

Never gave a flying fuck.

With a roar of nearly a decade's worth of pain ripping from my chest, I unload the rest of the bullets into his chest and skull. I keep pulling the trigger, even once the magazine is empty, unable to stop the outpouring of emotions that are flooding through me. He deserves more than death—he deserves hell. When the red haze of hate finally lifts, I watch with morbid satisfaction as the blood—crimson and thick—around his ruined body seeps into the expensive carpet. My chest is heaving, I'm dripping in sweat, and the room reeks of a pungent coppery odor of both a monster and his last victim.

"Who's the pussy now, old man?" I mutter to his corpse.

I take one last look at poor, bloody Krista before turning back to him. With all the disgust and hate from a decade of his punishments rushing through me, I spit on him and then kick his body.

It's finally over.

And one thing is for fucking sure.

I'm *not* weak.

Not anymore.

II | Gabe

The Present

"JOHAN," ALEJANDRA PLEADS, HER OLIVE-COLORED hands clawing at my chest. "Don't leave me."

I'm an animal locked in a goddamned cage.

Pacing and angry.

Unfuckingcontrollable.

I push her away from me and stalk toward the window over the kitchen sink. It's my stalker post. Most days, I spend hours and hours praying they'll go down to the beach. And don't even get me started on when it rains. When I don't see them. Those days, I can barely hold it together.

"Our time is through, Alejandra," I say as I grip the countertop and peer out the window. "I have unfinished business. Business that doesn't involve you."

Her continued sobs grate on my nerves. I clench my jaw and squint my eyes. From this distance, I wouldn't be able to see her face. Not that she's out there this afternoon anyway. Sometimes, I climb up on their back porch after dark and watch them through the glass because I need to see her. Tonight will be one of those nights.

I close my eyes and envision her bouncy blonde curls. She gets bigger and smarter every day. Her laughter, which I can hear through the glass, is adorable as hell. Sometimes I feel like crashing through the glass, slaughtering the entire goddamn family, and taking her back home with me where she belongs.

I may be a psychopath, but I'm also her father.

To destroy her entire life would fuck her up. Just like my father fucked me up. And I will not be that asshole. Even I have some morals.

But lately, it's becoming harder and harder to stay put knowing she's growing up without my presence in her life. I know Baylee will love the child with all she's got. That's who she is, despite knowing I'm the girl's father. If the father was Satan, Baylee would still love her all the same.

"Johan…"

I tense at Alejandra's teary pleading. "You know that's not my fucking name," I say with a growl, refusing to look at her. It's been a little over two years since I stepped foot in her old kitchen where she brought me back to life. Where she slipped me right into the role of her late husband. We never discussed my real name. The crazy bitch just went right along living in her pretend bubble.

Well, I'm tired of fucking pretending.

"My name is Gabriel Sharpe."

She wraps me in a hug from behind and it relaxes me a bit. Whenever her big tits are smashed against me, I tend to get distracted. "I'll call you Gabriel if that makes you happy. But please don't leave me. I love you."

I turn to regard her. Her palms slide up my chest to my cheeks, which now sport a thick beard. She practically digs her nails into my flesh to make me look down at her. Brown, bloodshot eyes behind wet lashes look up at me.

"Don't leave me."

Inhaling a deep breath, I attempt to calm myself. I'm comfortable here. If I took the girl, I'd be on the run. Baylee wouldn't stop until she found her. I would have to kill the child's mother and that just isn't fucking happening.

I close my eyes. But perhaps, I could take them both…

"Gabriel," Alejandra whispers in desperation. "Stay."

Blinking my eyes open, I regard the beautiful woman. I'd miss her. I don't know what to do but this peeping Tom bullshit isn't cutting it. My daughter turned two a few months ago, and she doesn't even know me.

"Why? I'm not your real husband, love. You know this. My heart is there," I grumble and point at the window. "With her."

Tears stream down her face and she stands on her toes to reach me. "Your heart can be in both places. Besides," she murmurs and threads her fingers into my hair. "I have a reason for you to stay."

She tugs me lower and her hot breath tickles my ear as she whispers her reason. Her words have their intended effect on me because another moment later I'm on my knees worshipping her.

Kissing.

Adoring.

Thanking.

Alejandra's right. I can have the best of both worlds. And I will.

Hannah

Nearly sixteen years later...

NATURE VERSUS NURTURE. THE DEBATE THAT MY ELEVENTH grade Psychology teacher Mr. Collins couldn't seem to stop talking about last year. Over and over again. Were our behaviors as humans learned? Did the people who raised us teach us and mold us into the adults we were all becoming? Or, was it ingrained in us since birth. A simple genetic code woven together the moment our fathers spurt their seed into our mothers. A delicate pattern of traits and characteristics meshed together to create a unique human.

Mr. Collins believes in nurture. He was a child born to a crack whore and spent his entire life in the system, bounced from one abusive foster home to the next. It wasn't until he landed in a little old lady's home that he finally learned how to behave. He learned kindness and love. She taught him to be a man of integrity. To be accountable for his actions. To own up to his shortcomings and conquer this life.

I can remember the way his brown skin would glisten with a sheen of sweat as he lectured us with the passion of a thousand men charging into battle. It was mesmerizing and beautiful. His dark brown eyes would narrow as he snared each one of us in his gaze. He would preach about how it doesn't matter who you were born to—or the blood running through you—that you could become whoever you wanted.

To say he inspired me with his lectures was an under-statement. I loved Mr. Collins. Loved the way he would place a hand on another student's shoulders as he worked out a problem with him on his assignment. Or the way he'd high-five the basketball players in the hall when they'd win a game. I even loved how he'd attend every softball game I played in with his wife and two kids. How his smiles never waned.

But as much as I loved Mr. Collins, he was wrong.

My parents have brought me up in this world with fierce love and protection. They've doted on my brothers and I. Pro-vided us with everything we should ever need. Been there through good times and bad.

I believe human nature runs in our blood. That no matter what we do to change who we are, we'll always be a fragment of who are parents were. At least. Mr. Collins will always be the boy who came kicking and screaming into this world ad-dicted to crack. That despite not knowing his real parents, he carries on their traits and behaviors. Maybe even unknow-ingly.

My father, Warren McPherson, has psychological prob-lems. I know this because, despite my parents' desire to hide every single bad thing from my siblings and I, some things just won't stay swept under the rug. They can't hide the way my father counts seconds. His mouth always moving. His eyes darting back and forth as various scenarios torment him from the inside. He can flash me a grin and tickle my middle, but I see the struggle within him.

It's in his blood.

It's in *my* blood.

My mother has dozens of bookshelves at home filled with the works of Freud and Jung and Horney. Books I've taken into my room and studied. Books that have both torn apart Mr. Collins's beliefs or supported them. Many of her books are highlighted, the pages frayed and torn from overuse. They talk of such things like obsessive compulsive disorders. Delusional disorders. Trauma related disorders. Personality disorders. And so on and so on.

Panic attacks used to seize me. Started when I was twelve years old, not long after the accident. I'd sit up in bed at night gasping for air that didn't seem to exist. Clawing at my throat until my dad would burst in, turn on my lamp, and speak calm words to soothe my mind. Mom always tried, but it was Dad who could reach me. Dad who always pulled me from my own inner darkness. Dad who, in the end, physically saved me.

Mom keeps a constant lock on her emotions. She hides them away with her smiles and her love. Never reveals what makes her who she is—what hides the true person within. She shelters my brothers and I from the world. Keeps us in our happy little bubble. Nurtures us.

But my nature always wins out…

I see a glimmering in my father's eyes—a certain recognition. Often, he tells me I remind him of his mother. His jaw clenches and his lips stay sealed, but I can tell he wants to grab me by the shoulders and explain the history that runs through me in greater detail. Explain how it taints my mind and heart.

My brothers don't understand. They're too much like Mom. Fierce and strong.

It's Dad, though, who recognizes I'm different.

"Mom would kill you if she saw you wearing that, Han."

My thoughts are ripped from the forefront of my mind and dragged away, back into the dark corners, as I affix my brother Ren with a devious grin. "Good thing she's in Italy then, huh?"

My overprotective younger, but taller, brother waves his phone at me with a smirk on his face. "I could show them. What do you think, Calder? Should I send Mom and Dad a picture of our underdressed sister?"

Calder, our fourteen-year-old brother, doesn't even look up from his phone as he inhales a slice of pizza and shrugs. When our parents aren't around, which isn't often, we tend to do crap they wouldn't approve of. Like eat foods we're not normally allowed to eat, go to parties we shouldn't go to, and dress like we've been threatened not to. Typical teenagers.

But it's Ren who keeps us all in line, despite me being the oldest. Ren is like Mom's secret spy. Lets us get away with just enough but pulls rank when we do something our parents would flip out about. It's irritating. And what's even more irritating is that after the heat of the moment is over, I can admit he was right to do so.

I'm the rash one—although Dad prefers brave.

I'm the quickest one to get angry—although Dad calls me passionate.

I'm the one always questioning why there are certain

rules—Dad calls me intelligent.

"I'm almost eighteen," I bite at him in defense. "God, ever since you got your driver's license, you act like you're some big man. You're not Dad, little brother."

Nobody could ever be my dad. If anyone is like him, it's me. Not Ren. Ren is just like Mom. Definitely nature with him too.

"You look like a slut." His harsh words sting, and I flip him off.

The last person to call me a slut was Mrs. Collins after Mr. Collins was fired from our high school. I'm not a slut, though. She'd been sadly mistaken. I'm still a virgin. I don't mess around with boys, or girls for that matter. I'm just me. It wasn't my fault he fell in love with me.

You're delusional, he'd said that day.

You need help, he'd hissed that afternoon.

But the heart wants what the heart wants.

My heart wanted Mr. Collins. And he wanted me too, no matter how much he tried to deny it. I saw the way his eyes would turn molten when I'd bend over his desk to ask him a question. The way they'd darken when my cleavage was hanging in his face. The way his cock would harden between us when I'd throw my arms around him and hug his neck before class each day. The way his breath would come out in a sharp gasp when I'd whisper something inappropriate.

He'd been nurtured to be a good, faithful man to his wife. To follow the norms of our society and obey the rules. Because that's what the old lady had taught him to do.

But he couldn't deny his true nature.

His eyes refused to say no when I unbuttoned my shirt and revealed my breasts to him one day after class. His fisted

28

hands and barely controlled restraint were proof his blood was running hot. That it wasn't a matter of nurture—it was his true nature surging wildly through his veins. He wanted me. Badly. Had we had more time, I could have been the one to give him a real lesson on the subject of nature versus nurture. To prove his trivial theories wrong.

All it took was one moment, though. One irritating moment, for someone to be in the wrong place at the wrong time and become a "witness" in the way he "leered" at my breasts. The way he'd "used his power of position over me." That he was staring at the tits of a "victimized, under-aged girl."

Mrs. Simms cried for me that day. Held my shirt together and ushered me out of that classroom and straight to the principal's office, despite the begging and cursing of Mr. Collins behind us. Stood on her soapbox and defended my honor against "that predator." I still miss Mr. Collins. Later that spring, it was Mrs. Collins who marched out onto the softball field at one of my games and told me I was a slut. That was after she slapped me. Took both coaches and my mother to drag her off that field.

I'm *not* a slut.

"Screw you," I snap and flip Ren off. "And you're an asshole."

Storming out of the kitchen, I stomp back toward my bedroom. Ren thinks he can judge me, but I don't see anything wrong with my black skirt and pink halter-top. I'm going to a college party so I should look at least college age. It's not like I'm trying to seduce my teacher or anything. My best friend, Kiera, will be wearing something no doubt way sluttier.

I am *not* a slut.

Once I'm in my room, I stand in front of my long mirror to look over my appearance. The short skirt shows off my long, toned legs—legs I work my ass off for in the gym and on the softball field. And the halter-top, thanks to a great push-up bra, makes my boobs look bigger. I look sexy. Ren can fuck right off.

With a huff, I switch on my hair straightener and set to smoothing out my long blonde hair. Once I'm satisfied that it's sleek and frizz free, I apply some makeup. Ren can get his panties all up in a wad after he sees me when I'm all made up. Tattle to Mom later if he wants.

You're rebellious and impulsive, she'll say.

But Dad will say I'm strong-willed and determined.

I smile at the mirror, and my blue eyes flicker with excitement. I've given myself smoky eyes, darkened my thick lashes with mascara, and applied some dark lipstick on my full lips. I look older. Definitely college aged. Tonight, I'm going to get laid.

That is, if I don't wuss out again.

My mind drifts to my last boyfriend, Brody. We'd dated for a while, and I was ready to lose my virginity to him last fall. But then, at the last minute, I freaked. God, he was furious. He'd said that for a rumored slut, I was a cocktease. When I gripped his bare balls in fury and gave them a tight squeeze, I forced him to take back his words. I am *not* a slut. With tears in his eyes, he retracted his words. Brody Stephens vowed to never say another word on the subject. And Brody's been true to his promise. Kid doesn't even make eye contact when we pass in the halls.

Sometimes I wish I would have just slept with him. I wish I would have just gotten over the worry of the painful loss of my virginity, and we could be dating as we speak. Who knows, maybe he'd have even wanted to marry me after we graduate. Most women these days want to go off to college and have successful careers before they get married or start their families. Not me. I want love…and I want it now.

My mind is lost to visions of me in a white dress with a handful of sweet-smelling daisies in my grip when my phone alerts me. When I pick it up, I see that it was Ren.

Ren: I'm sorry I was a dick.

Letting out a sigh, I type out a response.

Me: I'm not going to get pregnant. I'll be fine.

Ren: Call me if you need a ride home. I don't care how late it is.

I smile. He's so much like Dad, even named after him—Warren or Ren because it's much cooler. And while I appreciate my brother's protectiveness, sometimes he's overbearing. I wish he'd find a girlfriend, so he'd stop harassing me. Actually, scratch that. Thoughts of his last girlfriend have me shuddering.

Me: Thanks, Dad, but you'll have your hands full keeping an eye on Calder.

At this I laugh. Our younger brother is a zombie. While I'm athletic with softball and Ren's always on his board in the ocean, Calder doesn't get up off the couch. Mom says he's a techie like Dad. I just think he's a lazy ass.

Ren: Fuck off…but be safe while you fuck off.

Grinning, I start tucking everything into my purse, including my phone.

Before I leave my room, I take one last look in the mirror. Dad would say I was beautiful. I just hope some guy at this party thinks so, too. Starting college as a virgin is not on my list of things to do.

I'm going to do everything in my power to pop the proverbial cherry.

I may even have to act like a slut.

But I am *not* a slut.

"Oh my God," Kiera yells into my ear over the loud thumping music. "The guys here are all hot. And big. I bet they all have big cocks too unlike those losers we go to school with."

I laugh and peruse my friend's appearance. Her black hair is cut into a chin-length blunt bob. She's half Korean and has elegant features. Creamy skin. Almond-shaped eyes. High cheek bones. Super petite frame. But her eyes are the palest blue you've ever seen. That comes directly from her father's Scandinavian decent. She's gorgeous and pretty much lands any guy she smiles at.

"I feel out of place," I groan, and self-consciously run my palms down the front of my skirt. Earlier, I'd thought I looked hot. Now, I worry that I've made a damn fool of myself by trying too hard.

Kiera swats me on the butt, causing me to giggle.

"We're both hot so shush. Let's go find Corey," she says, grabbing my hand and guiding me through the throng of dancing bodies.

Corey is a guy she met at work who goes to college at the University of San Diego. He'd boasted that his fraternity was holding this end of year blow-out party and he invited her. Told her to bring her hot friends.

"Kiera!" A tall, lanky guy calls out. His brown hair is kind of long and hangs in his eyes, like in a young Justin Bieber kind of way. "My Asian angel!"

She laughs and swats at him, her flirt game in full effect. I flash him a fake smile. He's not that cute, but she seems into him. She always had Bieber Fever…

"And who are you? Malibu Barbie?" he questions with a half-grin. His brown eyes are rimmed bloodshot red. The guy's higher than a kite right now.

"Han McPherson," I say politely and hold my hand out to him.

His gaze lingers at my chest for a brief moment before he takes my hand. "Like Han Solo?" He laughs as he kisses the top of my hand. God, what a nerd. Kiera is in trouble for this crap. I thought we were coming to meet cool college guys, not Star Wars geeks. Older, more refined men. Someone who was going to take my virginity with style and finesse.

Refraining from rolling my eyes, I give him another tight smile. "Something like that."

"Come on," he says, never letting go of my hand. "Let me introduce you two ladies to some friends of mine."

Kiera laughs from beside me as Corey drags me through the frat house. We end up in a dark living room of sorts. People are lounging all over the place. It reeks of weed, and I think a couple over in the corner may even be having sex against the wall. I'm already over this party. Ren would be pissed, but he'd come get me if I called.

"Cheer up. We'll get a beer or something and then you can relax. You're wound up way too tight," Kiera says into my ear. "God, Corey is so hot. I'm going to get him drunk and then make crazy love to him."

I snarl my lip up in disgust. "With him? Are you sure?"

With a big grin, she nods. Then, she bounces off after him, leaving her best friend standing in the middle of a roomful of strangers.

"Pretty lame, huh?" A deep voice rumbles from behind me.

I turn to see a good-looking guy towering over me. He has hair as black as Kiera's, but it's long in front and styled to stick out in every which way. His grey T-shirt hugs his broad shoulders and massive chest. And his biceps, all the way to his wrists, are covered in tattoos. I drag my gaze from his body to look into his eyes. Bright green. Curious. Mischievous. And older…by several years. I bet he could pop a cherry without calling a girl a cocktease when she showed apprehension. I bet he would make a girl beg for it. I'm completely enthralled by him.

"I'm Julian," he tells me with a wide, crooked grin that makes my knees wobble a bit.

"And I'm Hunter."

Another guy, around the same age, comes to stand beside Julian. Hunter, as he calls himself, is even more beautiful than Julian. He's wearing a red polo shirt that barely fits him. The guy is ripped but he's missing all the tattoos Julian has. And Hunter has bright blue eyes and blond hair. Typical All-American guy. Abercrombie & Fitch models in the making. They're both hot as hell and Kiera's missing out.

"Uh, I'm Hannah."

They're both smiling at me, and I feel like melting right here on the floor in front of them. I'm so out of my league, but I won't deny I don't love the way they both devour me with their gazes. Their attention is on me. Consuming me. Drinking me up. I hope they get drunk on it.

"You look like you could use a beer or something. Loosen up, babe," Hunter says with a grin before walking away.

"We were just about to leave this lame party but then…"

I lift my gaze to meet Julian's twinkling jade orbs. His eyes are kind. Despite his outward, rugged appearance, he looks like the kind of guy you definitely would one day bring home to Mom. "Then what?"

"I saw you. Just standing there looking beautiful and bored. I figured misery loves company," he says in a low tone. He dips his head closer to mine and brushes his lips against my ear. "Plus, I knew I couldn't leave this party without hearing your voice or seeing your smile."

My cheeks heat and a shiver ripples through me. *God, Kiera is totally missing out!*

"You're a real life Romeo, huh?" I tease, my attempt to keep my voice light and playful fails. A tiny tremor of excitement makes my voice wobble. Would he be a gentle lover or like one of those guys who tied up a woman and spanked her until she came?

He reaches up and brushes a strand of hair that's stuck to my lipstick away from my face. His fingertip sends jolts of desire coursing through me.

"Babe, you have no idea."

I'm saved from any more stupid remarks on my end when Hunter returns. He hands us each a red solo cup. In an effort to hide my embarrassment, I take several chugs.

"Wow!" I choke out. "That's so strong. What did they put in it? Gasoline?"

Both men—*and God how they are men*—laugh at me. My mind briefly imagines a scenario with both of them. I'm sandwiched in between while each one of them fights to pleasure me. Their fingers and teeth scraping along my flesh as they both vie for their own piece. Heat burns from my cheeks, along my neck, and to my chest. I'm probably way out of my league, but I've melted into a puddle of want and desire. The only way I'm leaving these two is if someone drags me out of here.

I take another sip of the gasoline to hide my reactions to the sex on sticks standing before me. Neither of them seem to mind and continue their blatant staring. The heated level of interest in both of their eyes excites me and gives me hope about how the rest of the evening will go.

"You go to school here?" Hunter questions, standing too close for comfort. I can smell his delicious cologne, and I try not to inhale him.

"No. A different college," I lie.

They exchange a look. Julian grins and leans in to whisper in my ear again. "Don't lie, babe. Your eyes darken when you do it. A dead giveaway. You're in high school aren't you?"

Defeated, I nod.

Maybe I won't be losing my virginity after all.

The downfall with older men...they're too afraid to pursue the carrot dangling in their face for fear of society's rules and labels.

His palm finds my lower back, and he chuckles. The deep reverberation ignites every nerve ending in my body. "That's okay. You seem pretty mature to me. I won't tell anyone. Our little secret."

Maybe this one likes the carrot...

I flash him a thankful smile before chugging down the rest of the disgusting contents of my cup.

"Damn, girl," Hunter says with a smirk. "Slow down or some stupid frat boy's going to come steal you away from us. You'll wake up in the morning with an STD and pregnant or some shit."

When I gape at his crudeness, Julian growls from beside me. "Fuck off, Hunter. We'll look after her. I dare any of these asshole punks to take advantage of her. Fucking dare them."

Hunter shrugs his shoulders in defense. "I got your back, bro."

He takes my cup before sauntering off somewhere. When I turn to thank Julian for sticking up for me, I'm ensnared by his heated gaze. My eyes drop to his full lips. His lips are much more delicious looking than Brody's or Mr. Collins's ever were. I want to kiss him. He's so beautiful. I'm not sure I'll ever get the opportunity to kiss someone this good looking ever again. Standing on my toes, I swallow down my nerves and make my move. Closing my eyes, I brush a soft kiss against his perfect lips.

When I reopen my eyes, he's almost glaring at me. But the good kind of glaring. The kind of glaring that makes me think he wants every single part of me. Another shiver courses through me.

He gently grips my chin and stares at my lips. "That will never be enough." Then, his mouth descends upon mine. His kiss is urgent, but expert. It's as if he's kissed me a thousand times and knows exactly what I like. I let out a small, satisfied moan, running my fingers through his hair.

"Maybe she should be afraid of *you*," Hunter jokes, causing Julian and me to reluctantly pull from our kiss.

With a wink, Hunter hands me another cup. We spend the next few minutes discussing which classes they take here at the college. Julian's going to school for business, and Hunter's studying pre-law. They seem older—as if they are closer to Mr. Collins's age than mine—but I don't question them. Nobody lies about going to college. Well, unless they're younger and wish they were in college.

I don't miss the fact that while we talk, Julian stands close to me, almost possessively. Hunter seems to see it as a challenge because he touches me as often as he can. By the time I've finished my second glass, I'm dizzy and having a hard time keeping up with the conversation.

But one thing's for sure, they're both pretty to look at.

"You don't look so well, babe," Julian says, taking my cup. "I'm cutting you off."

I nod and relinquish the remnants of my gasoline.

"Come on, let's get you some fresh air. Do you have someone you want to call?" he questions.

He all but drags me out to the front porch where people are everywhere making out. It makes me want to make out with him, too, but I am afraid I'll puke. And that would be too ridiculously embarrassing.

A gust of cool air whips around me and I inhale the refreshing air.

"I really wanted to get to know you but you're about to pass out, babe," Julian says, nervousness in his voice. "There's no way in hell I'm leaving you at this party in this state. Some fucker will mess with you."

His words are like molasses. Sticky. Messy. Sweet. God, I'm so confused.

"Let me see your phone. Want me to call your mom? Dad?" he questions.

I have the sense to shake my head. "P-Please, no," I slur.

"C-Call Ren. That's my bro—"

The last thing I see is Julian's worried gaze before the world turns black.

IV | Hannah

"**H**ANNAH," A DEEP VOICE RUMBLES. "CAN YOU HEAR me?"

I blink my eyes open slowly. Dark green eyes are focused on mine. "Mmm."

He frowns and glances somewhere else before looking back at me. "I think you have alcohol poisoning or something. I've been calling your brother over and over, but he's not picking up. Even tried a Calder on your phone. Should I call your parents?"

I'm shaking my head, but it only makes me dizzier. "No—Italy—Ugh."

I fade out once again. When I reopen my eyes, Julian is carrying me.

"Shhh," he whispers. "I'm taking you someplace safe. Hunter's dad is a doctor. He'll make sure you're not going to die on us, babe. Just try to rest."

His words are like a lullaby, and I fall back asleep.

"Hannah."

I crack open my eyes. I'm trying to take stock of my surroundings, but I don't recognize anything around me. The room seems expensive. And I'm lying on top of a bed. My heart rate spikes, but Julian's tender touch on my forehead calms me.

"Relax, babe. You're safe. Hunter's talking to his dad now, downstairs. We're going to get you well."

I nod but can barely keep my eyes open. He leans forward and presses a kiss to my lips. Stupid me had to get too drunk to kiss back the hottest guy I've ever seen. Kiera's probably worried sick about me. I try to ask for my phone, but it's too much of an effort.

"He said to give her this," Hunter says from the doorway. He stalks over to my side and looks down at me. His eyes don't have the same kindness Julian's have, and a tremor of fear paralyzes me.

"N-No," I tell him, eying the syringe warily.

Julian clutches my hand. "Babe, you're sick. We're going to help you."

My eyes close the moment the bite of the needle stings my thigh. I'd expected a rush of awareness. Not more grogginess. I try to sit up, but my body fails me. I'm panicking, but Julian's comforting voice is once again at my ear.

"Shhh, rest now."

My entire body feels numb. I can't even wiggle my toes. When I go to open my eyes, it's a struggle. Words are garbled in my mouth. Nothing makes sense.

"So damn sexy."

This deep voice warms me, but I'm also confused. When I finally manage to open my eyes, I see Julian sitting beside me, without his shirt on. My gaze flickers over his hard chest for a moment before looking back up at him.

"You're such a good little girl," he tells me calmly. His fingertip tickles my inner thigh. I'd shiver, but my entire body feels useless. "You went along with everything so well. I think you should be rewarded."

My eyes widen, and he chuckles. His laugh now freaks me out. I don't like it. "L-Let—"

"I like it when you're quiet," he tells me. Then, his fingers slide up under my skirt. My heart thunders in my chest as he slides my panties down my thighs. He's gentle as he removes them completely. "This should work."

I'm horrified when he pushes my panties into my mouth. I start to gag, and he laughs.

Shit!

What have I done?

Everything goes black again. I'm not sure how long I'm out for. But I wake with a start.

Two green eyes look up at me from between my legs. I'm naked. *Shit, I'm naked!* I can't really feel what he's doing to me. His tongue is on me, that much I can see. Tears streak down my cheeks as I attempt to scream through my panties. All I hear are muffled moans and the disgusting way he slurps at me.

"So sweet," he growls. "Are you a virgin?"

Terror immobilizes me, and our eyes meet. Gone is the handsome guy I met earlier. His true colors come out, and I'm staring into the eyes of a monster.

I watch helplessly as he rips the foil off a condom and slides it on his thick cock. He grabs my thighs and pushes them apart. And then, he's inside me.

"Fuck!" he hisses as he thrusts into me. "You're so god-damned tight."

I'm crying hysterically, but I'm unable to move. *I don't know what they gave to me!*

"You're such a pussy," Hunter laughs as he saunters in without a shirt. "You always make love to them. Maybe she just wants to be fucked rough and hard."

Julian ignores him as he pounds himself into my body. I thank my lucky stars that at least I can't feel him. Beads of sweat form on his wrinkled brow and his once styled hair is now disheveled. His mouth parts open to let out a groan.

"I want her again after you're done," he says to Hunter as he slides out of me.

My eyes fall to the condom on his dick. It's blood tinged, which makes me gag.

"Pull the panties out of her mouth," Hunter instructs with a growl. "I like to hear them scream."

Julian yanks them from my mouth, and I do find my voice. Words don't form, but a garbled scream does roar from me.

"Scream all you want, bitch. Nobody's coming for you."

Hunter sheds his clothes and puts on a condom. I start screaming some more when he flips me onto my stomach. He yanks my thighs apart and laughs. "Ever been fucked in the ass before?"

I finally find words. "Y-You can't d-d-do this!"

He grabs a handful of my hair and jerks my head back. His mouth finds my ear. "Why? Because you'll tell them we raped you? Just try it, bitch. After we've had our fill of fucking you, we're going to put your cum dumpster ass in the tub. We'll wash you clean. Then, we'll drop your unconscious body on the bed of some shithole motel. When you wake up, you'll remember shit. And if you try and tell the police, they'll have no physical evidence. Jesus, you teenage whores are all the same. Fucking stupid and easy. Newsflash, Hannah. You've been had. You fell for our shit and now you must deal with the consequences of your stupidity."

My tears are just a continuous stream down my hot cheeks. This can't be real. He releases my hair and drops me back to the bed. I'm crying so hard I think I might suffocate, which is preferable to letting two monsters rape me.

"Don't fuck her ass, Hunter," Julian warns. His warning infuriates me. As if what he did to me was any better.

"Why? Because I don't have any lube? That's what her pussy is for. You already lubed it up for me, man," he says with a dark chuckle.

It's then that I feel him push into me. Hours ago I was a virgin and now, I'm not. Hell, earlier tonight I'd wanted to lose my innocence, but certainly not like this. Not for two men to have had me. This is so screwed up. I wish it were a dream!

"Still so tight even though fuckwad over there popped your cherry. But that ass is mine," he growls. "You just—"

A sickening crunch has Hunter stalling.

"What the fuck? Who the fuck are you?" he starts, but then I hear another sickening crunch.

Wetness splatters on my back where I've regained some feeling. Hunter, who was filling me just a moment before, is suddenly ripped from inside me. I wonder if Julian decided to be a man and put a stop to this. The crunching sound won't stop, though. Over and over again it replays inside my mind. I want to make it stop.

"Jesus," a gravelly, deep voice hisses. "What did those motherfuckers do to my sweet girl?"

I'm gently urged onto my back. My eyes meet the fierce chocolate brown ones of an older man. His dark eyebrows are furled together, and he looks pained. Is he a cop? He scowls, but for some reason, I'm not afraid of him. I know. He's my savior, not like the villains who were taking advantage of me only moments before.

With a huff, he wraps me in a sheet and pulls me into his arms. My eyes flit around the room. Two bodies. Two rapists with their heads smashed to gory bits by a baseball bat that lies in the middle of the floor. Blood is everywhere. So mesmerizing. Beautiful. I should be horrified by the sight, but all I can think about is how they got what they deserved. Someway, somehow, I had an angel looking out for me. One look in his protective eyes, and I don't feel an ounce of fear.

He would kill for me.

That's what his eyes say.

And he did.

Twice.

I'm completely in and out during the drive. I don't know where he's taking me. A part of me momentarily shudders imagining he's a monster too. But he saved me. He killed those assholes to get me out of there. Monsters don't rescue raped girls. Do they?

Mom and Dad are going to kill me. Right after Ren gives me the longest *I-told-you-so* speech known to man. God, I'm the dumbest person on the planet. I fell for such a stupid scheme. And now I'm a statistic.

"We're almost to my house," the deep voice assures me. "I'd take you home, but your parents aren't even there, are they?"

I stiffen at his words and cut my gaze over to him. "How do you know that?"

He offers me a comforting smile. "I live about a half mile up the beach—can even see your house from mine. Your parents and I go way back. My wife Alejandra is a surgeon. You should let her take a look at you when we get there. Then, in the morning, we'll get you back to your house. Unless you want to go home in the state your in…"

I close my eyes and can imagine the horrified stares of my brothers. Hell no.

"You could be lying to me," I say with a tremble of my voice. "Those guys who took me—"

"They're dead. You don't have to worry about those maniacs anymore. I promise you're safe here. Do you want to call your parents and tell them what happened?"

I don't have my purse so I can't text them. I'd have to call them from this guy's house, and I definitely don't want them leaving Dad's business trip in Italy because I was the big dumbass who got herself raped twice in one night.

"Did you say you know my parents?" I question.

His eyes meet mine and with absolute honesty he says, "I know them very well. In fact, I've known your mother since she was seven years old."

A weight is lifted from my shoulders and I nod. "I'd like to get myself together then, before I tell them what happened if that's okay with you. I want your wife to make sure I'm okay. Those assholes gave me something. I couldn't fight them off or even move."

He clenches the steering wheel as if he's furious on my behalf. Once again, I'm warmed by my savior's presence.

"Sir," I say in a whisper. "What's your name?"

"My name is Gabriel Sharpe. Call me Gabe." He smiles at me. "Pleased to officially meet you, sweet girl."

Maybe I will let this man and his wife help me.

"We're here," he says as he pulls into a driveway to a beautiful home on the beach. A home that is not far from mine. So he was telling the truth. "See," he points through the window. "Your house is that way."

I nod as he climbs out of the car. When he opens my car door, I attempt to move my legs. They're still useless, and I look up at him with tears in my eyes. "They paralyzed me," I hiss out in frustration.

He kneels down in front of me and furrows his eyebrows together. I can tell he was handsome in his younger years. Hell, he's handsome now. Much more handsome than Mr. Collins.

"It's probably only temporary. Alejandra will know what they did. My wife is good at what she does. Let her help you."

He slides his arms beneath me, and I shiver. Now that my mind is clearing, parts of my body are prickling back to life, too. I can smell Gabe's scent—something spicy maybe—and I like it. He holds me like my dad does. As if he wants to protect me from the entire world. If it weren't for him showing up when he did…

"How did you know to find me there?"

His eyes flicker down to me, and he frowns. It mars his beautiful face, and I wonder what it'd look like if he smiled. My fingers twitch out of need to touch his beard. God, what is wrong with me? I don't even know this man. "I was driving by and saw two men carrying you into that house. I kept driving, but something niggled at me. Told me it wasn't right. I'd made it all the way home when I decided I needed to ease my conscience. Turns out, the feeling in my gut was accurate. I'm sorry I didn't get there sooner." Sorrow whispers over his features, causing my belly to ache for him. Out of a need to comfort him, I give in to my curiosity and touch his beard. It's coarse and wiry with a few grey strands sprinkled in. I like it.

I wonder what it would feel like against the soft, fleshy parts of me. Would it feel scratchy or would it tickle? A wicked shiver ripples through me.

He doesn't remark to my touching him and silently lets us into the home. Once inside, he turns on the entryway light. The home is well-decorated and smells nice. Like cinnamon and nutmeg. Family pictures on the wall once again put me at ease.

"I'm going to have to wake her up and explain what happened so she doesn't panic. Would you like to bathe until then?" he questions.

My heart patters in my chest as he climbs a flight of stairs. But once again, I'm met with more family pictures. He's here to look after me. Gabe knows my parents. I'm safe.

"Um, what're their names?" I blurt out as he enters a large bathroom. "My parents, I mean." A girl can never be too safe.

He smiles, and it's as brilliant as I imagined. "Baylee Marie Winston was your mother's name before she married Warren McPherson. Your grandfather is Loveland McPherson. And you, my dear, are Hannah. Let me guess," he says with a chuckle. "Your mom hates cucumbers." His laughter is even more beautiful than his smiles. It warms me to my core.

I return his smile. "Well, she's allergic. Dad is too, I think." Both of my parents shudder at any mention of cucumbers. One time, when I was younger, while she was shopping for produce, I pulled one from the bin and chased my little brothers with my "wiener" as I called it. She yanked me up so quick and spanked me right there in the store. I'd never seen her so mad before.

He winks at me. "Trust me now?"

Nodding, I relax in his arms as he carries me into the bathroom. He sets me on the toilet seat while he starts a bath. I check him out from behind while he fills the tub and pours bath salts into the steamy water. His dark jeans hug his muscled frame well but are stained with blood. The white T-shirt he's wearing is fitted and splattered with more blood. Gabe is all man—hard and chiseled and hairy in all the right places. Made Mr. Collins look like a pussy wannabe. Gabe should probably look scary, but to me he screams comfort and safety. And something else I can't quite put my finger on… Another shiver.

"Can you get in or do you need my help? If you need my help, I can assist. Don't worry," he says with a growl. "You could be a daughter to me. I'm not interested in what's under that sheet if that's worrying you."

His words both disappoint me and relieve me. Disappointment because I don't want to be thought of as a daughter to this man. But at the same time, I know I wouldn't even know what to do with a man like him. I'd be way in over my head. So definite relief that he doesn't want me because I'm not sure I could deal with any more stress in one night. I'm going to need some serious therapy after this night...

"I need your help," I tell him bravely. He may not want me, but it doesn't change the fact that I want him...to help me.

He nods and strolls over to me. For his age, he's incredibly fit. His chest is defined and ripples with every movement. I should be embarrassed that after such a horrifying night, I'm lusting over my savior. Has to be some sort of PTSD or something. Whatever it is, my mind likes the way his eyes assess me and wash over me, as if I'm precious to him. It makes me want to see more of it. He kneels in front of me. His eyes meet mine as he slowly peels the sheet from my shoulders. Our eyes meet, and he silently asks my permission. A slight nod is all I give, and he doesn't waste any time removing it from my body. I shiver as the cold air meets my naked flesh. I continue to study his features with interest. Even though he was my savior, I'm not blind to the fact that his dark eyes hold villainous secrets. Secrets I want to unlock and discover.

He stands back up and then slides his arms beneath me. The hairs from his forearm tickle the underside of my thighs, a signal that my feeling is coming back.

"Don't drown," he says with a chuckle as he lowers me into the water.

It's hot, and the parts of my flesh that are coming back to life sting. Whereas the dead parts still feel nothing. What a bizarre feeling.

His gaze flickers over my body as he assesses me. "Did they hit you?"

I shake my head as tears well in my eyes. "Nope. Just… raped me." I let out a harsh laugh. Of course, my first time would be against my will and unenjoyable. Fit for a slut. If only Mrs. Collins could see me now…

A murderous glare paints his features, and I like it. I like that he hates those men just as much as I do.

"They'll never hurt anyone again," he says with conviction, his eyes meeting mine.

Blinking back my tears, I nod. "Thank you, Gabe. You saved me, and I can't thank you enough."

Our eyes meet for a long moment. A million different emotions flicker in his eyes. I want to reach inside his head and pull each one out. Ask him about each and every one of them. Find the part of him that wants me too and dissect it. Make him look at it with me. Explore it alongside me where I feel safe and cared for.

His jaw clenches and he tugs off his shirt, revealing his exquisite chest. My eyes inspect a mottled scar on his chest, and I wonder how he came to get such a nasty wound. "Bathe. I'm going to take a quick shower and talk with Alejandra. She can be a little over the top when she's upset. And this is really going to upset her. Just warning you," he tells me as he wads up the bloody shirt in his strong hands. I want to look in his eyes, but I can't help but stare at his rigid chest and broad shoulders. Dark hair between his pecks and another patch just below his navel. I'm completely mesmerized. I bet Mr. Collins had a soft, protruding belly. Maybe even man boobs. He'd never look like the god of a man before me. All Gabe would need is a staff and a toga, and he'd be right out of the Greek mythology we studied freshman year. He doesn't look like he'd be Zeus or Poseidon. No, Gabe looks like he could be Hades. Splattered with the blood of his enemies. Evil and sinister, yet powerful and protective. Knows what he wants and destroys all those in his path. And I could be Persephone. He could steal me away and take me to the underworld where I belong. With him. My black thoughts would be welcome and normal there. Gabe certainly doesn't look like he belongs here. Neither do I.

When our eyes meet, his dark ones are like molten lava. Heat straight from the depths of hell. I'm spellbound by that look and want to see more of it.

"Relax, sweet girl," he instructs before stalking out of the bathroom, leaving me alone to my bizarre thoughts and inner ramblings of a madwoman.

With a sigh, I do just as he says. Now that I'm alone and rational thought begins to seep in, I finally come to terms with what happened to me. They raped me. Those assholes raped me. Neither asked, they just took. And as each moment passes and feeling begins to return to my body, I am more and more aware of their violation. Tomorrow, bruises will mottle my thighs and belly. My sex will be sore and hurting. But it'll be my mind that suffers the most—as if I could afford the extra affliction there. The drugs will clear my system, and I'll be fully aware of the gravity of what happened.

This is going to severely fuck with my head.

V | Gabe

"YOU DID WHAT?" ALEJANDRA SCREECHES AS SHE slings on her robe.

I lean against the doorjamb, running a towel through my wet hair, and glare at her. "They fucking raped her, woman. What the fuck was I supposed to do?"

She yanks the ties on her robe and knots it at her waist. "You took her. You took your daughter. They'll come for you, Johan."

Our eyes meet and her chin quivers.

"Gabe," I seethe.

Nodding, she swallows down her emotion. "*Gabe*, they will come after you. Your past is—"

"Is in the past," I hiss. "Now's the time I can have a relationship with her. All these years, I've dealt with the pain of not having a relationship with my daughter. She's almost eighteen. If she likes me, it won't be up to Baylee anymore. Hannah and I can finally be together. She's my daughter, Alejandra. You know this. And by default, that makes her your family too. So cut the shit and help me."

My wife storms past me in a huff. But before she can pass, I snatch her bicep and squeeze. "Accept this. It is a part of me. If you can't deal with this, then I can't deal with *you*." Her eyes widen at my threat. We both know what I mean. I won't leave my life here. However, if she thinks she can ruin this, I'll fucking ruin her.

"Fine."

Leaning forward, I press a kiss to her forehead. "Thank you, beautiful."

She relaxes marginally and pulls away. I follow her as she gathers her medical bag. Together, we enter the bathroom.

There, an angel sleeps.

My angel.

Perfect and gorgeous.

An exact replica of her mother.

My heart aches inside of my chest.

"Hannah," I whisper as I sit on the ledge of the gigantic tub that seems to swallow my daughter. "This is my wife, Alejandra."

Her eyes flutter open and her panicked blue eyes fly to mine. Upon seeing me, she calms. It only makes me more protective over her. Our connection is natural.

"Sweetheart," Alejandra says in the tone she reserves for her patients, "tell me what happened."

I start to leave, to give them their privacy, but Hannah yelps and reaches a shaking hand for my arm. "Please don't leave me."

Her gesture fills me with a warmth I didn't think my cold, hollow insides were capable of anymore. With a nod, I sit down on the floor beside the tub and hold her hand. Her voice wobbles as she retells the entire painful story of those bastards who hurt her, but she doesn't cry. She's angry and embarrassed. I'd expected tears and horror, not the vengeful look on her face. Alejandra, being the professional she is, is efficient in diagnosing her problems and assessing her for injuries.

"You shouldn't have bathed her, Gabe," Alejandra chides. "The hospital won't be able to process her for DNA."

Hannah splashes in the water as she tries to sit up. "No! If you take me to a hospital, then he'll go to jail. He saved me!" Her terrified blue eyes meet mine, and I see a flash of adoration in them.

My heart swells in my chest, and I squeeze her hand. "I'm not going anywhere."

Alejandra sighs. "You're right. After your bath, though, I want to check you for vaginal and rectal tears."

Hannah's face grows bright red and her plump lip wobbles in horror.

"Go grab her some hot tea and something to eat. You're overwhelming her," I snap at Alejandra, flashing her a warning glare. "I'll get her out of the bath."

Alejandra flickers her gaze to Hannah for a moment and I sense jealousy radiating from her. She better back the fuck off and remember her place around here.

"Alejandra," I say with a low growl.

She has the sense to jump and nod. Understanding once again softening her face. As soon as she rushes from the bathroom, I stand to hunt for a towel. I locate a large white one and bring it over to the tub.

"How are you feeling?"

Her teary eyes meet mine. "I'm starting to hurt. I guess

that's a good thing. Means my feeling is coming back."

The washcloth is fisted in her hand. Her body quakes as she desperately attempts to hold her tears in. This girl is brave. Tough as shit.

"Were you able to clean yourself?" I question, my voice hoarse with emotion. If those assholes weren't already dead, I'd fucking gut them this time and let her watch them as they bled out. I would pull their beating hearts from their bodies and lay them at Hannah's feet so she could crush them until they stopped twitching.

"Not like I wanted to." Her eyes flicker with something I don't fully recognize or understand. Not sadness or frustration. Something else.

She hands me the cloth, and I nod my understanding. With clinical efficiency, I clean her in the places they violated her. Once I'm satisfied those motherfuckers are no longer on her, I meet her gaze. Her full lips are pressed together but she stares at me as if I'm her entire world.

I want to be her entire world.

Always.

Our connection is thick. You could cut it with a knife, but now that I've had her in my home, I won't ever let anyone sever the way we seem to be tethered to one another.

"Let's get you out of there, sweet girl," I coo as I help her stand on shaky legs. Quickly, I wrap the towel around her. She may be able to walk, but I don't take any chances, scooping her light frame into my arms.

I carry her downstairs to the guest bedroom. Once inside, I lie her on the bed and then find the switch to the lamp. As soon as the light floods the bedroom, I see that her wide blue eyes are once again on me.

"How old are you?" she questions, her slender fingers reaching out to touch my bare chest. Her touch, so innocent but curious, warms me.

I clutch her hand and pull it to my heart so she can feel how it beats for her. "Old enough to be your father."

Releasing her, I start toward the door.

"Don't leave me," she begs, her entire body shivering.

"I'm going to find you something to wear, sweet girl. I'll be right back."

When I come back, Alejandra is sitting at her bedside, stroking her hair and trying to get her to sip some tea. My wife will be rewarded later for helping me. I'll make her cunt weep all over my lips when we finally get back to bed. After murdering those fuckers and rescuing my Hannah, I'm desperate for some sort of physical release.

"Hey," I say gruffly as I stride over to the bed.

Hannah reaches for me and frowns. I take her hand and turn my gaze to my wife. "Now what?"

Alejandra's eyes become sad. "I really need to check you, sweetheart. To make sure you aren't bleeding inside. Since your body is numb, you may not be able to feel how hurt you could be. Were you a virgin? Did they use condoms?"

Hannah nods at her.

"Just close your eyes," Alejandra says calmly, "and it'll all be over soon."

Hannah's eyes fly to mine. "I'm scared."

A fierce growl rumbles in my chest. "I'll be right here, baby."

At this, she smiles at me, as if I've given her the moon right from the sky. If it were possible, I'd reach right up there and pull it down for her.

Sitting beside her, I half pull her onto my lap. I stroke her soft hair as Alejandra sets to work. She positions Hannah's feet flat against the bed so her knees are up. Then, she slides on some latex gloves.

"Will it hurt?" The shivering girl in my arms claws at my forearm, as if I might try and leave her during such a time.

"No," Alejandra assures her. "You'll feel some discomfort, but I need to check you out." My wife lubricates her fingers and begins to examine her.

I close my eyes because I can't watch. I'd much rather think of the surprise in that sick fuck's eyes when I swung that baseball bat at his face. How his skull cracked the moment the bat made its impact. The minutes pass by quickly.

"You're inflamed, which isn't uncommon for someone with no prior sexual history. However, there aren't any tears that could become infected or need stitching. Your rectum seems untouched. We can thank God both men used condoms. Considering the circumstances, you were very lucky."

I shoot Alejandra a relieved look. "Thank you."

"Of course. Gabe, can I talk to you for a minute in the hallway?"

Hannah twists in my arms, her eyes wide with fear and her fingers gouging holes in my chest. "What's happening? What's wrong?"

I stroke her cheek with my finger, hoping to calm her. "Nothing's wrong. I'll be right back. Promise."

She relaxes, and I slip out from beneath her to follow Alejandra out. Once the door is closed behind us, she flips out.

"This is deep shit, Gabe. We have a victimized girl, your daughter whom you stole, in our house. And, you murdered the two men who raped her. This is bad, Gabe. Very bad."

I glare at her and seize her throat. She gags when I haul her down the hallway and into the kitchen. Pushing her against the cabinets, I get in her face.

"It was bad when you rescued me all those years ago. You knew what you were getting yourself into. Now, get the fuck over yourself, woman. I'm going to help her. I'll spend every waking minute with her until she asks to go home. I need this. You know I need this. For my goddamned sanity. Either get on board or get the fuck out of my way. I won't bring the law to our house if that's what you're worried about. Do you understand me?"

She nods. "But what if you leave me for her? What if you run away to live your life with your daughter? I can't lose you."

Same song and dance with us.

"Keep pissing me off, and I'll do just that," I threaten.

She lets out a pained sob. "What do you want? I'll do whatever you want."

"Go to sleep. This will look better in the morning," I assure her.

Her lips find mine and she kisses me. I don't kiss her back. She's already left a sour taste in my mouth. "I left two pills on her bedside table. One is a muscle relaxer and one is a Xanax. She'll need to sleep. Other than that, she's going to be okay. By tomorrow, she should be able to walk around like normal. Her mind will be ruined, though, Gabe. She's been through a traumatizing event. I'll do what I can to help her."

Sliding my hands to my wife's generous ass, I give it a squeeze. "Thank you. I owe you so much for this."

She leaves without another word, and I make my way back to the guest bedroom. When I peek inside, Hannah's still wrapped in the towel. Her wide eyes soften once she sees it's me. Relief floods her pretty features.

"You should dress," I tell her as I come into the room and close the door behind me. "You're shivering. Do you need help?"

Her eyes fall to the scar on my chest and linger there.

"Yes."

I stride over to the silky gown I stole from Alejandra's drawer and slide it over her head. She pokes her arms through the holes as I tug it down over her bare breasts and stomach. Once she's covered, I drag the blanket over her quivering body.

"Do you want me to leave so you can sleep?"

She shakes her head wildly. "N-No. Can you sit with me? Tell me stories of how you knew my mom. She's never mentioned you."

My chest squeezes and a flash of anger surges through me. It pisses me off Baylee never told her about me. Not one single thing.

"Sweet girl," I say as I sit down on the other side of the bed. "Not all the parts of my story are good. In fact, most of it is awful. I guess to understand my relationship with your mom, you'll need to understand me."

She lifts the blanket urging me to get under the covers. I'll probably suffocate with these sweat pants on, but that's the kind of shit you do for the one who belongs to you. With a sigh, I slide underneath and pull the covers up over us. As if it's her instinct to do so, she snuggles up against my side. I hug her to me. It's as if a missing part of me has finally been reconnected. I feel whole and invincible. One tiny moment of her in my arms will never be enough. I'll need her here over and over again.

"To understand me, we're going to need to start from the beginning. Back when I was about your age," I tell her.

Her fingers flutter over my chest hair and she nods. "I want to hear it. All of it."

"I once fell in love with a girl named Krista. She was beautiful and feisty," I murmur, "just like you."

My mind escapes to the past and I tell her all of it. What my father did to me, the sex ring him and his friends were a part of, and finally every gruesome detail of how I murdered my sick father. She doesn't flinch. She doesn't recoil. She doesn't cry.

She just keeps drawing hearts on my chest, over and over again, until I wonder if her fingernail will eventually cut right through my flesh. Now that's a scar I'd wear proudly.

This girl is brave and unflappable.

This girl is mine.

VI | Hannah

WHEN HE STOPS TELLING HIS STORY AND REGARDS ME with the saddest eyes I've ever seen, it breaks something inside of me. As a child, he was molested. It's sickening.

"I'm so sorry," I tell him, my voice a shaky whisper. "He deserved everything he got. Everything."

And I believe that wholeheartedly. I should be worried that this man killed two men to rescue me and admitted to killing once before, but I'm not afraid. In fact, I'm dying to know more.

"Did you love my mom once?" I ask bluntly.

He strokes the back of my arm with his fingertips, causing me to shiver. "My love for Baylee has morphed and transformed over the years. At first, it was a fierce need to protect. Kind of like with Krista. And like you. But then, she grew right before my eyes and became this beautiful piece of art. My love for her changed. It became distorted, but it was real nonetheless. I can even admit that there was a time I thought I hated her. Now I know it was just a fleeting emotion. I was simply angry with her."

"Why?"

"She fell in love with someone else."

"My dad?"

He stiffens in my arms and changes the subject. "Are you hungry?"

I shake my head and sit up. "Do I look like her?"

His eyes skim over my face, causing him to frown. "Exactly, baby. Almost exactly."

A smile plays at my lips. I'm not sure why, but I like the fact that this old friend, maybe even boyfriend, of Mom's who was so in love with her says I look like her. It makes me wonder if they slept together. Was he a good lover? Did she scream his name in pleasure?

"Do you think I'm pretty?" I ask, batting my lashes at the handsome older man.

His lips pull into a half-grin. He pushes the hair out of my eyes. "Beautiful, actually. So fucking beautiful."

My heart thunders in my chest. "She never talks about her father. I've asked a lot but she always changes the subject. Did you know my grandfather?"

His dark eyebrows pinch together, a painful expression painting his face. I want to reach into the air and pull the words back. To apologize for making him sad. To go back to him telling stories that make him growl and tense, not ones that make him upset.

"I'm sorry. I didn't know—"

He surprises me by hugging me tightly. "Shhh. I'm going to tell you everything. I just miss Tony. He was my best friend."

My throat aches with emotion. He's the one gutted, and

yet here I am the fool trying not to cry against his warm, firm chest as he holds me. "Tell me about him."

He chuckles, the sound thick and rich. It blankets and soothes me. "He was big. Had one of those Viking beards and a perpetual scowl. Everyone was afraid of him. Well, aside from Baylee and her angelic mother. Did she ever tell you about Lynn?"

I nod. "She talks about her often. That's why I don't understand why she doesn't mention my grandfather, Tony. I don't know much about him."

The room goes silent, and I wonder if I'm bothering him by asking too many questions. If he sees me as a curious child rather than an inquisitive woman who looks like an old love of his. Eventually, he lets out a sigh before launching back to the past.

VII | Gabe

MY PAST FOLLOWS ME WHEREVER I GO. NOT A DAY GOES BY when I don't think about the night that ended it all. The night I dispatched my father who killed Krista in cold blood after brutally raping her. Her blue eyes haunt my nightmares. For thirteen years, I've thought about her non-stop. Every time some asshole tries to pull a fast one over me, I think of her.

That night, after I sought my revenge, I found my father's friends still in our house. I showed them what Grant Sharpe had turned me into. Naturally, they were scared. Not just from me but afraid of what would happen if I were caught. Their shitty deviant ways would be dragged out into the open for all to see. It was in their best interest to help me.

And so from that point on, my father's best friend, Lance, became my mentor. He gave me money until my twenty-first birthday, where I was given access to my trust fund my mother set up and my inheritance that went to me after my father's death. Anytime I got into too much trouble, Lance was there to guide my way back out of it.

I'm not going to lie. I went through a dark phase. Did things I certainly regret. But now I'm attempting to turn over a new leaf. Which is exactly why I'm headed to a boring house in a boring suburb on a boring day.

Lance says I can't keep blowing through my money or I won't have any left. He also says my bullshit is leaving a trail that leads back to them. So, in an effort to chill the fuck out, I'm trying to start a new life. Who knows, maybe I can meet someone and settle down.

I'm squinting to read the addresses on the street when I lock eyes with her.

A woman.

Her shoulder-length golden hair blowing in the wind as she makes her way to her mailbox. When she sees me, she grins and waves.

Krista?

I slam on my brakes, but I can't peel my eyes from her. Not to be a dick, I wave back. She turns and bounces back up toward her house. It's then I realize her address is right next to the one I'm moving into.

Talk about fate.

With a smile on my face, I pull into my driveway. I'm climbing out of my car and about to call out to the woman making her way up the porch when someone steps out of her home. The Viking motherfucker zeroes in on me and glares. He's massive and borderline psychotic looking. Our eyes stay on one another as he pulls the woman into his arms and hugs her.

Well, fuck.

My first instinct is to climb back into my car and haul ass out of here. The last thing I need is a territorial war with some fuck face over his woman. I've spent a lifetime being fucking *bullied by kids from school, my father's friends, and my father himself. I don't need this shit.*

"Are you the new neighbor?" Her voice is like a musical breeze—soft and tantalizing. It instantly threads its way inside my head and takes root there. "I'm Lynn Winston. This is my husband, Tony."

I'm snapped from my daze to see them walking toward me. Shutting my car door, I saunter over to them with false bravado. In actuality, I wish there were a hole to crawl into instead.

"Gabriel Sharpe," I say in a deep voice and extend my hand to the Viking.

He grunts but takes my hand. "Good to meet you."

Next, the angel takes my hand. "Welcome to the neighborhood. I was marinating some steaks if you want to come by for dinner tonight. Tony and I'd love to give you a proper welcome."

Tony's gaze lingers on where she grasps me, and I quickly jerk my hand from her grip. "Uh, sure. I'll bring over a case of beer. I mean, if that's okay. Do you drink beer?"

Tony growls and Lynn chuckles. I like her laugh. "I don't, but this brute here does. Could you pick up a two-liter of orange soda too?"

I'm nodding. I find that she could ask me to donate my skin and I'd cut it right from my body. Something inside of me wants to give her what she wants.

"It's settled then. See you at, seven, Mr. Sharpe."

I laugh. "Gabe. Please call me Gabe."

I'm still wound up thinking about her as I drive back to my

new home from the store. This Lynn lady looks so much like Krista it's scary. But she's happy. Unlike poor Krista, Lynn has a life worth living. She doesn't have to run or to fear men like my crazy dad.

She's safe.

And that makes me happy.

Happy is an unfamiliar emotion. Sometimes, I'm satisfied. And hell, with the right woman, I can feel pretty damn good. But never do I feel a thumping in my chest like this. The way my blood rushes to my ears and I can't fucking think straight.

I wonder if she would leave the Viking for me.

Pulling into the driveway, I let out a huff of frustration. The woman is happily married. I'm not going to fuck with that. No way. I turn off the vehicle and head to the trunk. Once I pull out the case of beer and two-liter of orange soda, I shut the trunk and flicker my gaze to their porch. Staring back at me is the mini version of Lynn. A small girl. Beautiful and innocent.

Mine.

The thought, so sudden and fierce, startles me. Fuck that! I'm not some sicko. But it's nothing like that, I assure myself. It's much different.

"Did you get my orange soda?" she asks, her voice sweet like cotton candy.

I'm grinning like a goddamned fool. Walking up to her, I hand her the big bottle. "Is this for you?"

She beams, her blue eyes twinkling, and reveals a couple of missing teeth. "It's my favorite. What's your name? How old are you? What's your favorite television show? Do you like to swim?"

My heart squeezes. Maybe fate sent me here because I need normalcy. If I can get past the Viking, having Lynn and this little girl in my life could be good for me.

"Gabe. I'm thirty-one. I don't really watch much television but I do love to swim. What's your name little girl? How old are you? Do you interrogate strangers often?"

She giggles, and I swear it's a salve to my burned soul.

"Baylee Marie Winston. I'm seven. What does interrogate mean?"

I kneel down in front of her. "It means to ask questions. You ask a lot of them."

She scrunches her nose up. "Daddy says I'm nosy. Mommy says I'm curious. What do you think?"

Does it make me a fucking creep that I want to hug her to me and never let go? Deciding that it does, I push the thought from my head.

"I think you're inquisitive. And that's a nice trait to have," I tell her with a grin.

Her blue eyes sparkle. "I like you, Gabe. Will you take me swimming?"

Ruffling her hair, because she's too fucking cute not to, I shrug. "I don't know, sweet girl. Maybe one day you, me, and your parents can all go. We have to convince your dad to like me first. I don't think he cares too much for me."

She leans in to tell me a secret. "Daddy doesn't like anybody, but Mommy will make him."

At that, she bounces off with her orange soda in hand. Her pigtails, almost white in color, flop back and forth as she runs up the steps.

My life is finally starting to look up.

Thanks to a couple of intervening angels.

VIII | Hannah

"So my grandpa was grumpy? That's why my mom doesn't speak of him?" I question. The two pills I took earlier have relaxed me and sleep keeps dragging my lids down. "I don't understand."

He strokes my hair in such a way it makes me even sleepier. "There's more. I'm not sure you want to hear about it, though. Your mother and I sort of went to war. It was your grandpa who did some unforgivable things to her. She hated him for what he did."

My palm splays on his toned belly, and he covers my hand with his. "You were just my grandpa's friend? What was my mother to you?"

"She was my everything." His tone is low and gravelly. The way he says it, in such a possessive way, has a sliver of unwarranted jealously trickling through me.

"Oh."

"But then…" He trails off.

I look up at him and his chocolate-colored eyes are liquid

love. "Then what?"

"Then you came along."

"Me? I'm nobody to you."

His chuckle warms me down to my toes. "Sweet girl, you became my everything."

Furrowing my brows together in confusion, I let out a sigh. "I don't understand. You don't know me."

His fingers slide through my hair near my cheek as he murmurs his words. "I've watched you grow and blossom into such a brilliant, beautiful young woman. I've been to most of your softball games. Watched you from afar. The team is nothing without you, by the way."

His words of praise wash over me like a cold spring rain and cleanse me. But then, my blood turns to ice when I wonder if he saw *her*. Mrs. Collins. When she went psychotic in front of my entire team and family.

"I'm not that good."

"Better than Jameson, Cartwright, and Brown," he argues.

If he knows the three best players on my team, then he *does* come to our games. So why is it he's never revealed himself until now?

"So the Viking eventually became your friend because you get sad when you talk about him. Am I right?"

He laughs. "That he did. They became the family I never had. Lynn was so…" He trails off as if to think of the perfect word. "She may have looked like Krista, but she was gentle and kind. Krista would have ripped your throat out with her teeth had she had the chance. And then little Baylee grew up right before my eyes."

"You fell in love with my mom?"

His body grows tense. "It was way more complicated

71

than that. You see, Lynn was dying. They didn't have a lot of money. I'd exhausted most of mine from acting like a jackass all those years, so I was no help. My sexual tastes were outside of the norm and that forced me to satiate that need in ways my father would have been proud of."

This time, it's me who is the one hardening at his words. I sit up on one elbow and frown at him. "What sort of sexual tastes?"

His fingertips drum at his stomach and his eyes darken. With every breath he takes, his nostrils flare and his jaw clenches. "Depraved. Devious. Sick sexual tastes," he breathes. "Nothing a little girl should know about."

"I want to know."

He's quiet for a moment. "I bought and sold girls. When I needed cash, I took them, trained them, and made a quick buck."

"Just like your father," I say in astonishment.

Nature versus nurture.

It's in Gabe's nature to be like his father.

My theory remains hole-proof.

"Yes," he growls, "just like my goddamned father."

Instead of shuddering at his angry tone, I snuggle back up against his warm, hard body. I wasn't judging him. Simply stating a fact. I'm like *my* father, Warren McPherson, and his mother. Certain parts are just broken inside our heads. The good parts of me intricately twisted with the bad. Struggling every day to keep my head above the water so the black abyss doesn't suck me down forever. I've had a few dips into darkness over the years. I have no right to judge anyone.

"Then what?"

"Well, after going to these trades over the years, I took

notice of the ones who sold for the highest. Once I had a game plan, I was able to bring in higher profits. Every day, Lynn grew more and more sick. Tony became depressed. And my sweet Baylee was so sad. I wanted to fix them all. They were my family."

I smile and begin drawing hearts on his chest again.

"One day, your mother was bouncing through the house, in nothing but a red swimsuit, hunting for sunscreen. I wanted her so fucking bad in that moment. She was no longer the daughter of my friend. She was a woman. Curvaceous. Beautiful. Her body was ripe. An untouched virgin. I wanted her for my own selfish reasons."

"She looked just like me?" I can't help but remind him.

His fingers stroke my hair. "Exactly."

"Did you sell her?"

He flinches at my words. "How could you possibly come to that conclusion?"

"Grandma Lynn needed money. You wanted my mother. If you were smart, you could have had the best of both worlds. You could have slept with her, trained her, and then sold her. Then you'd have the money to save Lynn. But since you loved my mom, you could then rescue her afterward." I expect him to laugh at my hypothesis, but he doesn't.

His eyes narrow and I can see him attempting to peel back the layers inside my head. *Good luck.* "You're a smart girl, Hannah."

"I understand true love."

"Do you now?"

I nod and wait for him to continue.

"Well, your mother wasn't the happiest camper. Once Tony reluctantly agreed to the plan, I was to take her right from her bedroom window. I took her and…"

"Did you make love to her?"

He rolls over onto his side and glares down at me. "Among other things, Hannah. When I say little girls don't need to hear these things, I mean it. Eventually, after I broke her in, I sold her. The plan was to swoop right in and take her back. But everything went to shit after that. Her ex-boyfriend killed Tony for his involvement. Lynn passed away, the grief was too much to bear. And Baylee was nowhere to be found. The man who bought her went to expensive lengths to keep his name out of it. My girl was lost, in the hands of some monster, and I didn't rest until I got her back."

"So you *did* rescue her," I say with a smile. My fingers once again rise to touch his beard. "You were her hero."

His eyes clench closed. "I tried, but fuck if her ex-boy-friend wasn't a pain in my ass. Not to mention, your mother fell in love with her captor. Stockholm Syndrome bullshit."

"But you loved her, and she loved you. Ever since she was a little girl," I argue, my voice rising several octaves.

He opens his eyes back up and skims them over my features. "She didn't love me anymore. I was angry and lonely and heartbroken. My friends were dead and my sweet Baylee no longer belonged to me. Not truly. When her psycho ex tried to kill her, I put a bullet in his skull. She seemed so relieved to see me—for what I'd done. I knew we could put all the heartache behind us and move on together. That she would be my wife one day. But…"

His hand grabs mine and he drags my fingertips over the scar on his chest. Our eyes meet and what I see in his breaks my heart. Tears well in my eyes but don't spill out.

"But what?"

"She stabbed me. She stabbed me because she loved him instead."

"Her ex?"

"No, Warren McPherson," he bites out with a sneer, "your father."

I'm stunned silent. "My father *bought* my mother?"

"For millions."

A tear streaks down my cheek as I attempt to put together what he's saying. It explains my parents' secret love story they never divulge. It explains a lot actually.

"I'm so sorry," I blurt out. I love my mother and father, but right now my heart aches for the man whose heart thunders in his chest beneath my fingertips.

"Don't be sorry," he says with a smile and leans forward, kissing my nose. My stomach feels as if it does a flop inside of me. What would he do if I parted my lips and kissed him on his handsome mouth?

"But, my family hurt you," I murmur.

"Shhh," he whispers. "I'm fine. Look at me now."

"Gabe, why am I everything to you then? Why do you follow me and watch my games? Is it because I look like her? Do you want me, too?" I question, hope filling my voice.

His gaze softens. "Of course I want you. I've always wanted you since day one. But I also wanted you to be happy. I never wanted to hurt you or ruin your life."

I bask in his warm gaze. "But you have a wife. Won't she be upset?"

"She'll have to deal with it, sweet girl."

Mrs. Collins didn't have to deal with it. *I* had to deal with it. This time, the roles are reversed. It thrills me.

He rolls onto his back, and I can't help but slide my knee

over his hip. My fingertips skim over his hard torso as I attempt to find the courage to make my move. I lean forward and kiss his cheek near his ear. "I want you too," I whisper. Then, I kiss along his jawline until my lips hover over his. They barely brush over his soft mouth when I'm flipped over on my back and am staring into his furious brown glare.

"What the fuck are you doing?" he barks.

I frown and try to run my fingers through his hair. My efforts are thwarted when he grabs both wrists and pins them to the bed. His body is heavy on mine. I should be afraid. Terrified, like I was when Julian and Hunter were having their way with me. Instead, I'm hot and needy and desperate. If he weren't so heavy, I'd wrap my legs around his hips just to feel his erection against my clit. Just the vision of such a perfect scenario sends a quiver of excitement pulsating through me.

"We want each other," I tell him.

We have a silent stare off for a moment before he speaks again. "Not like this, sweet girl. Jesus!"

I squirm against his grip, but he only tightens his hold. The way he devours me as if I'm his entire world has me desperate to come at his touch. He's strong and powerful and wicked. His wickedness attracts me. Gabe truly is Hades. I want to be his Persephone. I want us to explore the depths of the darkness together.

"You said I look just like her," I argue. "You said I was pretty."

His glare becomes murderous. "Beautiful. You're fucking beautiful."

The anger in his voice, so fierce and sure, makes me smile. "So why won't you make love to *me*? Why won't you kiss *me*?"

The fury is wiped right from his face as shock settles in.

"What?"

Wiggling my legs free, I hook them around his waist and drive him against me with the heels of my feet. His body is warm against my tingling, needy sex. "I can be her. Krista or Lynn or Mom. But this time, nobody stands in your way. Don't you feel this connection? I want you inside of me, erasing what those bastards did. You, Gabe."

His cock between us comes alive at my words. The sweatpants between us feel like a punishment, and I wish they were gone.

"Baby," he murmurs and buries his face against my neck. "Fuck, I should have said something sooner." His grip on my wrists is gone so he can slide his arms around my body to hug me. I'm completely trapped in his heavy hug. "We can't do that."

Tears of rejection sting my eyes. "Why not?"

His hot breath is once again on my ear. It sends desire zapping through me. I wiggle my hips in hopes of feeling his cock rub against my clit—anything to relieve this fiery need.

"We can't do this because…" His words are hoarse and ragged. He bucks against me, just once. Stars blind me as pleasure surges through me.

"Do it again," I mutter.

He's panting into my ear. The uneven breaths make me crazy. I want to hear them as he splits me in two with his massive cock that's simply teasing me now.

"Please," I beg.

His groan is a painful one—as if touching me is the hardest thing he'll ever have to do in his life. But he heeds my wishes. He grinds against me so hard, I think his cock may tear through the material and find its way inside of me.

"Oh God," I gasp. I've never felt so alive and wanted by a man. My mind is going crazy with images of him fucking me forever.

"Fuckfuckfuckfuck," he chants into my ear. "Fuckfuck-fuckfuck."

His entire body shakes as if he's trying desperately not to give in to what we both want. He surprises me when he thrusts against me slowly, but not as hard. With each movement, his cock presses against my clit in just the right way.

"Please don't hate me after this," he murmurs against my ear.

"I swear it."

With my vow still hanging in the air, he suckles gently on my earlobe as he uses his cock to drive me closer to orgasm. I've come many a times with my own fingers but never at the hand of another. My entire body tenses as my climax nears. I'm desperate for it. So needy for the release.

"Come, sweet girl. Soak my pants with your juices," he growls.

His words are enough to send me over the edge. The darkness I tried to avoid swallows me whole. I'm no longer Hannah McPherson—the weird little girl who does inappropriate things. I'm no longer the girl who falls in love with teachers and doctors and coaches. I'm no longer the girl who runs a razor along her wrist simply to watch the blood spill all over the perfect white bathroom tiles. I'm no longer the girl who tries to drown on purpose so the lifeguard will save her. I'm no longer the girl who spent three weeks two summers ago in a mental health facility for delusions and obsessions and a multitude of other things.

My orgasm consumes me, and I cry out his name.

I'm no longer that girl.
Because now I am his.
I belong to Hades.
I am Persephone.

IX | Gabe

LOVE IS A WICKED LITTLE CREATURE. IT SLITHERS INTO your life and sinks its teeth into you whether you like it or not. Love doesn't care about morals or social norms or familial boundaries. Love takes whatever the fuck it wants.

And right now, love has me crazy with the need to rip my sweatpants off so I can sink my throbbing cock inside of her. I'm so desperate to do so, I think my chest might explode at any minute. Fucking insane with need.

Somehow, though, I manage to enjoy her sweet orgasm until it subsides and then pull myself up off of her. When I sit up on my knees, I can't help but admire how fucking beautiful she is. Her blonde hair is a halo around her soft features. With each ragged breath she takes, her chest heaves. Tiny nipples poke through the sheer fabric, and it makes me want to bite them. Her legs remain spread apart. My eyes fall to her sweet pussy, which glistens with her arousal.

This is so wrong…

But it feels so right.

Tearing my gaze from her cunt, I meet her blazing blue eyes with a stern look. "We can't ever do that again." My words cause her to frown. Rejection mars her pretty features and her lip wobbles.

"Was I not good? Do you not want me?"

The way she whispers those questions, so unsure and sad, has me wanting to give her whatever the fuck she wants—morals be damned.

"You were perfect," I tell her with a smile. I can't help but reach out and stroke a blonde strand of hair away from her pretty face. "I'm just a sick bastard who takes what he wants even when it's the wrong thing to take. I'll go to hell one day for all of this."

Her brows furl together. "I'll go with you."

My heart beats to life in my chest, and I can't help but smile at her. "You don't belong in hell, sweet girl. You're an angel."

She sits up on her elbows and gives me the evilest grin I've ever seen on a woman. My goddamned traitorous cock strains in my pants.

"I'm no angel."

Running my fingers through my hair, I attempt to spill the words that need to be said. "Baby," I say with a sigh. "There's a reason I followed you all these years."

She blinks at me innocently. Not an angel, my ass.

"I'm your father."

I expect tears and screams and fists. What I don't expect is for perfect, angelic laughter to fill the room. She laughs until tears of amusement stream down her cheeks. I watch as her tits jiggle through the silky material.

"You are not," she argues, a huge smile on her face.

I grab at the hem of her nightgown to cover her still wet cunt. It's fucking distracting me. "I am too. When your mother stabbed me, she'd said she was pregnant. It had to be mine."

Hannah reaches for the waistband of my sweatpants. Once she has it in her grip, she tugs it down and my cock bounces out enthusiastically. My dick weeps at the way she licks her lips hungrily. It takes every ounce of humanity left inside me to push away from her and tuck the eager thing back into my pants.

"Hannah, no."

I climb off the bed and take several steps away. "I'm your biological father. What we just did was wrong. It certainly can't happen again."

She sits up and draws her knees to her chest. Her pretty features fall as sadness takes over. "I have a father."

Her words sting, but I shake them off. "I know, but I'm the one who gave you life. It's my DNA inside you. I'd like to have a relationship with you, though. To take you places and buy you things. To spend time with you."

At this, her face lights up with a breathtaking smile. "Really? You want to see me again?"

"I want to see you every goddamned day for the rest of my life. And not from afar. I want you close to me. I need to make up for lost time."

She relaxes in the bed and stretches out. "I'd like that too. But my parents can't know. They'll forbid it. I just know it."

I reach for her and pat her thigh. "Our secret."

"I'd plug your name into my phone but I think it's still at that house."

Squeezing her thigh, I wink at her. "Get some sleep. I'll get your phone back."

She nods, and I go to leave the room. When I get the door open, she calls out for me.

"I love you," she mutters, her eyes flickering with a thousand emotions.

The words infect my heart and disease me with her—all of her. "I've been waiting eighteen years to hear those words. I love you too, sweet girl."

Going back to that house was probably smart. I'd left clues and shit everywhere. After several hours of cleaning, collecting her things, and disposing of the bodies, I felt much better about not getting caught. The last thing I needed was the police to take her away from me again. Now those fuckers are swimming in the Pacific. My hope is the fish and saltwater will take care of any lingering evidence.

By the time I got home and cleaned up, the sun was rising. Not one to miss a workout, I've been lifting weights ever since. My mind is focused on her. My sweet girl. I finally have her. Sweat pours from me as I power through an exhausting workout after no sleep. I can't sleep knowing she's in the other room. I'm not sure I'll ever sleep again.

I curl the barbell to my chest and let out a grunt. My dark eyes find their reflection in the mirror. Every muscle is flexed and hardened. Sweat drips from each strand of my hair as it hangs in my face. I'm wired and high on adrenaline. I'd go up and fuck Alejandra to relieve some of this energy, except I don't want to. My focus is elsewhere. And, just as Alejandra feared, it might never be back on her again.

"Gabe?"

The sweet voice is music to my ears. With a groan, I set the barbell down and turn to find the voice. Hannah stands in the doorway to my home gym, wearing that thin little gown with no panties and a mischievous smile on her face. She plays with the hem of it, revealing her creamy thighs, and I force myself to look back up at her face.

"Good morning, beautiful."

She beams and then runs to me. Apparently, my sweat doesn't bother her because she throws her arms around my neck and kisses my cheek. "Good morning, beefcake."

Chuckling, I look down at her. She's all smiles and bright eyes this morning, despite what a fucked-up night she had. "Beefcake?"

She smirks. "If my brother saw how ripped you were... he'd be so jealous. He's sixteen and spends all of his free time working out. The poor kid has a few muscles but he's got a long way to go."

I stroke her soft hair and inspect her features. "Did you sleep well? How does your body feel?"

Her eyes drop to my mouth and she sighs. "A little sore but I'll be okay. I'm going to have to go home, though."

She lifts her gaze to mine, and it's sad. I can tell she doesn't want to leave, which makes my heart fucking soar. "Yeah, sweet girl, you're going to have to go home. But," I say, breaking from her warm grasp, "I got you a present."

Sauntering over to the countertop along the far wall, I retrieve her purse and phone. She takes them from me and lets out a sigh of relief. "You went back."

I nod. "There's no evidence left of you being there. Or me for that matter."

Her fingers tap away on her phone. Then, she looks up at me. "What's your number?"

I snatch a towel from the bench and dry my face and hair. Once I locate my phone, we exchange numbers.

"Put me in your phone as Persephone," she instructs, mischief painting her features. "You'll be Hades in mine."

Lifting up an amused brow, I do as I'm told. I'd rather have aliases in the event her mother ever got ahold of her phone.

"Are you ready for me to take you home, Persephone?" I question, one corner of my lips quirking up.

Her cheeks turn red, but she shakes her head. "Not really. I want to stay wrapped up in your arms with you telling me stories forever." She bites on her bottom lip and sends me a look no daughter should ever send her father.

Clearing my throat and hiding my reaction with the towel, I start toward the door. "We'll find ways to hang out, sweet girl. Trust me. And one day, if you want, you can come live with me. We have to be careful, though. Your mom will get me sent me to prison if she ever finds out."

Twenty minutes later, after I've had her dress in a pair of Alejandra's yoga pants and a tank top, I walk her out to my car. She's quiet as we get in. The sun is finally above the horizon in the east.

"This isn't over, baby," I tell her and reach over to squeeze her hand. "This is the start of something we had stolen from us. Nobody can take that away from us now."

She smiles at me. "I'll probably drive you crazy."

"Never."

"I'm kind of a stalker."

"So am I."

At this, she grins. "I guess we have that in common."

"I guess we do," I agree and wink at her. "Don't ever feel afraid to call me or text me. Any time is the perfect time. All of the time is the perfect time. I'm yours now, sweet girl, and you're mine."

She shivers but nods. "Always."

When I drop her off in front of her house, she turns to look back at me, shielding her eyes from the sun. I can see her nipples through the tank, and I hope she finds something decent to wear before she traipses around in front of her brothers. She blows me a kiss that melts my fucking heart before bouncing back into her house.

My sweet girl.

All mine.

It's been five days since I saved her from those monsters. Since I brought her into my home and nursed her physical and emotional wounds. Five days since I fell in love with the most beautiful girl in the world.

Alejandra isn't pleased with my leaving every day to take Hannah to dinner or to a movie or for a walk along the beach. She wears a wary expression but doesn't speak out against me. Wise woman. I do as I please. I make up for lost time. I hug my girl. I spoil her rotten.

"What do you want to do today?" I question as we weave down the road, the warm air whipping around us through the open windows.

She has her toned legs stretched out and her bare feet

propped up on the dash. "Let's go find a secluded beach and swim. I haven't been swimming in ages, and it's hot today."

"Did you bring your swimsuit?"

"Nope." She flashes me a wide grin, but I can't see her eyes behind her shades. This girl grows naughtier by the day. Like finding her biological father suddenly gave her a license to behave badly. I don't mind if she's bad, though, as long as she's bad with me. Where I can protect her and look after her.

"When do your parents get back?"

"Tomorrow," she says with a groan. "They're not going to let me leave all of the time like I've done this week. I don't know what we'll do then."

Anxiety makes my chest ache. I've grown used to seeing her every day as soon as she gets out of school. Today, she skipped school altogether, so we could spend the entire day together. "We'll find a way, sweet girl. Even if I have to steal you away."

Words like that should make her fearful, but she only giggles. "It's not stealing when your victim willingly goes with you."

Arching an eyebrow at her, I look at her in question. "So you're my victim now?"

"I can be your victim if you want me to be." Her lips pout out, and she runs her fingers through her wild blonde hair.

"What do you want for your birthday?" I question to change the subject from the dangerous territory it had gone to as I turn onto a gravel road I know leads to a quiet part of the ocean.

"Hmm," she ponders as we park. When I turn off the car, she turns to look at me. "I want you."

"You have me."

"That's all I want," she murmurs. I want her to elaborate, but she climbs out of the car. Before her door even closes, I'm already out of the car and trudging through the sand after her. The wind picks up and whips her hair off to the left. She'd worn a loose summer dress, which flaps in the wind. With every gust, it gives me a glimpse of her round ass barely contained in a pair of pink panties.

Swimming is a bad idea.

When she reaches the water's edge, she grabs the hem of her dress and peels it away. I freeze in my tracks. My jaw clenches as I watch her shed her bra and then finally those tiny panties. Her body is perfect—exactly like Baylee's. My traitorous cock agrees.

Swimming is a very fucking bad idea.

"The water's warm," she calls out, flashing me a grin and a view of her perky tits before she sinks into the ocean. "Come swim with me, Gabe."

I tear my shirt from my body and lose my shorts. The wise thing to do would be to leave my boxers on so I don't get carried away with Baylee's twin in the water.

I've never been a wise man.

I'm a man who thinks with his cock.

And my cock thanks me the moment I shove down my boxers and charge after her. The water is warm like she said.

"I'm a bad influence on you, sweet girl," I tell her and grab her wrist to pull her closer moments before a wave nearly drowns us both. When we reemerge, sputtering water, I pull her all the way to me.

"How do you know I wasn't bad before?" she questions, her arms snaking around my neck.

"Because I've been watching you this entire time. You're

a good girl."

She leans her forehead against mine. "Did your stalking reveal the time my parents put me in a mental hospital?"

I tense at her words. "They fucking did what?"

She leans back and holds her wrist up for me to see. "Do good girls cut their own wrists just to see the blood?"

I press a kiss to the scarred flesh there. "Why would you do that?"

"Because I don't think like normal people. My brain is wired differently."

"Different is good. Hell, I'm as fucking different as they come."

"Good girls don't steal and tell lies to their friends, so they'll hate each other. Good girls don't watch their younger brother stroke his cock at night. Good girls don't take their shirt off for their forty-year-old teacher and try to break up his marriage. Good girls don't want to fuck their…" she looks down at my lips but doesn't finish her statement.

I close my eyes because she's driving me fucking crazy. "We can't fuck, sweet girl. I know I seem like a fun friend who showed up when you needed him most. But I'm more than that. Your creator. Your father. A piece of you."

Her eyes cloud over and she looks past me down the beach. "If I could prove you weren't my real father, would you make love to me?"

A growl rumbles from my chest and I squeeze her to me. "You're mine."

She brushes her lips across mine. "I know. Whether you're my father or not. I'm yours. I became yours the moment I heard the sickening crunch of that baseball bat."

Another wave hits us, and my palms find her ass to keep

her from going under. She wraps her legs around my waist. My cock presses against her sweet center, desperate to push inside of her.

"Why are you doing this?" I grumble.

"Why are you fighting this?"

"I'm a bad man who does very bad things," I snarl, my restraint holding on by a precariously thin thread. "I'm better when I'm with you. Let me be a better man."

Her eyes mist over and her lip wobbles. The rejection she wears on her face cripples me. "I don't want you to be a better man. I want you to be you."

Slipping my thumb into her mouth, I grip her jaw with my other fingers and hold her so I can look at her. "Don't make me cross that line, sweet girl. There's no coming back once it's been crossed. I'll never let you go. Ever."

Her teeth sink into my flesh as anger flashes in her eyes. I yank my grip from her and glower at her.

"You let *her* go," she snaps.

I grab a handful of her hair. "Because of *you*."

When her hand clutches onto my cock, black bleeds into my vision. The sunlight is snuffed out as darkness creeps in. Out here in the water, we're two halves of a whole. Society's rules mean fucking nothing. I'm about to cross that line when someone hollers at the shoreline.

I jerk my head over to see some asshole. "You can't swim here. Private property. You've got five minutes to get out of here, or I'm calling the police."

He stomps away. I wonder if I could choke the life out of him in those five minutes. If I had my knife, I'd slice open his gut and drag his entrails into the water for the fish to feed on. This fucker just ruined our moment.

I take a deep breath.

A moment that would have changed everything between us.

A moment that would have killed something before it even began.

"Come on," I tell her and forcefully rip her from my body. "We need to leave." I all but drag her out of the water.

She pouts as she pulls her clothes back over her wet flesh. I brood while I dress. Neither of us says a word. We're both pissed and frustrated and confused.

"Now what?" she questions once we're settled back in the car.

"I take you back home."

She scoffs. "I don't want to go home."

Slamming my fist into the steering wheel, I turn to glare at her. "And I don't want to fucking lose you because I fucked you during a moment where I let my dick do the thinking. You're mine, Hannah."

"Not yet," she murmurs.

I clench my jaw but don't argue. She's right, though. This girl won't be mine until we're far, far away from this hell hole where our families, and the negativity they bring, are in the way.

"Not yet," I agree and squeeze her hand. "But soon."

X | Hannah

OON.

Soon.

Soon.

That was several months ago. Ever since the day I almost got him to fuck me, he's been strangely resilient to my advances. Mom and Dad have long since come home. And as predicted, my time with Gabe has diminished to mostly on weekends. Our phone calls last until the wee hours of the morning and our texts never stop. I just wish we could have more.

But at least he watched me graduate. When I'd walked across the stage, I found him in the crowd and blew him a kiss. My parents would never see him in the sea of people. It was my public promise to him. A proclamation of my love. And I didn't miss the way his dark eyes lit up with love.

"Your move," Dad reminds me.

I blink away my daze and skim my eyes over the chess pieces. No matter my play, he'll win. Dad always wins. "I'm thinking," I stall, twisting my peace sign necklace in my fingers my dad gave me when I turned sixteen.

He smiles and leans back. "What's there to think about, Han? I'm going to win. May as well get it over with."

Ignoring his taunting, I lean forward with my elbows on my knees. After a moment, I look into his navy blue eyes. My dad is handsome and sweet. And my *real* father. One hundred percent. I'd wanted to explain that to Gabe, but then I feared he might not want to see me after that. That, I couldn't bear.

"Do you remember that time I cut myself?" I question, my voice even and unaffected.

His eyes close and his face blanches. "All too clearly."

"We have a rare blood type."

He swallows and nods. "Rarest of them all. O negative. Only six point five percent of the population has that blood type. But you and I both have it."

"Is it weird your blood flows through me?" I question. His face is pale and his shaking hands draw into fists. "That it mixes with mine and somehow works?"

"I'm thankful. It saved you."

"Dad?"

His eyes open, and I see the darkness flickering there. He's thinking about it. He's calculating the probability of how I should have died. That a girl with a rare blood type's chance of living after such a traumatic "accident" should be dead. Not alive and well and happy playing chess with him. The numbers practically dance out of his head into the air. It's painful for him, that much I can see. Not just thinking about what happened to me. The close call. What's painful is his need to keep a lid on his darkness.

For years I tried to keep my lid on too.

93

But now I don't like the lid.

I prefer the darkness to the light.

I want to free it.

"You know I love you, Dad. No matter what."

"I know, Han."

Scanning the board, I find the most satisfying move. The most satisfying win for my dear father. Once I move the rook, opening up my queen, I stand and give him a kiss on his cheek. "You win, Daddy."

His smile is wide and the love in his eyes chases away the darkness that lingered there only moments ago. "I always win." He winks. "Why don't you get off to bed? Tomorrow the five us can take a beach day. Soon you'll go off to college, and we'll miss you. Get some rest and tomorrow will be just us. Ren can surf. Your mom can run. Calder and I can take turns dunking you like old times."

Laughing, I give him a quick squeeze around his neck. "Sounds perfect."

"Night, honey," Mom says from the doorway.

I look up from my phone where I was texting Gabe and smile. "Night."

Her brows furrow together and she stares at me for a long time. "Where'd you get that ring?"

A pink diamond on a platinum band sits on my ring finger. Gabe gave it to me for my eighteenth birthday a couple of months ago. He'd put it on my right hand, but when I'm alone, I wear it on my left and pretend he's my husband. I never wear it at home, though, for this very reason.

"Um," I start, slightly shocked at her taking notice. Lately, she's too wrapped up in everyone else to notice something like my jewelry. "It's from my boyfriend."

Not totally a lie.

Gabe just doesn't know he's my boyfriend.

Details.

"What's his name?"

Crap.

"Julian Hunter," I blurt out. As soon as I say the names of my rapists, I wish I hadn't.

Her eyes narrow and she purses her lips together. "Is he good to you? Why haven't we met him?"

I sit up and twist the band around my finger. "You've met him plenty of times. Not my fault you can't remember him." I can't help but fuck with her.

She frowns. "When did you meet him?"

"While you were in Italy."

"I see. How old is he?"

"Older," I challenge.

Her arms cross over her chest and she gives me the sternest look she can muster. "I want to meet him. Invite him over tomorrow for our family beach day. I'm sure he's lovely, but I don't feel comfortable with you seeing him without us having met him. You know how we feel about these things."

"Why? Did something happen to you to make you worry about me so much?"

She swallows and her hands ball into fists. "No."

I challenge her with my gaze. She's lying straight to my face.

"Why don't you talk about Grandpa?"

95

"Hannah, you're not—"

"Were you raped when you were younger?"

"No, I—" Her eyes widen in shock, and I can see the wheels turning in her head.

Another lie. "What, it's not rape when you have feelings for your attacker?"

She storms over to me and slaps me. "Don't you dare talk to me that way ever again. You know nothing, Hannah. Nothing."

A cruel laugh escapes me. "No, *Mother*, you know nothing."

We glare at each other for a long moment. My phone buzzes. Before I can yank it away, she has it in her grip reading our texts. Invading my privacy.

"I miss you, sweet girl," she whispers aloud. "Is his name really Hades?"

I snatch my phone from her. "Privacy, Mom!"

"Get some sleep," she seethes. "Tomorrow we're discussing what's gotten into you. I'm going to call Dr. Gibson. The medication isn't working like it used to. Your moods are all over the place."

In a fit of rage, I throw my phone as hard as I can at her. It misses her face because I *made* it miss her face. If I wanted it to hit her, she'd have a broken nose as we speak. Instead, my phone now sits cracked and dead on the floor.

She doesn't say another word, just slips out and closes the door behind her. Tears stream down my cheeks. I'm not going to see Dr. Gibson again. Last time, he asked me questions about my sexuality. Had I ever had anal sex? Did I watch porn when I was alone? How many times did I masturbate a week? All questions to help him diagnose me, he'd said. His words danced the line between helpful doctor and perverted old man. I didn't miss the way he eyed my thighs every couple of minutes. I refuse to let that man give me more medications that'll have me as a vegetable on his black couch ready and waiting for his wrinkly fingers on me and in me.

Hopping off the bed, I find my duffle bag I use when we travel for softball. I stuff as many clothes that will fit inside. Once I've thrown in my makeup and medications—just in case—I zip it up and plan my escape. Before I leave, though, I pull open my laptop and send Dad an email.

Daddy,

I can't stay here anymore. Mom wants to medicate me, and I don't feel like myself on all of those medications. Summer's here now, and college is around the corner. I'm going to stay with a friend until I get myself sorted out. I love you.

Han

I know Dad won't read the email until morning. Once I send it, I snatch up my bag and push open my bedroom window before they set the alarm for the night. I'm outside and halfway to Gabe's before I give in to tears. The walk takes about thirty minutes. Soon I'm standing at his front door with my fist poised to knock.

Ever since that first night, we've never come back to his house. I've only ever seen his wife once. I'm nervous about seeing her again.

With a sigh, I knock softly on the door. A few moments later and it opens. I stare into the eyes of a girl no older than Calder. Her brown hair is pulled back into a ponytail, and she eyes me curiously.

"Can I help you?"

I vaguely remember her from the family pictures on the

wall from that first night. "I'm here to see Gabe," I tell her.

Just then, Gabe's massive frame fills the doorway behind her. He takes one look at my tearstained face and crushes me with a comforting hug. I let out a sob as I grip his T-shirt.

"What happened?"

"I left. I thought maybe we could…"

He pulls away and looks at the girl. "Brie, go on up to bed."

"Who is she?" she questions.

"Someone very special to us. Go to bed now."

When she disappears, he hauls me into the entryway. I set my bag down and swallow down my emotion. "What's your blood type?"

His brows furrow together. "AB positive. Why?"

My smile is so big it hurts my face. "Can I stay here to-night?"

"Of course, sweet girl."

He hefts my bag from the floor and guides me to the bed-room I stayed in the first and only time I was here.

"Will you stay *with* me? Like last time?"

He nods. "I'll be right back."

While he's gone, I undress and then find an oversized T-shirt in my bag. Once I've pulled it over my head, I climb into the warm bed that somehow smells like Gabe. Rubbing my thighs together, I wonder what it'll be like to have him.

I *will* have him.

Closing my eyes, I part my legs and touch my bare pussy. I lean back against the pillows to relax. My fingers massage my sensitive flesh while I dream of the dangerous man I've become so close to. With each swirl of my touch, I get closer and closer. But it's not close enough. It's not good enough. It's not *him*.

"Mmm," I whine.

A soft click of the door has me reopening my eyes. He leans against the closed door, his dark eyes shadowed by his hair that curtains around them. Somewhere along the way, he took off his shirt and dons only a pair of low-slung holey blue jeans. He's fucking hot, and I want him inside of me.

"What are you doing?" he grumbles.

I meet his gaze and then push a finger inside of myself. "Trying and failing to orgasm."

His jaw clenches.

"You could help me," I murmur and can't help but taunt him, "Daddy."

He closes his eyes and gives his head a shake, as if to drive the depraved thoughts from his head. I don't want them to go away, though. I want to see them and dance with them and live with them and make love to them.

"Sweet girl," he growls. His voice is low and angry. I want to unleash his fury. I want to be his victim.

"Why won't you fuck me?"

He storms toward me, furious and violent, and I nearly come at the sight because he's so beautiful. I part my lips to gasp with pleasure. "You're poking a bear that's been in hibernation for a long time."

Arching a brow at him, I give him a challenging stare. "Maybe I need the bear to maul me."

His eyes caress my flesh. "The bear would fucking hurt you. The bear is unstoppable. The bear is cruel."

"It's a good thing I'm not Goldilocks then. I'm not running from you, Hades. I'm running *to* you. We were meant to find each other. I can be her…Krista, Lynn, Mom. Just do it already. I'm dying for you."

He launches himself at me, causing me to cry out in surprise. His fingers grip my wrist and jerk me away from touching myself. "Stop it," he orders. His chest is heaving as he pins it to the bed. The way his fingers dig into me makes me fight him more. I like the bite of the pain.

"No."

"Fucking stop," he snarls. "I'm going to hurt you."

His mouth is close to mine so, I lift forward and bite his lip. My mouth is forced from his when he brutally grabs my jaw. I punch his side with my free hand, which causes him to lose his grip on my face. We struggle until I have him right where I want him.

Between my legs.

"There," I purr, my eyes meeting his enraged ones. "Much better."

His tongue flicks out, and he licks away the blood I drew from his bottom lip. I want to lick that lip too, but he won't release me. Both of us breathing heavily as we stare each other down.

"You're fucking with my head, sweet girl."

Smirking, I dig my heels into his ass. "I'd rather fuck *you* instead."

His growl melts my insides.

"That night, when those motherfuckers raped you," he murmurs, "they fucked your head up too. You think you want this, but you don't."

His words infuriate me and I explode. "Fuck you, Gabe!"

I squirm enough to free my hand and I claw at his face. As soon as my fingernails meet his flesh, he slams my hand back onto the bed. His breath is minty and sweet and just a hair from my lips. This time, I lean up and kiss him. I don't bite him, but instead run my tongue over his wound. When I let out a whimper of need, his little thread he clings so desperately to snaps.

Pop.

"So wrong," he hisses before spearing his tongue deep into my mouth. He kisses me expertly, as if he's been practicing his entire life just for me. We're no longer fighting against one another. Now we're fighting to climb into each other. My fingers rip at his hair as he kisses me like I might disappear.

"I won't disappear," I voice my thoughts against his lips.

"Fucking damn straight you won't."

His mouth swallows mine again. I lose all sense of reality as the beast consumes me. I need him inside of me. I'm trying to voice this need, but his kiss is too powerful. He doesn't stop nipping and sucking and tasting me until he lifts up briefly to undo his jeans. I don't get any sort of warning to the fact he's made his decision until I feel the tip of his cock against my wet pussy.

Gabe isn't slow or sweet or gentle.

He just drives into me with one powerful thrust that has me screaming—a scream he swallows with a kiss. His cock is thick, so thick, and I feel like he's going to split me in two. Thrust after thundering thrust, he fucks me like it's his right to do so. I've never felt so wanted or loved in my entire life. It's as if he wants to live inside me.

I want him to live there too.

"Don't stop," I manage to murmur when he lets me gasp for air.

"I'll never fucking stop," he snarls.

His fingers slip between us, and he massages my swollen

clit. The sensations are too much. I try to clench my legs together, but this beast between my thighs makes it impossible.

"I want you soaking my cock, sweet girl. Make that pretty pussy juice all over me. I want it all. Fucking give it to me," he orders with a growl.

The sensations mixed with his words drive me wild. But I need more…

"I want you to look at me when I come," I tell him bluntly. "Look. At. Me."

His eyes turn nearly black, but he heeds my request. I stare into his dark, vicious eyes and I see me. I see my own monster staring back at me. Oh, what a beautiful monster she is too.

"You're so fucking perfect," he huffs, "and mine."

I let out a choked sound of pleasure as an orgasm takes hold of me with force. My body jolts and quivers as I climax hard. His grunting only lasts another moment before scorching heat fills me. Every inch of my insides are coated by the beast on top of me. He slows his bucking into me until the twitching of his cock subsides. Then, he buries his nose into my hair at the base of my neck.

"I have no moral compass, Hannah."

I laugh. I'm sure his words were meant in warning, but they only comfort me. "Neither do I."

"What the fuck?" he grumbles. "That was so fucked up, but I loved every second of it. I'm waiting for my dick to wake back up so I can fuck you again. I want inside every single one of your holes. Those motherfuckers may have taken your virginity, but I'm going to take your ass one day. Every tight inch."

Shivering, I scratch my fingernails down his spine. "Run

away with me. Let's leave this town."

He lifts up and indecision paints his features. "I have Brie to think about too, sweet girl."

His words irritate me. He has *me* to think about. I try to push him away from me, but he's like a brick house. After several unsuccessful attempts, he chuckles.

"Are you pouting?"

Not meeting his eyes, I shake my head. "No."

"Liar."

"I'm not pouting."

"Look me in the eye."

My gaze snaps to his, and I hope he sees the jealousy and anger in them. "I didn't think about my family when I ran to you."

Guilt morphs his features and he peppers kisses all over my face. "No, you didn't. You're reckless and irresponsible and uncaring of others."

I glare at him. "Okay, Mom."

His gaze darkens. "I'm your fath—"

"Yeah, about that," I interrupt. "You're not."

He doesn't blink. Just stares at me. I watch with amusement as his jaw clenches several times. "Impossible."

"Possible."

"But I know—"

"Well, you're wrong. I have the rarest blood type. So does my father," I whisper, "Warren."

He flinches at the name. Instead of arguing, he pulls out of me and climbs off the bed. He pulls up his jeans over his hips and points at me. "Get dressed. Now."

Frowning, I shake my head. "No."

"Don't test me, sweet girl."

With tears springing in my eyes, I climb off after him. When I'm near him, I throw my arms around his neck. "I'm sorry. I didn't mean to taunt you. Please don't make me leave. I love you." A choked sob escapes me. "We can pretend. I can be her. Please let me be her."

His fingers tangle in my hair and he jerks my head back to the point of pain. I let out a whine when his mouth sucks on the flesh just to the left of my throat. "When I said you were mine, I wasn't fucking joking. You think I'm going to let you go? Now? Fuck that. *We're* leaving. Tonight."

I sag in his arms, relief washing over me. His mouth is all over my neck marking me as his. With each nip and suck, I grow hungrier for him. I need him inside of me again.

"Will she try and stop you?" I question.

His chuckle is downright evil and sinister. Straight from the depths of hell. I love how it warms me from the inside out. "She can fucking try."

Smiling, I slide my fingers into his hair and grip him.

"Grab a quick shower, sweet girl," he says and slaps my ass. "I need to go deal with Alejandra."

"How was your shower?" he asks as he hauls a suitcase to the front door.

"Would have been better *with* you."

He smirks at me. "Tomorrow I'll bathe you."

With that promise, he walks out the front door to load the vehicle. While he's preoccupied, I tiptoe up the stairs to see how he "dealt" with Alejandra. I wonder if he dealt with her by using a baseball bat to her beautiful face. Would her blood color the walls? Grinning wickedly, I peek my head into the bedroom doors until I find the master bedroom.

Inside, I'm sickened by what I see.

Fucking sickened.

Alejandra's wild eyes meet mine, and she whimpers through the gag in her mouth. She's been tied to each poster of the bed. But she's *alive*. Unharmed.

Eyeing the knife he used to cut the rope, sitting on the nightstand, I walk over to it. She implores me with her eyes to use it to free her. To cut her loose so she can stop Hades from dragging Persephone into his hell.

I don't think so.

Persephone *wants* to be dragged into the dark underworld where she belongs. With her love, her life, her Hades.

Alejandra is a complication. A complication we don't need.

"He's mine now," I tell her as I sit beside her on the bed. "I hope you enjoyed him while you had him."

She glares at me but can't speak through her gag.

I hold up the knife. Sharp. Serrated. Long. Wide. A knife like this could really hurt someone. It would make such a mess.

Dragging the tip between her breasts, I watch with glee as the knife tears through the fabric easily. I wonder if it tears through flesh, muscle, and bone all the same. Her muffled screams are beautiful. A symphony of sadness, anger, and jealousy. I love her screams because they're a means to an end.

I want Gabe to tie me up and make me scream too.

But my screams will only be the beginning.

"Did he tell you he was my Daddy?" I taunt.

Her eyes widen and she nods.

Leaning in toward her, I grin. "Did he tell you he fucked me earlier? Made me come all over his cock? That we're going to run away together so we can fuck all of the time?"

Tears well in her eyes and she shakes her head in denial.

"True story," I tell her. "He's been waiting for me all this time. And now I'm here. Ready for him. He's all mine now."

Our eyes are glued to each other when I drag the tip of the knife up her chest to her throat. She starts to cry when I find the giant artery that pulsates in her neck.

"What happens if I poke a hole here?" I question. "Does the good doctor bleed out?"

Not waiting for her response, I push the tip of the knife into her flesh above the pulsating vein. She garbles words through her gag. The small hole I poked gushes for such a small hole. Crimson leaks out around the tip of the knife soaking her pillow behind her.

I'd always heard when you slice the carotid artery, it sprays everywhere.

They never educated us on what happens when you poke it.

But what about when you twist your knife into the thick vein? Do I get a bloody spray then? Will it be as climactic as I'd hoped?

The knife twists slowly in my grip. Her flesh tears against the blade. A bigger gush seeps out, but still no spray. The movies were all wrong. I'm severely underwhelmed.

Releasing the knife, I slide off the bed and stand.

"I'll take good care of him," I promise. And I'll never break that promise.

With that, I hurry down the stairs toward my future.

My love.
My life.
Mine.

XI | Gabe

AFTER SIX HOURS IN THE CAR, WE FINALLY PULL OFF THE old highway down a dirt road situated between two mountains just outside of Tucson. Hannah is asleep, and the sun is just barely coming up over the desert horizon. A few years ago, I took some of the money I had stockpiled away from when War bought Baylee and purchased this private land. It was always my hope to whisk Hannah away one day. To convince her to stay with me.

What I didn't anticipate was her revealing that I'm *not* her father.

At first it made my heart fucking bleed, but the animalistic craving for her just wouldn't go away. I'd needed her in some primitive way since the moment I scooped her bloody body from that rapist's bed. It grew and morphed into something I refused to unleash. I love her and crossing a line like that could have been detrimental. Turns out, I worried for nothing.

I can now have her any fucking way I want her.

The drive down the narrow road takes another thirty minutes until I arrive at the stucco home I'd had built for this moment. It's not a large house. Just a couple of bedrooms. But it's new and has all of the amenities we could ever need. I'd even had the builders put in a pool. This will be our paradise. Our home. Our forever.

And now I don't just get to take care of her, I get to fuck her too.

Talk about happily fucking ever after.

My mind drifts to Alejandra. I'd meant to end her life. It's what I should have done. But then I thought of Brie. My sweet little Brie. She'll need her mother. One day I'll come back for her, but not until the aftermath our departure will bring dies down. Brie doesn't need to leave her school or friends. Alejandra will be a good mother to her until I come back.

I park inside of the garage and look over at Hannah. She stirs, rubbing her palms in her eyes. Her blonde hair is messy, but she's still perfect.

"We're here," I tell her.

We climb out, and I take her hand before we enter. A cleaning lady comes once a week to keep the place free of vermin and dust. On the way here, I'd given her a call to ask her to bring a few things to the house. I'm pleased to see a bowl of fruit on the island as we enter the kitchen. I know the refrigerator and cabinets will be stocked with food, too.

"Cute place," Hannah praises as she prances through the house touching everything in sight. I follow after her, watching her tight ass jiggle every time she moves.

"The best part is outside."

She pulls open the sliding glass door and squeals when she sees the sparkling pool. "Let's swim!"

I chuckle and hook my arm around her waist before she dives in fully clothed. "It's six in the morning. Let's rest and we'll swim when the sun's out."

She pouts but relaxes against my chest. "What will we do until then?"

"Sleep," I propose.

Not giving her a chance to argue, I clutch her hand and guide her through the house toward the bedroom we'll be sharing. I'd had the other room set up for her, but now I don't want her anywhere but in my bed.

"Take off your clothes and get in the bed," I order, pulling off my own shirt.

Her eyes darken and a smile plays at her lips. "Do you like tying girls up?"

My cock twitches at her words. Visions of my sweet girl bound and at my mercy twist my mind up. Dirty, dark thoughts have my body dying to do so many things to her.

"Yes." My voice is husky and dry.

"Are they bad girls?"

"Sometimes."

"What do you do to them?"

I smirk. "Whatever the fuck I want."

"Would you do that to me?" A golden eyebrow arches up in challenge.

I'm not sure what she wants from me. "Only if you ran from me. There's no getting away now, sweet girl."

Fear doesn't flicker in her eyes. Desire does.

She edges over, taking a few steps in my direction. "So if I ran from you, you'd drag me back and tie me up? What would you do then?"

A low growl rumbles in my throat. "I'd whip your ass for

leaving me." I unbutton the top of my jeans and kick my shoes off.

She looks down at her tennis shoes and sends me another challenging stare. "Then what?"

"I'd fuck you until you begged me to stop."

"What if I didn't want you to stop?"

"Trust me, you can't handle what I would do."

She closes the distance between us and licks her lips in a seductive way that has me fisting my hands at my sides to keep from mauling her. "I bet I could. I bet I'd want it."

"I don't think so."

Both of her palms run along my pectoral muscles. "I'm not Krista or Lynn or Mom. I'm better," she snips out. "You'll see."

I'm about to argue back when she shoves me as hard as she can. I lose my footing and fall on my ass. It's then that I see a flash of blonde as she bolts from the room. That bad, bad girl.

Clambering to my feet, I don't hesitate as I chase after her. The backdoor slams as she runs from me—fucking runs— fully knowing the consequences of such an act. Her blonde hair flies out behind her like she's some kind of flying fairy.

I'm going to catch her.

I'm going to hurt her.

The Arizona dirt under my feet stings as I tear after her, but I ignore the bite of the tiny pebbles against my soft flesh. All that matters is catching that girl so I can fuck her.

"Getting slow in your old age?" she taunts over her shoulder.

Letting out a growl, I power after her. She may have played softball, but I work my ass off at the gym. Her legs are no match for mine. Soon, I'm close to her. I reach out, but she zigs hard to the left and then zags quickly to the right. I'm momentarily stunned but catch back up. This time, when she's close, I tackle her. She cries out when her knees hit the dirt.

"Don't fight me," I hiss.

But, boy, does she fight me. Her fist swings up and clocks me in the jaw. Amazingly, she rolls out from beneath me and starts to take off again. I grab her ankle to yank her back to me. I fucking maul her like the bear I am and press her chest into the dirt. She lets out a moan, but still fights me as I tear her shorts from her body. Once I have them to her knees, along with her panties, I don't waste any time pulling my cock out. I'd expected her cunt to be dry, but she's wet, and it greedily sucks me into her body.

"Oh yes," she moans and clenches around me.

I grab her hair and yank her head back. "Why'd you fucking run from me?"

"To see if you'd catch me," she pants.

Grunting, I drive into her hard and fast. I'm going to come inside of her. As soon as I get off, I'm going to give her the ass whipping of a lifetime.

"Of course, I'd fucking catch you. I'll always catch you."

She moans as if my words please her. "This feels good, Gabe."

"Are you going to come with my dick inside you? I can't reach your needy clit from here, sweet girl."

Her body writhes beneath me. "Yes!"

And, boy, fucking does she. Her pussy clamps down around my cock, which makes me explode inside her. I come so hard, I think I might pass out. An old guy like me does not need to be running through deserts chasing little fuck dolls. I'm too old for this shit.

"Jesus!" I hiss as I spurt out the last of my seed. "You trying to fucking kill me?"

Her fingers clutch the dirt, and it's then I notice she's wearing the ring I gave her on her wedding finger. It makes my chest swell with manly pride. She's mine.

"You promised to bathe me," she murmurs, her back heaving with exertion. "And I'm really dirty."

Groaning, I slide out of her and stand on shaky legs. My dick still drips with my release, splashing her white ass—an ass I'm going to royally fuck up later. I tuck my cock back into my jeans and fasten them before helping her to her feet. She drags her clothes back up over her dirty body. When our eyes meet, I love the way hers shine with pleasure. Her little monster has been sated.

"You're bleeding," I point out and gesture to her knees.

She shrugs. "I'm guessing it won't be the last time you make me bleed."

I turn away from her, so she can't see just how fucking crazy she makes me. "Come on."

Hand in hand, we walk back to the house. When we reach the back door, we strip out of our clothes so we don't drag dirt into the new house. I guide my dirty girl to the massive bathroom and start the walk-in shower. Once it warms, I pull her under the hot spray with me.

"That was stupid," I tell her. "After everything I've told you about me. About what I've done, who I've killed, people I've taken and tortured. You still poke the bear. What happens when I hurt you? Will you wake up one day and realize you've had enough?"

She wraps her arms around my waist. "I'll never have enough. That was the single most exciting moment of my entire boring life. I don't want to quit you."

I smile and hug her to me. "It's a good thing. Because there's no getting away. Ever."

After our shower, I can tell she's dragging. Her eyes droop and she practically stumbles into the bed. I sit on the edge of the bed watching her until she passes out. Then, I make my move. With quiet efficiency, I bind each of her wrists and tie them to the headboard above her head. She doesn't stir, and I bite back a laugh.

Once I'm sure she's secured, I jerk her knees apart and stare at her pink pussy.

"Wake up, sweet girl," I coo.

She mumbles and then lets out a needy whine once she realizes her predicament. "What are you doing?"

"Punishing you."

She laughs—fucking laughs at me. "Like you punished your wife? I peeked in and saw her all trussed up. Did you give her pussy a little fuck before you left?" Her eyes darken with jealousy.

Now it's my turn to laugh. "She was always a placeholder until you came back to me. And no, I didn't fuck her. I just wanted her to stay."

"Like a good dog."

Her pupils are dilated and she looks wild with fury.

"Are you on drugs?" I demand, my fingers biting into her

thighs so I can part her for me.

She smiles wide and her tits jiggle as she laughs. "Not anymore."

My fingers slide down to her cunt and sure enough, when I push a finger into her, she's wet for me. "What do you mean, not anymore? Were you using?"

Her body bucks as I finger fuck her. I almost stop to force her to talk to me, but she speaks before I have to. "Unless you call antipsychotics and antidepressants a drug addiction, then no, I wasn't using. Just doing as Mom and those doctors asked. But now that I have you, I don't have to take them anymore."

I clench my teeth together and push another finger into her. She moans as I stroke her G-spot. "You *only* need me," I agree.

Her eyes brighten with adoration. "Only you."

Now that I have her full attention, I feast upon her sweet pussy for the first time. The scream of pure bliss fills the room and she bucks against my face, greedy for the pleasure I intend on giving. I suck on her throbbing clit as I fuck her tight pussy with my fingers. Her cunt tastes of sin, and I gladly enter the dark side with her juices running down my chin.

"I need…I need more…"

I insert another finger inside of her, but not to fuck her with it. I want to get it wet. Once it's sufficiently drenched, I slide back out. When my finger probes the tight hole of her ass, she cries out in surprised shock.

But I don't give her a moment to argue. I push into her virgin hole slowly. My tongue continues to assault her clit while my fingers do their magic on her pleasure holes. Soon, she's screaming like a demon as she comes all over me. Her body tightens around my fingers, to the point that I wonder if I'll ever get them back out of there.

"Oh, God, that was…"

"I'm not finished, sweet girl. There is no 'was.' This is all happening *now*. I'm going to own every part of you until all you think about is me one hundred percent of the time."

She shakes her head. "I already think of you all of the time."

"When you're hungry and you think of my cock, when you're thirsty and you think of my cum, when you're tired and you think of my chest as your pillow, when you're needy for a fuck but I'm already pushing inside you," I bite out. "Then you'll be where you think of me all of the time."

"Right now, I could mention your mother or father or brothers and you'd think of them. I want your thoughts, sweet girl. Every single fucking one of them."

"Untie me," she begs, her breaths shallow. "I need to touch you."

Growling, I twist her until she's on her stomach. Then, I drag her legs off the bed so her ass juts out at me. "I'm not done touching you first."

"What are you going to do?"

I lean over her and growl in her ear, "Don't you remember? I owe you a whipping."

She starts to argue but I hit her ass hard with my palm. It stings my flesh. Her yelp gets my cock hard as fuck.

"Did that hurt?"

"Yes!"

"Want me to do it again?"

"No…"

Lying little girl. I can tell by the way her body shudders

with need that she doesn't want me to stop. Her monster inside is begging for it. Begging to be beat into submission.

"Beg me to hurt you."

"Only if you call me Persephone," she bites back.

I laugh and hit her ass harder this time. The bright red mark of my hand will no doubt turn into a bruise later.

"Do you like that, Persephone?"

"Yes, hit me again, Hades."

Smirking, I step away to find my belt still looped around my jeans. Once I slip it from my pants, I make my way back over to her red ass.

"Beg."

"Hit me again! Please!"

Thwap!

She screams and wriggles away, but I dig my fingers into her thigh to pull her back to me.

Thwap! Thwap! Thwap!

At one point, she kicks backward and narrowly misses my balls. Despite her begging, she doesn't like it.

"You wanted me to hurt you," I snarl and whip her several more times. "But now you want to kick me away?"

"Stop!"

"No!"

She twists back around onto her back and kicks me right in the jaw. I stumble backward until I fall on my ass. Her wild eyes are dilated to the point they almost look black. That caged monster is running free.

"What do you want me to do then?" I demand, my chest huffing.

"Release me so I can claw your fucking throat out," she screams.

117

With a full-bellied laugh, I throw my head back. "Not yet, sweet girl. Not yet."

This time when I stand and head for her, I'm prepared for her attack. When she kicks, I grab her ankle and twist her back onto her belly. Her ass cheeks clench together as she prepares for the next blow. But it doesn't come. I crush her with my weight and suckle on her neck. My palms slide underneath her and pinch at her nipples. I thrust my cock against her sore ass until she's whimpering.

"Please…"

"Please what, my beautiful girl?"

"Please fuck me."

I chuckle. "I want to take your virginity."

"My ass?" she whimpers.

"If you're good and you relax for me, I'll reward you like you would not believe."

Her entire body goes limp. "Okay."

With a grin, I lift up and push my rock-hard cock into her cunt to wet it first. Despite this girl wanting to kill me moments before, her pussy is fucking drenched. Bad girl.

I pull out of her wet hole and then press against her much tighter hole. Her screams are otherworldly as I inch into her slowly. Everything in me begs to slam into her, but I love her and hurting her more than she can handle right now just isn't on my list of things to do. I want her to enjoy this. She cries against the mattress but remains deathly still as if moving one single bit will make it worse on her.

"Such a sweet, sweet girl," I praise. "Take my cock in your tight ass. Tell me how much you love it."

"I love it," she moans.

I wrap a hand around her waist until I locate her clit.

With soft circles I bring her to the edge of bliss while I slowly pump into her. "Does that feel good?"

"Yes."

"Want me to stop?"

"God, no," she hisses. "Don't stop. Oh my goooood!"

As soon as her climax overtakes her, her quaking body clenches around my cock like a vise. I'm helpless to make it last any longer because the moment she loses control, my release gushes deep inside her, filling her up.

"Fuck!" I snarl as my cock drains inside of her. "Fuck!"

My cock softens after a moment, and I slip it carefully out of her. She's limp as I untie her hands. Her body remains unmoving when I scoop her into my arms to carry her back into the shower. Those pretty blue eyes refuse to meet mine as I set her to her feet inside the shower and start cleaning her.

Finally, I've had enough of her games.

"Open your eyes and look at me."

When she finally opens them, I expect to see fear with a little bit of hate. What I don't expect is hunger and possession and love.

Clenching her jaw in my grip, I make her look up at me. "I love you, sweet girl. Don't you ever forget it. Even when you feel like you can't take it anymore. When you think you hate me. When you consider running away for real. Remember, I love you. I have since before you were born."

Her fingers claw at my shoulders as she draws me closer. "Every second with you only binds my heart more intricately with yours. You're the one who will want to run away in the end. I'm difficult and hard to handle. Just ask my parents."

At this I laugh. "I'm difficult and hard to handle too. Seems we were meant to find each other."

XII | Hannah

THE HEAT OF THE AFTERNOON SUN WARMS ME. I'VE BEEN out here for hours and should probably go inside, but I don't want to. I'm relaxed and happy. In heaven. With my king of the underworld. My Hades.

I peek an eye open and watch him over the top of my sunglasses as he drags a net along the pool surface gathering bugs and debris from the water. Every muscle in his body flexes with each movement. Large biceps and forearms are bite-worthy, complete with bulging veins and just enough arm hair to make a girl go crazy. He dons a pair of swim trunks that hang low on his waist, revealing a sexy little V with a trail of dark hair right in the middle that leads straight to his hidden massive cock. I'm hungry and want to rip those shorts right from his body.

He kneels by the edge and scoops a handful of water into his palm. His hair had fallen into his eyes but now he splashes it with the water so he can slick it back. The water droplets run down his face dripping onto his solid chest. I lick my lips. I'm thirsty too. Men who look this good should be rich and ridiculously famous with big breasted women hanging all over them. Not secluded in the middle of the desert with a girl who barely knows her way around the bedroom.

Yet, here we are...

I've been rewarded by some higher power, that's for sure.

When I go to sit up, I let out a whine that has him jerking his head toward me. His black aviators on his nose hide his dark eyes, but I know they flicker with desire. Despite the pain he doled out earlier, I'd come so hard. I'm still in a post-anal-sex stupor. After he whipped me and then fucked me until I lost my sanity, he'd cuddled with me. So much so that we'd slept through the morning, and most of the day away. I'd made us a quick meal before we came outside to enjoy the sunshine before it disappeared.

"Your ass hurt, sweet girl?" he calls out as he returns the net to its hook on the wall, his full lips quirking up into a half grin.

I stand and amble over to him. "Maybe."

"Want me to kiss your bruises?"

Our mouths meet for a quick kiss. "Do I really have bruises?"

His chuckle heats me from the inside out. "There's no doubt, baby. I didn't go easy on you."

Pulling away from him, I walk over to the water's edge. Then, I look over my shoulder at him giving him a wicked smile as I drag my toe in the warm water. With my eyes on his, I inch the bottoms of my black swimsuit down my thighs, baring my ass to him. The reaction is instantaneous, and his cock strains through his swim trunks. I love the effect I have on him. So immediate. So greedy and needy and downright possessive.

"Is it bad?" I question, a slight pout in my voice.

He charges for me and palms my breasts as he hugs me to him, letting me feel his throbbing erection against my sore ass. "So bad," he growls. "But fucking beautiful too. Purple and blue. Like a goddamned masterpiece."

I twist in his arms and palm his pectoral muscles, making sure to turn him right where I want him. "Will this earn me more?" With a hard shove, I push him backward into the pool. The splash is loud. His dark form lurks in the deep end and his aviators flutter to the bottom. I pull my bottoms back up and wait for him to resurface with my hands on my hips.

But he doesn't resurface.

He just sinks to the bottom.

He's fucking with me.

We play chicken. Each of us waiting out the other.

My heart races in my chest while I wait for him to gasp for air and chase after me. For him to spank me and call me his bad girl.

But he doesn't resurface.

He just remains still at the bottom.

He's fucking with me.

Right?

"Gabe," I yell. "Not funny!"

Nothing.

Did he hit his head on the bottom?

Panic seizes me. Do I still remember CPR from tenth grade?

He's fucking with me.

"Gabe!"

Time ticks by quickly and he doesn't move. At all. Not

one tiny bit.

He's not fucking with me.

"No!"

Without another moment of hesitation, I dive into the water. I swim quickly to him and wrap my arms around his waist. He doesn't move or jerk or anything. His body is heavy, but in the water, I'm able to drag him toward the shallow end. When I can touch, I roll him over to his back. Dark hair clings to his eyes and his mouth hangs open.

"No!" I screech and slap his face. "No!"

I drag him over to the steps so I can attempt to feel for his pulse. When I can't seem to find the thumping that should be there, I start to panic. I need to do CPR but I don't know how I'll get him out of the pool. A sob rips from my chest and interrupts the quiet desert air. My mouth hovers of his. I press my lips to his and blow air into his mouth. This isn't how they taught me to do it in gym class, but it's the best I can do.

"Breathe, goddammit!" I beg.

I'm so busy trying to force air into his lungs, I barely register his palm cupping my breast. As soon as I realize this, his tongue spears into my mouth while his other hand grips my hair.

"You're not dead!" I scream at him.

But he will be for freaking me out.

Fisting my hands, I rain punches down against his hard chest until he grabs both wrists and immobilizes me.

"I don't die, sweet girl." He winks. Smug motherfucker.

"I hate you!"

He releases my hand to grip me by the throat. With his fierce, smoldering eyes on mine, he walks me out to the deep end by my neck. I'm not choking because the water makes me practically weightless and I can still touch. But when we get out to where I can't touch, it becomes a struggle to stay afloat and the grip on my throat does start to choke me.

"Take it back," he seethes, his lips inches from mine.

I kick at his balls but the water thwarts my efforts.

"So help me, Hannah. Take it back or I'll drown you right now."

"Fuck you!"

His eyes flicker with rage, his fist squeezing around my throat. "Say it."

When I don't, he begins pushing me under the water. My hand grips his wrist that's clasping my throat. He dips me to my chin.

"Fucking take it back," he orders.

"No!"

Dunk.

I'd barely gotten a breath of air before he submerged me. I kick and struggle, landing a knee to his stomach. His grip loosens, and I rise to the surface. I've barely sucked in a deep breath when I'm pushed back under.

"Take it back!" he roars above the water.

Reaching forward, I grab his nipple and twist until he lets me go. I swim away from him, deeper into the water. When I think I might get away, a firm grip around my ankle yanks me back. My lungs burn with the need to breathe air. His handle on me is loose enough that I could get away, but I'm assaulted by memories of the accident.

Jace Friedman is twenty-three and beautiful. He's thirteen years older than me but surely a man like him could want a girl like me. I haven't developed breasts yet but I'd be a great kisser, I just know it. If only I could convince him to even look at me.

I'm sure once I got his attention, I'd have it forever.

The waves are super choppy today. Mom told me to stay in the shallow part but she's got her hands full with Calder. He's crying because there's sand in his juice box.

Would Mom even notice if I drowned?

She only notices when I do something bad.

Drowning is bad…

"Mommy! Watch this!" I call out moments before I do an impressive cartwheel in the shallow water.

She doesn't look up. She babies my brother instead.

Pouting, I wade out into the water. The waves are crazy and try to swallow me whole. Some days I wonder what would happen if they swallowed me. Would I become a mermaid and live at the bottom of the sea?

Maybe Jace is a merman…

I'm lost in a daydream where Jace and I swim along the ocean floor, collecting pretty shells for my daddy, when a gigantic wave crashes over me. It yanks me back with it, and when I go to reach my toes out to touch, I can't find sand. Only water.

Panic seizes me, and I thrash in the water.

Jace will save me.

Don't swim.

If you drown, he'll have to come out here and rescue you. He'll have to wrap his big, muscled arms around you and put his lips on you.

Thrashing to the surface, I splash and scream. I'm proud of my act, but then another wave hits me sucking me under. This time, I don't care about the slow lifeguard. This time, I try to swim to the surface. But I'm confused and I can't tell which way is up.

My lungs hurt and I want to breathe!

I'm fading out when something grabs my arm.

Jace?

The grip is tight, and I'm dragged to the surface. As soon as I gasp for air and choke out seawater, my eyes meet the terrified blue ones of my mother.

"My baby girl," she coos and hugs me to her chest. "You scared me half to death, baby."

I start to cry and hug her tightly as she swims us back to shore.

Maybe she pays more attention than I realized.

"Sweet girl," a deep voice rumbles through my daze. "Where'd you go, baby?"

I look into a pair of dark brown eyes in confusion. "Jace?"

Those dark eyes swirl with rage. "Who the fuck is Jace?"

Reality swoops in and settles around me.

Gabe. My Hades.

"A lifeguard when I was ten," I tell him, my voice hoarse. "I was confused."

It's then I realize that I'm in his arms, and we're sitting on the steps in the pool. My thoughts are murky and the past still lingers.

"Look at me," he orders, his chocolate-colored eyes swirling with emotion. Anger and rage and fear and sadness and love. And me. "Take back what you said. We're not leaving this pool until you do."

Tears well in my eyes and I wrap my arms around his neck. I straddle him and press my lips to his. He squeezes me against him as if he never wants to let me go. I'll die if he ever does let me go…

"I don't hate you. I couldn't ever hate you," I murmur

against his mouth. It's the truth. He scared the shit out of me. All I could think about was being alone. Without him. A world without him simply doesn't exist anymore. Nothing else matters but him.

"I'm sorry I held you under. I'd never let you drown," he says. "You know that."

Our teeth clash together as we kiss with the need to devour the other. His fingers rip at my swimsuit, both top and bottom, until I'm naked in his arms. He somehow manages to squirm out of his trunks and one breath later he spears me with his cock.

"Oh God!" I shriek.

"He can't hear you now that you're with me," he growls and nips at my bottom lip.

I tilt my head back as he bucks into me. His mouth finds my neck. Teeth and more teeth. Biting and tearing and scraping. He hurts me. He may even make me bleed. The bruising, the cuts. I love it. I need it.

All it takes is his fingers on my clit while he fucks me, and I'm lost. Gabe is this dark thunderstorm that came up over my horizon, decimated everything in his path, and swept me away with his torrential presence.

Who needs light when the dark nourishes your entire being?

Not this girl.

"Yesss…" My words trail off as I climax hard enough to see glittering stars in the middle of the day. His heat fills me as he roars like a bear tearing apart his prey.

Gabe tears me apart.

Rips and shreds me.

And then he somehow puts me back together better than

I was before.

It's magic.

"I love you, sweet girl," he murmurs against my throat. "Too much. A love like this will eventually kill one of us."

Gripping his hair, I tilt my head down to look into the sated monster's eyes. My eyes zero in on his perfect lips, and I lick mine. "I hope it's me then. What a way to go…"

His features harden and he grips my jaw, his thumb biting into the soft flesh below my cheek. "A life without you is no life at all. I can assure you, I will die before you. Not because of my age, but because I can't mentally fathom something happening to you or being here without you. My mind would crush in on itself. If you needed to breathe, I'd give you my last breath. All for you, sweet girl."

We remain conjoined, his cock soft inside of me. I bury my face into his neck and cry. His words scare me. I don't like thinking of a life where one of us exists without the other. I only want to know a life where the two of us live together. Alone. In the desert. Secluded from society and reality. A piece of heaven.

He climbs out of the pool with me in his arms, kicking out of his shorts the rest of the way. I shiver when we make it inside and the air conditioning chases away the warmth from outside. He doesn't set me down until we're standing in the shower and the water turns hot. Then, he slides me off his cock and onto my feet. I'm shuddering from the cold, but also from fretting about his words. They haunt me.

I'm obsessed with them.

I'd give you my last breath.

Tears choke me up, and I hug my middle.

Well, Gabe, I would suffocate before I accepted it.

Powerful arms wrap around me. I'm safe and warm in his embrace. No threats or stress or heartache. Only happiness and love.

XIII | Gabe

E'VE BEEN LOCKED AWAY IN OUR SECLUDED PARADISE for days. The time passes slowly and quickly, and sometimes I think it simply stops. I've given up caring about what day of the week it is, or anything else for that matter, because she's all that matters.

But sometimes, late at night, after I've fucked her pretty much until she passes out, I think about other stuff. I think about my Gabriella. Little Brie. So sweet and smart like her mother. Beautiful. Too innocent for this world. Soon, she'll be old enough for boys and shit. That makes me crazy fucking furious. She'll need me to look after her and protect her.

I could bring her here…

But what about Alejandra? She doesn't fit into this equation. Hannah is my love, my fucking angel. Alejandra doesn't fit.

Fuck.

My conscience, some bastardy intangible thing that seemed to vine its way through my mind from the moment

Alejandra told me she was pregnant. No matter how hard I try to cut it away—to leave it in the past—I can't. It's still there sprouting beautiful little flowers named Brie.

She's probably upset and confused at how her daddy could abandon her. And I *did* abandon her. I left her without a goodbye because I'd had Hannah on the brain. I'd let my obsession fuel and guide me.

I'd left my own flesh and blood because my dick told me to do so.

Hannah stirs beside me in the dark. My thoughts are interrupted when the blanket slides down my stomach past my cock and down my thighs. Warm lips wrap around my soft dick, but it wakes right the fuck up. She's been practicing late at night, so I can't see her face. I think it gives her confidence to try weird shit. Like, just yesterday, she tried to stick her finger up my ass. That ended when I flipped her over and drove my dick inside hers instead. Tonight, she's not trying to get in my ass, but instead tongues the tip of my cock like it's a lollipop. She's fucking teasing me on purpose.

She distracts me.

My moral compass is obliterated in her presence.

As long as she's touching me. Laughing. Chatting my ear off. Just looking at me. I'm completely focused on her. Nothing else exists. I'm blissed the fuck out on her. Only when the world goes silent does my conscience slowly wake.

I'm not this man.

I don't have complications.

Life is simple. I take what I want. I get what I want.

But what happens when what I want threatens to tear me apart and drag me in opposite directions.

Hannah's teeth sink into my cock causing me to hiss. She

doesn't bite hard enough to make me bleed, but she bites hard enough to force my attention back on her. My sweet girl hates to be ignored. She hates it when she's not sitting pretty on her pedestal.

In fact, she goes a little crazy.

We discovered that yesterday when I made her stay at home while I ran to the store. I didn't need anything, but I needed to check in on Brie. At the house, there's no signal whatsoever so I had to find out. Brie didn't respond to my text. I'd even dragged my ass around town for an hour. Nothing. Crickets. Alejandra, even though I left her tied up, would have gotten loose eventually, or Brie would have released her. So when I bit the bullet and called my wife, I had expected her to answer. Nothing.

It's been bothering me ever since.

What really bothered me was when I came home. Hannah's face was red from crying. She'd thrown all of the lawn furniture into the pool. I'd found her sitting with her legs dangling in the water. Naked. Crying. Furious.

It took a lot of soothing words and finally an ass whipping followed by an angry fuck to calm her ass down. Then she just cried until she fell asleep. While she slept, I found her empty duffel bag under the bed. The medications sat there untouched. I'm fucking worried as hell that she truly does need that shit. She doesn't act like the girl I met. The girl I met was subdued. An animal, yes. She was caged, though. Then, I set her free.

Now, I don't know how to cage her back up when she acts like a madwoman.

I'll simply have to force her to take the meds again. She'll get over it. It'll piss her off, but she'll calm the fuck down eventually.

"Fuck!" I snap when she bites me again. Yanking at her hair, I pull her away from my dick. "Bite me again and I'll tie your ass to the bed for a week. Don't test me, sweet girl."

She laughs like a fucking lunatic and goes back to sucking my dick like a motherfucking pro. When I'm about to come, she grips my balls to the point of pain before taking me deep in her throat. The girl's a wicked vixen, and I come without abandon. All down her warm little throat. And when she gags, I push on her head so she'll take it deeper.

I release her when the last of my cum spurts out. She slips away and straddles me. Not because she wants to fuck but, because she wants to be the center of my world. Grabbing her elbows, I pull her to my chest to hug her and press a kiss against her hair.

"I want you back on your meds in the morning." My words hold no room for negotiation.

She stiffens in my arms. "Why?"

I let out a sigh. "Because you need them."

"Says who," she bites out.

"Says me."

"You're not my dad."

I growl and flip her over onto her back. "No, you're my fuck doll, sweet girl. You're my woman, my soul, my motherfucking other half. But you need them and you'll do as I say, or I'll force them down your throat just like I forced my cock down it."

She rages beneath me, further proof that she needs the shit. Thankfully, I'm stronger than her little bad ass. Eventually, she gives up and relaxes.

"You think I'm crazy too. Just like Mom. Just like those

doctors."

Pressing my lips to hers, I kiss her softly and breathe my words against her. "I don't think you're crazy...I just don't want to lose you to your impulses."

She wiggles. "Fine."

"That's it. Just fine?"

"You want to control me? Control me. I'll take the pills. I'll be your little zombie girl until the end of time if that makes you happy."

I let her curse and rage and hate for the rest of the night.

And the next morning, she takes the fucking pills.

Things have gone back to normal once she got back on her medication. No more wild child moments. No more tantrums. No tearful breakdowns.

Just her.

And me.

In motherfucking bliss.

But I have to know how my daughter is doing. I need to check on her. To give her some sort of explanation and a promise that I will come back for her. She's probably beside herself with stress and worry. Brie's an innocent. Such a sweet, brilliant girl. As much as I belong out here with my Hannah, I can't help but feel torn. Her little heart will be broken.

"We almost there?" Hannah questions from the passenger seat, twisting her peace sign necklace between her fingers. "I'm hungry."

I learned my lesson last time and no longer leave her at

home alone when I go places. She rides shotgun and tells me a million different stories about her childhood—the ones I wasn't privy to being behind the glass and in the shadows of her life.

"Another fifteen minutes and we'll be on the outskirts of Tucson. We'll find a diner or something once we get there."

She nods and sticks one of her feet out the open window, wiggling her bare toes in the wind. Her dress lifts up and shows her pale pink panties which makes driving fucking impossible when I want to pull over and fuck her with my fingers instead. The girl likes to fuck. A lot. She's giving this old man a run for his money.

Dragging my gaze from between her thighs, I wonder if I'll be able to buy some gym equipment for this house. I'd not considered it when I had it furnished but after a week of not working out, it's driving me crazy. Running through the desert and swimming laps in the pool simply aren't cutting it. My body is used to a more rigorous regime.

"Do you think they're worried about me?" she questions, her head rocking to the beat of the music.

I think about how Baylee has hovered over her children over the years as if they may vanish at any moment. How War is always glancing at exits and people as if everyone is a potential child kidnapper. They're obsessed with their children's safety. And even though their oldest daughter is eighteen, I can imagine they're stressing the fuck out.

"Do you want to call them?" I blurt the words out before I can stop myself.

She bites on her lips and shrugs her shoulders. "Maybe. Can I think about it?"

Smiling, I reach over and grab her hand. "You can do

135

whatever you want, sweet girl. I'm going to check on Brie so I don't care if you check in, as long as you don't tell them where you're at or that you're with me."

She jerks her hand away and glares at me. "Why are you going to call her?"

Passing a slow car, I gun it before answering her. "She's my daughter. I need to let her know I'm okay and I love her."

Her mood darkens, and she crosses her arms over her chest. She's silent for the rest of the drive, and I wonder what's cooking inside of her head. I wonder what the fuck we're going to do when the meds need refilling and we don't have them.

Then, what the fuck?

"Pedro's Mexican Restaurant?" I ask when we pass a billboard boasting of the best enchiladas this side of the border.

"Sure," she says with a cold bite to her voice. "Oh, and I do want to call them. Thank you." I don't like her tone but I brush it off. I'll be sitting in on that conversation.

When we pull into a decrepit parking lot of the questionable looking restaurant, I pull out my phone and am thankful to see bars of service.

"You first," she says and clasps her fingers together.

With a sigh, I dial my daughter's number. No answer. Alejandra still doesn't answer either. I know she's pissed I left her tied up to the bed, but I could have done much worse. She of all people knows this. If she's keeping me from talking to Brie because of this shit, I'll make her pay dearly for it.

"No answer?" she questions.

"Nope. I'm going to try the hospital. Alejandra should be there."

She nods and gives me a beautiful smile. "Okay."

I dial the nurse's station where they can page her to talk to me.

"Surgery," a bland voice barks, "Nurse Brenda speaking."

"Hey, Brenda," I greet. "It's Johan. Is Alejandra available? I need to speak to her. It's urgent."

The line goes quiet for a moment. "Um, I, uh…" The phone is muffled as she speaks to someone else, but I can still hear her.

"What did they say to do if Johan calls?" she hisses to someone.

The response is muffled, but I understand. "Patch him through to Detective Larson."

"Um, yes, Johan," Brenda says with a shaky voice, "let me transfer you."

"Brenda, she doesn't have a phone there. You page her and she comes to the phone. Why are you trying to send me to a detective?" I demand with a growl.

"Do you really not know? I told them it wasn't you. You're good to her, and she loves you. But they didn't want to listen to me," she murmurs.

"Know what?"

"Alejandra was murdered a week ago."

Blood boils inside of me, and I shoot Hannah a scathing glare. She smirks. She motherfucking smirks at me. Swallowing, I let out a hiss. "I didn't fucking know this. Where's my daughter?"

"Well, since you weren't there and Alejandra has no other family in the US, she's been taken by child services. I'm so sorry. I thought you knew—"

She's cut off, and I hear a scuffle of voices. Then, I'm put on hold. What the actual fuck? Seconds later, the phone rings as it's forwarded. I hang up before it connects to this Detective Larson.

"What the fuck did you do, Hannah?" I demand.

Her eyes narrow and darken. "She was a complication. You said so yourself many times this week."

Running my fingers through my hair, I suppress the urge to throttle her. "What. The. Fuck. Did. You. Do?"

"I did what I had to do for us," she snaps and crawls over the console onto my lap to straddle me. Her wild eyes meet mine and she smiles like the devil. "I pushed that blade into her pretty little neck. Watched her bleed out all over the bed while you packed the car. She died before we even left the house."

I grab her by her throat and choke the shit out of her. She yanks at my wrist, but I don't let go. "You left my fifteen-year-old daughter home alone with her dead mother's body? You left her to find that shit by herself? What the fuck's wrong with you, Hannah?"

When she grows limp in my grip, I release her. She gasps for air but wastes no time attacking me. Her claws are bared, ready to rip my eyeballs out, but I snatch both of her wrists before she exacts any damage.

"She would have taken you away from me," she tells me, her voice defeated and her lip wobbly. "I didn't want her to come between us."

Closing my eyes, I lean my head back against the seat rest. "She and I were never truly in love, sweet girl. I would never have left you for her. Fucking ever. But letting Brie find her that way? You really fucked up, baby."

Her lips smash against mine and she threads her fingers into my overgrown hair. "Please forgive me," she breathes out her plea. "Please. I didn't think about what would happen. I just did it."

I slide my palms to her ass and squeeze. Her tongue finds its way into my mouth. She kisses me hungrily. When I've had enough of her apologetic kisses, I tug at her hair to pull her away from me.

"They're looking for me now. I'm obviously the main suspect. Of course, they're looking for Johan, not Gabe, but it won't take long to connect me, I'm sure."

A tear streaks down her cheek. She's not sad about the fact my daughter had to find her dead mother tied up to the bed. She's sad because she thinks the fucking police might take me away from her.

"No more bullshit, Hannah. You have to get your act together and do exactly as I say. If they're looking for me, then we're not safe here. You can make the call to your parents, but then we're getting rid of this phone."

She nods in agreement. I swipe the tear away with my thumb and kiss her nose.

"Be a good girl."

I hand over the phone and she dials a number.

"Put it on speaker," I instruct.

With another push of the button, the ringing can now be heard by both of us.

"Hello?" a kid answers.

"Ren?"

"Holy shit! Hannah? Where are you? Mom and Dad are freaking the fuck out!" he shouts.

She frowns. "I'm fine. I swear. How's everyone? How's Dad?"

"You know Dad. He's obsessed with locating where you're

at. You left your smashed phone here, but he's been on the hunt. They're super panicked because the day after you left, there was a murder up the road a little ways. I didn't think we had to worry about you since you emailed Dad but they still have been stressed about the whole thing. You should come home, Han. They won't eat or sleep or smile. They're sad."

I bring my lips to her neck and suckle the flesh there. My mind whirs with shit I now need to be aware of. Every trip to town is going to be a problem. Fingerprints are a problem. If they connect the two, it's a huge fucking problem.

"I'm not coming home, Ren. I'm in love."

He groans on the other line. "You're always in love, sis. At least talk to them."

When I nip at her flesh, she lets out a gasp. "Okay. Mom, though. I don't want to talk to Dad." I jerk away to read her features. Her eyes are teary. She's a daddy's girl and doesn't want to hear his disappointment.

"Mom?" Ren calls out. "Han's on the phone."

Not a second later, Baylee's breathy voice fills the line. My cock hardens from the sound of it I've missed for so long.

"Baby girl? Where are you? I'm so sorry we had a fight. Just come home and we'll work it out. God, I'm so glad you're okay."

Hannah grabs my wrist and guides my hand between her legs. Once she's shown me how wet her panties are, she gives me a wicked grin. *Finger me*, she mouths. I push a finger into her hot, tight center and revel in the way she gasps loudly.

"I'm better than okay, Mom. I'm in love."

Baylee sighs into the phone. My finger drives in and out of my sweet girl's cunt as she speaks with her mother. "You're not in love. With whom? That Julian Hunter?"

She smirks. "No, I lied. That's not his name."

Don't, I mouth to her in warning. I don't like the wicked gleam in her eyes.

"Is it your teacher?" Baylee questions, horror lacing her voice.

Hannah laughs, a little on the maniacal side. "Nope."

"Coach Phil?" Baylee's sigh is one of exasperation.

"Not this time."

"Stop playing these games and tell me." Baylee's voice is tight and fierce. It's a façade, though. I know when she hides her fear. She's fucking terrified for her daughter right now.

"You play games all the time, *Mother*," she snaps. "You lie and keep the truth from me. Truths I should have been told ages ago. But no, you hid it all in your obsessive stupid effort to protect me. A lot of good it did. I was raped by two men, *Mother*. Are you hearing me?" Hannah starts to cry, and I hug her. "Two men!"

"Hang up," I murmur against her hair.

"No."

I growl, but she pulls away from me and swipes at her tears.

"What are you talking about, Han?" Baylee asks, her voice a mere whisper.

"When you were in Italy, I was drugged, dragged away to some stranger's house, and they fucked me, *Mother*. They forced me and I couldn't do a damn thing about it because I was paralyzed against their attack. Maybe if you'd told me how *you'd* been kidnapped and raped, *I'd* have known what to do!" she screams, fat tears rolling down her cheeks. "You did this to me!"

Baylee starts to sob on the other end. "Where are you?

Who are these men who hurt you?"

"Julian and Hunter," she laughs, the sound sinister and harsh.

"Why didn't you go to the police?" Baylee demands. "Why didn't you tell us?"

"Because *he* saved me."

"Who?"

"Hades."

The line goes dead silent for a beat. And then, "Who is Hades?"

"He slaughtered those bastards and carried me out of that hell. He nursed me and loved me. He told me stories, *Mother*. Stories about my grandparents. Stories about *you*."

"No," I hiss and grab for the phone, but she wriggles away.

"No," Baylee's voice echoes mine.

"And then he made love to me, *Mother*. He showed me what true love is—love you threw away because you chose your captor over him! He's mine now, and I love him!"

"Hannah!" Both Baylee and I shout at the same time.

We wrestle for the phone, and I finally wrench it from her hand. I snag both of Hannah's wrists in my grip while she hisses and curses at me. Yanking her onto the console beside me, I hold her against me while I greet her mom. She squirms but isn't going anywhere.

"Miss me, sweetheart?" I growl into the phone. "And don't you worry your pretty little heart out. She's safe with me."

"YOU MOTHERFUCKING UNDYING MONSTER! I SWEAR IF YOU TOUCH MY DAUGHTER I WILL CAS-TRATE YOU AND—"

I hang up before she can finish the sentence. "Get your ass over there." Hannah tenses and lets out a gasp when I release her. "Don't speak. Don't move. Don't goddamned do a thing but sit there and think about the fucking mess you've made."

As soon as she scrambles into the seat, I climb out of the car and slam my phone into the concrete. I stomp on it several times until it's crushed and dead. I don't get to look at any pictures of Brie or *any-fucking-thing* because I don't need them tracking us here. I'll have to find a way to see Brie once I figure out what the fuck I'm going to do.

I climb back into the car and peel out of the parking lot. We're silent as I drive through and get some burgers from a fast food joint on our way home.

My heart is full with this girl. Fuller than it ever has been before. I love her.

But she's making me fucking crazy.

It's time to domesticate my wild animal.

I'm going to have to tie her ass up and teach her how to behave.

We're too far into this for either of us to back out now…

XIV | Hannah

H E REFUSED TO UTTER A WORD THE WHOLE WAY HOME. And the moment we pulled into the garage, he put on some running clothes and ran far, far away from me. I cried the whole time. I'd cut open Alejandra's throat *for us*. So she wouldn't try and steal him from me. So she wouldn't call me a slut like Mrs. Collins did. I did it *for us*.

But I suppose it ruined things.

Now he's wanted for a murder *I* committed.

And now, because I just couldn't help but taunt my mother, my parents know I'm with Gabe. I don't even want to begin to think what sort of means Dad will go through to get me back. As far as I know, he's probably already hacked into every surveillance camera in the US looking for footage of me to see where I'd gone off to.

Dad *will* find me.

Shit!

I chew off my fingernails as I wait for Gabe to return. It's growing dark, and I miss him. I want to throw myself at his feet and beg for forgiveness. I want to formulate a plan for us to become new people so we can hide away from those who hunt us.

He needs to come back home.

I need him.

Need. Him.

I fucking need him!

I find some Windex and set to cleaning every window and mirror in the house to distract myself from the terrors plaguing my mind. Once I've done that, I clean the toilets. Vacuum. Sweep. Scrub the shower. Then I count my pills. I obsess over how many I have left and what happens when I run out.

Will Gabe grow tired of me?

Am I too crazy for him?

Was I a fun fuck and now I'm simply a psycho, murdering thorn in his side?

I'm pacing the living room ripping at my hair when the back door opens up. When I drag my gaze over to him, he ensnares me with an evil glare.

A look that says, *I'm going to devour you.*

I flash him a wide, relieved grin. I *need* him to devour me—to promise me it'll all be okay. To comfort me. To erase this anxiety that's turning the inside of my head blacker than black.

My smile seems to infuriate him further, though. When I reach for him, he hisses at me.

"No."

His one word sends ice through me, chilling every vein in my body.

"What do you mean, *no*?"

He stalks over to me and snatches my wrist. It's painful and possessive. The way his thumb digs into my flesh sends relief fluttering through me. "I mean," he growls, "play time is over. Enough with this bullshit. It's time for your punishment."

Punishment last time was intense pleasure. He whipped my ass but made me come harder than ever before. His punishments don't seem like punishment at all. They seem like rewards. I'm confused because he doesn't look happy. He looks pissed.

"Okay," I tell him and then bite on my bottom lip.

He drags me into the bedroom. As soon as we're inside, he grabs up the rope he'd used before and binds my wrists together. Then, he once again uses a longer rope to tie it to the headboard. There's enough slack that I can easily stand beside the bed.

"What now?"

He tugs off his soaked T-shirt and tosses it to the floor. "You can wait there until I decide what I'm going to do with you."

"Are you mad at me?"

His jaw clenches and his eyes cloud over with darkness. "No, sweet girl, I'm not mad at you." He stalks toward me. His fingers dig into my hip as he draws me to him. I part my lips open when he lowers his face to mine. *Kiss me, Hades.* "I'm fucking furious."

Instead of kissing me like I'd wanted, he releases me and storms off into the bathroom. Anger surges through me. He can't just tie me up like some wild animal. I yank and pull at my bound wrists in an effort to loosen them. He's a pro, though. I'm not going anywhere. After several minutes of cussing and screaming, all of which he can't hear while in the shower anyway, I give up and sit on the edge of the bed.

My mind flits to Calder and Ren. I wonder if they miss me. Do they even notice I'm gone? Is it a relief not having their crazy sister there, fucking shit up as usual? Ren's probably free to have an actual girlfriend now. Without me there to terrorize her and sabotage their relationship. He's probably happy. Probably having sex with her as I sit here bound and helpless. She's probably a teenage whore. Just like that last girl he dated, Sidney. Sidney was perfect with her soft brown hair and bright green eyes. He doted on her. Treated her like she was the damn queen of the world. Ren stopped hanging out with me, his sister and best friend, so he could make out with the bitch. It pissed me off.

But I got rid of Sidney.

One day when she and Ren were out swimming, I snooped in her phone. Found all of these naked pictures she'd sent to Ren. So, I forwarded them to all of the male-sounding names in her contacts on her phone, along with some special messages to each of them, even making sure to add the stupid little tag she always puts when she texts.

Want to hang out later? xoxo Sid
My boyfriend doesn't kiss like you do. xoxo Sid
I'm horny. xoxo Sid
You're hot. xoxo Sid
I wish it were you instead of him. xoxo Sid

Including Calder. Calder, being the noble brother he is, later showed Ren the text Sidney had sent. *I wish it were you instead of him.*

I'd planned on drugging her and making a really racy video I could put on Youtube, but it never came to that. My brother broke up with her. She denied the claims and said her phone was hacked, but many of their mutual friends at school also confirmed receiving the text from Little Miss Innocent. Her reputation was ruined. And I had my brother back.

But now that I'm gone, is Ren glad?

Did he find another "good" girl?

Does he fuck her on my bed?

My fists ball up and my entire body trembles with fury. I've always been jealous of girls talking to my brothers, especially Ren. I don't know what I'll do if they ever get a wife.

Maybe she'll meet the same fate as Big Tits Alejandra…

"Have you had enough time to think about what you did wrong?" Gabe's deep voice drags me from my angry thoughts and into the present.

Jerking my head over to his voice, I find him standing in the doorway completely naked and drying his hair with a towel. He's no longer pulsating with rage. Instead, he seems amused now. One of his dark eyebrows is quirked up in question. A small smile tugs at one corner of his lips.

I want him to lie down on this bed so I can sit on his face.

I want to feel the way his recently thinned out beard feels against my inner thighs.

To have his tongue taste a part of me no other man but him has tasted.

I'm his and he is mine.

"Untie me. Let me touch you," I plead.

He chuckles, but it's not humorous. It's sinister. Dark. Deadly. It turns me right the fuck on. "Nope. We're only getting started, sweet girl."

Defeated, I hunch my shoulders and tear my gaze from his body that I'm positive was sculpted by gods with super powers. "I didn't mean to make a mess of things."

He finds a pair of sweatpants in a drawer and drags them up his muscular thighs, denying me the view of his nice cock. Then, he pulls on a shirt and some shoes. I guess we're not going to have makeup sex.

"You didn't mean to. But you did. Now, we can't enjoy our time here as a couple. Now, I have to make plans. I have to be vigilant. I have to keep a motherfucking eye over my shoulder twenty-four-seven," he seethes. "Not to mention, you murdered the mother of my only child and left her to find her by herself. No child should ever have to see their parent's bloody corpse. I have no idea where they've taken Brie because of you. You. Did. This."

Huffing, I snap my head up to glare at him. "For us!"

He stalks toward me, and I jump to my feet to meet him head on. His fingers thread in my hair, yanking my head back to look up at him. "You're out of control, Hannah. It's time you calm your ass down."

Sneering, I bare my teeth at him. "Good luck trying to control me. My parents and doctors couldn't. What makes you think you can?"

With a hard shove, he pushes me onto the bed. Before I can kick him, he anticipates my go-to move and grabs both shins immediately. "I can and I will. I'm going to run into town to buy a few supplies to break you in."

At this, I burst into tears. My blurry gaze finds his as my lip trembles. "Please don't leave me again."

He scowls and rests a knee on the bed between my spread thighs. The heat makes me rub my leg against his to seek relief and comfort. Then, he lowers himself over me to get close to my face. "You don't care anything about me breaking you in, do you? I could beat your ass until it killed you and you still wouldn't give a shit. No, you're afraid of something else entirely. You're afraid of being left alone. Afraid I won't talk to you. You're afraid of losing me." His eyes grow distant as he mulls this over. "Very interesting. Looks like we'll have to try something different."

"Don't leave me," I beg.

He grazes his lips across mine but doesn't kiss me. "That's exactly what I'll do."

Before I can plead my case any more, he jerks away from me and exits the room. I scream and cry for him. He's still in the house. I know because I can hear him rooting around in the kitchen. Finally, he comes back.

Holding a roll of duct tape.

"No," I sob. "I'll die. What if I hyperventilate and die?" My tears are coming out as steady streams now. With every ragged breath I take, my entire body quivers. "I'm scared."

Riiiip!

The tear of a strip of duct tape makes the same sound of my heart ripping from my chest. He's found a way to hurt me and it works. It hurts. So fucking bad.

"I won't forgive you for this," I murmur.

Our eyes meet and uncertainty flickers in his. But in the end, he wrestles me down and slaps the tape over my mouth. "Yes you will, baby. I need to do this."

If my eyes would do as I command them to, I'd scorch him with my fiery rage. Burn his body to the ground where he stands.

But then you'd be alone. Without him.

Tears spill over. Snot runs down the strip of tape. My heart ceases to beat.

"You're going to be okay. I'll be back. When you're fucking losing your shit, remember I'm doing this for you. For us. Just like you did what you did to Alejandra. For us. Sometimes we have to hurt the one we love in order to keep them," he says softly. His hand reaches out and he strokes my cheek. I lean in to his touch. "Sometimes we have to hurt them so they don't hurt themselves much worse. I'm doing this for us, sweet girl."

My entire world goes black with loneliness when he steps away. His footsteps thunder through the house until the door slams shut.

I'm alone.

All alone.

This is going to kill me.

"Wake up, beautiful. I brought you a present."

I stir from my fetal position on the bed to find Gabe stroking the hair out of my eyes. It's dark in the bedroom and the light from the bathroom illuminates his face in an eerie way. He leans forward and kisses my forehead. I need his mouth on mine. I need him to free me so he can make love to me. I need to touch him back.

His fingers grab the edge of the tape. With one quick yank, he rips it away along with probably a layer of my skin. I cry out, but he soothes me with his mouth on mine. He kisses me tentatively, but I try to maul him despite my bound position. My body seeks his desperately. I attempt to wrap my legs around his hips, but he stops me with his words.

151

"Don't you want to see your present first?"

I let out a whine. "No, I need you inside of me."

His growl makes my entire body quiver with need. "Later. First, I want to show you something."

He leaves me alone on the bed. Soon, I'm blinded by the overhead light. Squinting, I sit up on the bed to look for him. What I see at the end of the bed infuriates me.

"Her name is Maria."

Maria, an olive-skinned woman, stares at me with wide, bloodshot eyes. Her mouth is covered in duct tape and she's bound to one of the kitchen chairs. She looks terrified. Her brown eyes plead with me? Sympathize with me? Worry for me or with me, I'm not sure. All I'm sure about is the fact she's naked. Her big tits jiggle with each movement and her bushy cunt sits wide open by the way she's bound to the chair.

With a growl of my own, I snap my gaze to Gabe and spit out my words. "Why is there a naked woman in our bedroom?"

He arches a brow and shrugs. "She's your punishment."

"Did you fuck her?" I seethe.

His lips press together in a firm line. He shakes his head. "Not yet."

Animal. He thinks I'm a wild animal? He'll learn this when I escape and tear his eyeballs right from his skull!

"You cheating asshole! I will kill you for this!" I scream at him, sliding off the bed so I can stand. "I'll cut your cock off and feed it to the vultures!"

He smirks. Stupid man.

"So jealous," he tsks. "Are you jealous of every woman or just the ones in my life?"

I think about Ren and all the girls who talk to him. How I

hate them all. I think about when other girls would talk to Mr. Collins, and I wanted to choke them. I think about how Dad fawns all over my mother like she's the queen of England. But mostly, I think of Gabe touching Maria's hairy cunt with his perfect fingers—fingers that were meant for me and me only.

"I'm not jealous," I lie, my eyes cutting over to the woman, who now seems even more terrified. "Especially not of her. Is she a whore?"

Gabe laughs. "Not a whore. Just a lady who worked at the grocery store. A lady who couldn't say no to the proposition of sex with a man like me."

Hissing at her, I struggle at my bindings. "He's mine! How dare you?!"

Tears stream down her face and she shakes her head as if to argue his words. Gabe doesn't lie to me. The bitch wanted him. Wanted to sink her hairy pussy on his thick cock.

I want to hurt her.

To cut her throat like I did to Alejandra.

"I need to pee," I lie. Technically, I do have to pee, but I want him to cut me loose so I can get to her.

"I bet you do."

He saunters over to me, no longer wearing shoes or a shirt, and unties the part that's hooked onto the headboard. His grip is tight on the rope as he guides me into the bathroom. Since I'm bound, he has to slide my panties down my legs.

After I pee, he wipes my pussy for me but doesn't put my panties back on. I hope he compares our pussies and realizes mine is a thousand times better.

"Why are you so mad, sweet girl?" he taunts. "You're going to have to control your jealous impulses. You can't kill

153

every woman I pass on the street because you don't like the way she looks at me. We'd both end up in prison before the end of the week."

"You're mine," I snap. "She thinks she can come in here after minutes of knowing you and take you away from me. I hate her."

He pushes me against the bathroom wall with his hands on my hips. His lips descend upon mine in a soft kiss. I groan against his mouth and hike my leg around his hip.

"Make love to me, please."

"Not yet," he murmurs, his fingers fluttering over my rib cage toward my breasts. "Soon, baby."

I relax in his arms. "I don't want her here."

"I know. But you need to learn to deal with her presence without wanting to kill her. Prove to me you can go three days without cutting her throat, and things can go back to the way they were. I can trust you again."

The very idea of keeping her for three days makes me want to rip my hair out strand by strand. Instead, I nod. "Fine."

His hand slips around to my front and finds its way under my dress. He massages my clit in an almost reverent way that has me shuddering with excitement.

"See what good girls get?" he coos, his teeth nipping at my bottom lip. "Treats. Good girls get treats and rewards."

I moan and nod. "I'll be so good. I swear it."

His fingers make quick work, bringing me to orgasm in record speed. My pussy drips with the need to have him inside of me. Just when I think he's about to fuck me against the wall, he pulls away. "If you're good tonight, I'll untie you in the morning."

Ignoring his statement, I pout. "Why won't you fuck me, Gabe?"

His eyes darken as his gaze slides over my lips to my throat. "You have to work up to that reward."

With tears in my eyes, I nod. "I'm sorry."

"I'm sorry too, sweet girl. Just be good and we'll work through this. Then we can both have what we so desperately want. Each other."

XV | Gabe

W E SOMEHOW MADE IT THROUGH THE NIGHT. I SLEPT with my sweet girl in my arms and managed not to fuck her, despite every cell in both of our bodies begging me to. The bitch from the grocery store kept whimpering. It wasn't until I knocked her ass out I was able to sleep.

Hannah's still asleep but I promised her if she were good, I'd reward her. Carefully, I untie her wrists and set her free. I hope she doesn't disappoint me. She'd slept in her dress from yesterday since she was tied up, but now I want it gone. It'll be tempting not to fuck her once she's naked, but I'll have to refrain.

"Sweet girl," I murmur against her ear. "Wake up."

She moans, a sound so sweet and pure it wakes my dick up. I push her dress up her hips so I can see her pussy in the morning light. I'm desperate to taste her this morning. As I crawl between her legs, spreading her apart for me, I make the mistake of glancing at my captive. Her eyes are wide and repulsed by what I'm doing. But five bucks says when I finish, she'll be greedy for my tongue too.

Bringing my lips down between Hannah's thighs, I inhale her unique scent. I love the way she smells and tastes. So fucking delicious. Without further hesitation, I dive into my sexy breakfast. I nip and suck and taste every part of her that I know comes alive only for me. Hannah no longer sleeps, but instead bucks and moans on the bed. Her fingers, now very free fingers, rip at my hair to both beg me to stop and beg me not to all in one motion. I devour her until her sweet pussy soaks my chin with her orgasm. I don't stop my assault until she's relaxed and shivering on the bed.

When I lift up, our eyes meet and love shines in hers so brightly I wonder if it'll blind me. I love the adoration and dedication to me. It's addicting. Fucking perfect. She just needs to learn to control herself.

As she comes down from her high, her smile is wiped off her face when she sees Maria. I watch as her soft blue eyes blaze with rage, her entire body tensing with fury. Her little monster is jealous as fuck, and we need to deal with it.

"Sweet girl," I warn and slap her wet cunt with my hand. "Calm the fuck down."

Her wild eyes meet mine. "She watched us. That whore watched us."

Smirking, I push my finger inside of my woman. "Do you think it turned her on? Do you think our prisoner likes watching us?"

Hannah drags her gaze back over to the woman. "She better not have enjoyed it."

"But what if she did?"

She clenches her fists, and I swear she's seconds away from attacking the woman. But with incredible self-control, she relaxes. "I would want to punish her."

Good girl.

No psychotic rages or tantrums.

No fucking meltdowns.

She's using her words.

"I would want to punish her too," I agree with a smile. "Prisoners aren't supposed to enjoy what we did. They're supposed to hate us."

Hannah sits up on her elbows. "How would you punish her?"

"How would you punish her?" I counter.

Her eyes flit over to the bedside where I left my knife. For a brief moment, I worry I'll have to tackle her on the bed to keep her from cutting the hostage. Then, she gives me a sweet smile. "I'd whip her with your belt."

Grinning, I push deeper into her pussy with my finger before pulling all the way out. "Good answer, sweet girl." I suck on my finger and meet her eyes. "And how would we know if she got turned on or not?"

The woman whimpers from behind me.

Hannah's eyes widen, a wicked grin forming on her lips. "We see if she's wet."

"I guess I'll have to see—"

"No," she snaps, grabbing my wrist. "Don't touch her dirty pussy. I'll check."

I lift my brows in surprise as she crawls off the bed, bypassing the knife to make her way over to Maria.

"Do you want my man?" she demands.

Maria shakes her head no as tears streak down her cheeks.

"We'll see."

Smirking, I watch as Hannah bends over in front of the

woman. The woman's screams are muffled behind the duct tape as my girl shoves her finger inside of her. She doesn't remove her finger right away. Instead, she slides it in and out of the woman. Hannah's a sly one. She's not merely checking to see if the woman is wet. No, she's trying to make her wet on purpose. With the heel of her hand, she rubs against Maria's clit as she finger fucks her. The woman gasps and squirms. Pure horror lingers in her eyes. But the longer Hannah works her magic, the more the woman relaxes. It isn't until the woman shudders that I know Hannah brought her to orgasm literally single-handedly.

She slips her hand out of the woman and holds the proof in front of me. "She enjoyed it. Now let me whip her ass."

"I want to hear her scream," Hannah says as she drags the leather of my belt over Maria's big ass. "I need to hear her."

Sighing, I grab a handful of the woman's dark hair and yank her head up. "She'll beg us to free her. Say all sorts of shit to fuck with your head. Can you handle that?"

She nods that she understands. The second I rip the tape away, the woman begins her begging.

"P-P-Please l-let me g-g-go!"

Hannah cackles, the sound wicked and not from this world. "You're going to pay for lusting over Hades. He's not yours to look at."

The woman starts to plead again, but Hannah begins whipping her with the belt. Over and over and over again, I stare in wonder as my girl becomes the beast who lives within. Her eyes cloud over with rage. She doesn't stop or slow or hesitate.

She just whips and whips.

The woman screams but eventually passes out from the pain. Hannah just keeps doling out the punishment. The leather has torn the woman's ass up and it bleeds from several lash marks. I figure it'll slow Hannah, but she doesn't stop. Not when I order her to. Not when I shout at her. She only stops when I wrestle the belt from her hands. Even then, she struggles to get at the woman.

"You're done. Good girl," I praise, my mouth against her ear as I hold her tight.

Her body relaxes in my arms. A sob releases from her throat. She cries and cries. Not for the woman on the bed. She cries for us. Me and her. Hades and Persephone.

"Shhh," I murmur. "You were perfect, baby."

She lifts her head and kisses me hard. Our teeth bump together before we find our needy rhythm. Soon, her fingers are clawing at my sweatpants trying to free my cock.

"No," I snap, grabbing her wrist. "You're still being punished."

Apparently, my cock is being punished too. I'm dying to push inside of her slippery cunt and make love to her. But I need to calm her ass down first.

"Please," she begs.

"Soon." It's a motherfucking promise.

"Okay." She concedes easily, which shocks me. "Will you at least shower with me?"

"Not only will I shower with you but I'll also eat your pussy for breakfast, lunch, and dinner. Cheer up, sweet girl."

At this, she beams.

"Did you like the pancakes?" she questions.

She'd gone all out for breakfast. The girl is a great cook. I'll get fat if I'm not careful around her. "It was so good I think I need a nap now."

I must not have slept well because my eyes keep drooping. In fact, I'm really fucking tired.

"Come on," she purrs and helps me to my feet. "Let's get that whore out of our bed so we can lie back down."

The room spins when I stand. I stumble behind her, trying to understand what's going on. Confusion and disorientation cripple me. When we reach the bedroom, she yanks at the woman to push her to the side. Then, she undresses me and helps me lie down on the bed. I'm in and out of consciousness as she unties the woman's hands. Maria is rolled onto the floor with a loud thump. Hannah kneels out of view while she does something to Maria. I go to open my mouth and ask her what, but I pass right the fuck out instead.

"Wakey, wakey sleepyhead."

I crack open an eye to see the most devastatingly beautiful woman straddling my bare chest, naked. Her hair is wild and messy. She's spent some time doing up her makeup because I almost don't recognize her. Her eyes are rimmed in smudgy black liner, she's caked on black mascara, and shadows rim her lids, all of which make her blue eyes pop like two sparkly gems. She's painted her lips a dark shade of pink that makes them look fuller and more suckable.

I need to touch her.

But the moment I reach for her, I realize I'm in a bind. Literally. My sweet girl has bound each of my wrists to the top two corners of the bed and each of my ankles to the opposite end. I'm naked and completely at her mercy. My cock twitches with excitement, but unease trickles through me.

She's unpredictable as fuck.

"God, you look hot," I praise, my eyes once again falling to her pouty lips.

She beams at me, her eyes sparkling with delight. "So do you."

A growl rumbles in my chest. "Untie me, so I can fuck your pretty little cunt, sweet girl."

I can feel how wet her pussy is as she grinds it against my belly. A little lower and I'll make good on my promise.

"I thought I was still being punished," she says thoughtfully, her finger dragging along my chest. When she reaches my nipple, she twists it until I hiss in pain. She lets go and then leans forward to suckle on it.

"I don't give a shit about punishments right now," I mutter. "I just want inside of your hot, tight body."

She squirms above me. Her eyes dance with indecision. I can tell it excites her that I'm at her mercy, but the girl likes getting fucked. She likes it when I hold her down and force my dick into her ass while biting down on her shoulder.

"You left me," she pouts, her teary eyes finding mine. "You left me to find her."

My body stiffens, but I keep her gaze on mine. "Just to bring you closer to me. Just to try and show you you're stronger than your impulses." She tears her eyes from mine to look up at the ceiling. "Baby, look at me."

Her lip wobbles, but she meets my stare with a firm one. "You broke my heart leaving me like that. I'd have rather you'd hurt me physically. But leaving me tied up, that was cruel and torturous, Gabe. Now, I want to punish *you*."

My heart rate skitters to life at her words. "Sweet girl," I warn, my voice low and menacing. "Don't do something you're going to regret afterward."

Blonde eyebrows furrow together as she scowls. "I just want you to know what it feels like." Her voice is a fucking scary hiss. "I want you to feel the way you sliced my heart."

"I'm sorry," I whisper. "I didn't realize how fragile you were."

Her face falls for a moment. I think she might give in and untie me. Instead, she lifts her chin and meets my stare with a brave one of her own.

"I'm not just fragile. I was broken since the day I was born. You can't destroy what's already smashed and fragmented. All I've been searching for, my entire life, was someone to hold all the pieces together. Even if they had to bleed a little in the process. I thought you were that person, Gabe."

"I. Am. That. Person."

Unconvinced, she slides off of me, leaving a wet trail from her pussy in her wake. I want to hold her down on this bed so I can worship every inch of her flesh with my lips.

"I drugged you," she says as she reaches for the knife on the table. "Smashed those sleeping pills you keep in the cabinet to bits. I put them in your orange juice. Don't worry. I only put enough in there to knock you out, not kill you."

"I'm awake now, Hannah. Let me go so I can apologize

properly."

She sits beside me and drags the tip of the knife down the middle of my chest. A scraping sound can be heard, along with my ragged breathing, as she trails it along the lines of my defined stomach toward my cock.

I need to distract her.

"Baby…"

"What did you do to my mother?"

Both of my brows fly to my hairline in shock. Now is definitely not the time to talk about this. "I don't know what you mean."

She pokes the flesh of my stomach, just hard enough for a bead of blood to surround the tip of the knife. "I mean, you gave me the general gist. You raped her. The girl you loved so much. But I want details."

"Untie me and I'll tell you," I vow.

Her brows scrunch together as she contemplates my words. "Tell me and I'll untie you."

A motherfucking impasse.

"Hannah…"

"Did you hurt her?"

"Yes."

"Did you fuck her in the ass?"

"Yes."

"Did you tie her up?"

"Yes."

"Did you do that thing to her with your tongue?"

"Hannah—"

"JUST ANSWER THE FUCKING QUESTION!" she shrieks and slices my flesh along my stomach. Our eyes meet, and hers flicker with a mixture of curiosity and horror. She didn't cut me deep, but it's bleeding.

"I did. But I didn't love her like I love you. I didn't realize it back then. Not until I had you in my arms, did I realize what real love is." My words are honest and true, and I hope they fucking work.

She drops the knife back onto the end table and runs her fingertips along the cut on my stomach. Then, she brings her bloody fingers up to her face to inspect them. Her giggle is not cute or adorable—it's fucking wicked.

"Hannah," I growl in warning.

Her eyes flit to mine and she runs her tongue along her finger, tasting my blood. "Not as good as I thought it would taste," she muses aloud. Blood is smeared on her chin. She's wild and untamed. If she'd just fucking cut me loose, I'd bend her back into submission with the tongue she so loves.

"Where's the whore?" I question, distracting her.

She points to the corner. The woman is wriggling in the chair, but a blanket has been placed over her head.

"You got her in there all by yourself, baby?" I smile at her. "You're really good at being bad."

My praise washes over her like a cleansing rain. She flutters her lashes at me before climbing off the bed. Then, she pulls the blanket from the woman. Maria's mouth is still covered with the duct tape, but now tiny cuts paint her face. Blood trickles from each one. The woman's hair has also been cut crudely from her head. Her once long, almost black hair is gone. Just patches remain.

"She tried to escape," Hannah tells me, a slight waver in her voice.

"Good thing you stopped her, Persephone."

The name causes her to pause and jerk her head toward

me. Hunger flashes in her eyes. Her body lunges onto mine, her lips attacking mine as she tries to swallow me whole. I groan into her mouth and meet her tongue thrust for thrust.

"Get on my cock, good girl. Ride it like you own it because it's yours. Not that whore's or your mother's or Alejandra's. Only yours. Fuck me, baby," I order between our kisses.

She moans in agreement. My eyes roll closed when she sinks her tight heat on my aching dick.

"Such a good girl. God, you're so fucking beautiful. I've never seen someone so goddamned pretty in my entire life. Eyes as blue as the ocean, baby. Tits so perfect I have dreams of coming all over them. I love you, angel."

Her body quivers at my words. My little beast fucks me like the madwoman she is. With every bounce on my eager cock, I get closer and closer to coming inside my girl.

"I love your crazy, fucked up head," I tell her with a grunt. "Even when you do twisted shit like drug me, tie me to the bed, cut me open, and then fuck me. After I spurt every last drop of my orgasm into you, you're going to untie me so I can worship you. Do you understand, sweet girl?"

She whimpers at my words and quickens her pace. Her fingers dig into the flesh on my chest as she fucks me harder. When her pussy clamps down around my throbbing cock, I lose it before I can warn her. Thankfully, she's coming too, and we both cry out in pleasure.

My heat fills her.

Every inch of her.

I mark her as mine because she is. All mine.

Even when she's a crazy bitch.

When we both stop shaking with our explosive orgasms, she climbs off of me all too quickly. I don't like the sudden loss of her.

"I don't want her here," she tells me as she scrambles over to Maria. "I want her gone."

I sigh and shake my head. "Untie me and I'll get rid of her."

"She wants your cock."

"Baby…"

She rips away the duct tape from Maria's bloody face and begins untying her. The woman is shaky. Her terrified eyes meet mine in question.

"Clean his cock off with your mouth, and we'll let you live," Hannah barks at her. "Now!"

The woman nods frantically and scrambles onto the bed. "P-Please don't hurt me. I'll do as you say. L-Let me go, and I won't say a word. I promise."

Hannah smiles sweetly at her. An angel's smile with devilish intent. "I promise."

Gritting my teeth, I bite back words that will interrupt Hannah's plan. She wants to do this, so I'll fucking let her. It won't end well, but it's not like I expected otherwise when I lured Maria into my car.

"Suck it off of him."

My eyes lock with Hannah's as Maria grabs on to my cock. The touch makes it twitch back to life. I harden in her hands but don't lose eye contact with my girl.

"She makes you hard," Hannah seethes.

"No, you make me hard, baby," I counter. "*Your* dick sucking lips are what's making me hard. I want *your* lips on my dick, not hers."

She seems satisfied with my answer and climbs onto the bed. I groan when she reaches for the knife and then straddles my face, so she can face Maria. I'm blinded the moment she rubs the lips of her still dripping cunt on my mouth. Knowing what she wants, I lap at her pussy lips and tease her clit while I bury my nose between her ass cheeks.

Maria continues to suck our juices from my cock. I'm fully erect now and wonder how pissed Hannah will be if I shoot cum all over Maria's bloody face.

"Oh, yessss," Hannah purrs and rocks against my tongue. "More, Hades."

"Please, he's clean. Let me go," Maria begs. Stupid fucking woman.

"You're not done yet, whore!" Hannah's voice is a snarl as she leans forward toward Maria. "Take him down your throat!"

My eyes close when the tip of my cock slides down Maria's throat. I bite at Hannah's clit, which seems to drive her wild. She's grinding on my face while Maria deep throats my dick. This is hot as fuck. I'm going to come again.

"Fuck!" I hiss. "Fuck!"

Maria gags and Hannah screeches. "Stay!"

My dick is all the way down Maria's throat. Hannah keeps Maria's face pressed down against me, forcing her to stay there. Our hostage struggles and gags and a gush of hot liquid tells me she vomits too.

And my sick fuck ass comes so fiercely that I nearly black out.

"FUCK!" I roar against Hannah's cunt. I suck on her clit so hard, she screams loud enough to wake the dead.

More heat gushes around my dick as I drain the last of my seed into the mutilated woman's throat with the girl of my dreams quivering with pleasure on my face.

When the room grows silent, Hannah climbs off of me.

Maria's fucking dead as a doorknob.

Her vomit and blood soak my thighs and dick. The knife Hannah had sticks out from the side of Maria's neck, just below where my cock was only moments before. I snap my gaze to see Hannah smiling serenely. She yanks the knife from the dead woman's neck and turns her attention to me.

"Now, let's get you taken care of."

XVI | Hannah

"**A**M I TOO MUCH FOR YOU?" I QUESTION, WORRY tainting my words.

He reaches for me and pulls me into his arms, my back to his front, disrupting the calm water around us. Hot breath tickles my neck as he whispers his reply. "Not enough. Never enough. I'll always want every single part of you."

My eyes close and I lean my head back. His palms circle to my front so he can pinch my nipples. After a late evening of digging a grave and cleaning the big mess I made in the bedroom, we'd settled for a midnight skinny dip in the pool. Gabe didn't freak out or try to subdue me the moment I cut him free. Instead, he'd hugged me to him and whispered how perfect I was. How much he loved and adored me. How much he wanted to apologize.

I've been glued to him ever since.

Most of what happened with Maria is a fog. I don't want to think about it. I just want to forget it happened. To move on with my lover.

"Get on my cock, sweet girl," he murmurs against my earlobe, his dick nudging me between the cheeks of my ass.

I lift on my toes in the water. The tip of his cock pokes at my entrance making it easy to slide down over him. From this angle and behind me, he pushes against my g-spot in a way that makes me see stars without him even having to move.

"Mmm," I gasp.

He pinches my nipple with one hand and teases my clit with the other. "Mmm is right, baby. Fucking delicious with you on my cock."

I cry out when he begins to thrust against me. Each time, a pleasure-filled zing courses through me. It only takes a few pounds into me before I come with a shriek. Moments later, his heat fills me. He kisses the side of my neck but doesn't release me.

"What were you going to go to college for? Before…me." His words sound sad.

"I don't know. I figured maybe business so I could help Dad with his company. I'd not really considered it much," I tell him. Much to my mother's horror, I couldn't make a decision. Nothing interested or excited me. Until now…

He grabs my hips and pulls me off his cock. Then, he twists me so we're facing each other. "Why do I feel like saving you that night ruined your life?"

I frown and run my fingers through his wet hair. "You saved me for forever. I was drifting until I met you."

His eyes search mine for truth. That is the total truth. For once in my life, I feel complete.

"Everything is so fucked up right now," he murmurs, grazing his lips against mine. "But there's no other place I'd rather be."

He devours me with a kiss that steals pieces of my soul. His darkness, altogether different than my Dad's, complements mine. Together, we make twisted sense.

"Do you love me?" he asks.

"You know I do."

His lips trail away from mine, kissing my cheek and jaw until his teeth are nibbling at my ear. "Then do something for me."

"Anything."

"Spend the summer here with me. Together. We'll kiss and fuck and watch movies and swim. Just us." His lips move down to my neck, just below my ear, and he sucks on the skin there. "But then, let's go get my daughter."

I freeze at his words. My palms find his chest, and I push him away. Pain twists his handsome features. Even though he suggested it, he's not demanding it. With his molten chocolate-colored eyes, he's begging. My dark, delicious man is pleading with me.

Could I do that?

Share him with his fifteen-year-old daughter?

Would she hate me for what I'd done to Alejandra?

"I don't know…"

His jaw clenches and he gives me a clipped nod before tugging from my grasp. I watch, with my heart in my throat, as his naked form climbs out of the pool. He dries off quickly and then ties the towel around his waist.

"When people are in a relationship, they give and take. It has to be a team effort to make it work. If I learned anything from living with Alejandra, it was that a marriage could work as long as one of the partners wasn't being selfish. But," he growls, "if one of the partners has no regard to the other's wishes and feelings, resentment begins to form. And with resentment, dislike. Eventually hate." He looks me over with a cold glare. "I really don't want to fucking hate you, baby."

With those words hanging bitterly in the air, he leaves me.

I'm alone under the stars.

Sore from our latest fuck.

Heart aching from our latest mindfuck.

Fragmented and holding the bloody shards of myself in my own hands.

Loneliness is the worst demon lurking in my head. Eventually, that demon will be the one to kill me in the end.

I wade over to the steps and sit on the middle one. Burying my face in my palms, I think about what my life has become. What I've lost and what I've gained. What I could lose. Sobs overtake me, and I let my mind drift to other times I've been selfish. Times it didn't do anything but cause me heartache and pain.

"Your dad's so cool," Missy tells Brandi. "I can't believe he got us a hotel room for your birthday."

Brandi laughs as she turns off the lamp. "Not that cool. He's in the other room and won't let us lock the door."

A shiver quivers through me. "He's just keeping us safe."

My bed partner, Lana, has already passed out. She's the only girl on our softball team who can fall asleep anywhere. Coach has even yelled at her for napping in the dugout a time or two.

I stare up at the ceiling in the darkness. Brandi's dad, Coach Phil, may be cool but his new girlfriend, Stephanie, is not. She's much younger than him and walks around with her nose in the air as if she's too good for him. Truth is, he's too good for her.

After an hour or so of listening to the sound of my three favorite teammate's snores, I slip out of bed. I want to go watch Phil while he sleeps. At our games, he's always mad and his face is bright red as he barks out orders. When he's not at the games, he's more relaxed and even playful. I love him when he's playful. Sometimes I think he's even flirting with me.

Not that a man like him would be interested in a fifteen-year-old girl...but I still like to dream about it.

I've spent the night at Brandi's plenty of times and know Phil is cute when he sleeps. His full lips part as he sleeps with an arm slung over his eyes. Phil isn't one of those big muscle dudes, nor is he really hot. He's handsome in his own way. Fun smile, bright green eyes, messy hair. I love how tall he is. How he towers over me.

Sneaking into his bedroom is easy. The girls never wake. I pad over to his bedside and ignore dumb Stephanie, sleeping with her back turned to him. If I slept in his bed, I'd always cuddle with him.

The pale moonlight shines in through the window casting a glow on his sleeping face. My fingers beg to touch him. He hugs us all the time and pats us on the back when we make a good play, but we never really get to touch him.

I trace my fingertips over his lips and let out a slight sigh before dropping my hand. I'm about to go back to bed when his eyes flutter open. Confusion furrows his brows together before he expresses concern and sits up.

"Everything okay, Han?" he whispers.

Seeing his gaze on me, I want more. I shake my head. He slides out of bed, wearing nothing but a loose pair of boxers. When he goes to search for some clothes, I whimper. The sound has him glancing at the bed before gently grabbing my shoulders. He guides me into the bathroom. The light blinds us both.

"What's wrong?" he questions as he closes the door.

My eyes greedily devour his hairy chest. I never knew he had a tattoo. He's not trim or fit, but I don't care. I like his body. My gaze falls to his boxers. I've watched enough porn late at night on my computer to know he doesn't have a boner. But his penis seems big anyway because he bulges from his boxers. I wonder what happens when he gets hard.

"I think I pulled a muscle," I tell him with a whine, loving the way his concerned eyes wash over me.

"Your bicep from throwing? Do I need to rub some cream on it?"

"Actually," I tell him, biting my bottom lip. "It's on my thigh." I hoist my leg on the countertop and then lift my gown to show him. My eyes remain on his as I brush my fingers along my inner thigh. When the tip of my finger grazes my panties, I jolt with excitement. His worried expression darkens.

"Hannah, perhaps you should go to bed. We can see if it's better in the morning."

I massage the area in question and summon tears. "B-but it hurts now." My chin quivers and a tear snakes out.

He rakes a hand through his hair in frustration but his eyes remain glued to my thigh as if he's attempting to figure out what to do about it. A shiver of delight ripples through me when he takes a step forward.

"Let's see," he murmurs and kneels before me so he's eye level with the area in question.

A gasp escapes me when his strong fingers touch the flesh there. If only he'd move them a little in the opposite direction. Would he make me cry out like those women in the porn movies?

"Right there," I tell him.

His fingers deftly work the muscle and his brows remain furrowed in concentration. I sneak a peek and can't help but be excited to see his erection tenting his boxer shorts. He's turned on by rubbing my thigh. I'm turned on too.

"Does that feel any better?" *His voice is tight and strained.*

I grab hold of his shoulders to steady myself. "A little."

He lets out a sigh of relief when I drop my foot back to the floor. When he goes to stand, I grip his shoulders. Our eyes meet for a brief moment. With my toes, I touch his hardness through his boxers. A hiss rushes from him, and his eyes snap shut. He lets me rub on him with my foot for a few long seconds before he stands abruptly.

"No, Hannah." *His green eyes blaze with fury.* "You shouldn't have done that."

With his entire height above me, I cower away from him. On the softball field, he can be quite intimidating. But like this? He's terrifying.

"I'm sorry," *I whisper.*

His eyes skim over my body before he clenches his teeth and points a long finger at me. "This never happened."

My lip wobbles and I nod.

"You speak one word of this to anyone and you'll be off the team so fast you won't even know what happened. People won't believe you, Hannah."

Our moment was there, we both felt it. He was hard beneath my touch. His groans and breathing told me he enjoyed it. I want it again.

"Phil," I murmur and selfishly reach out to touch him. "I want you."

He huffs and takes a step toward me, snatching my wrist. Then, he leans forward, so close I think he might kiss me, but utters his hateful words. "You're a child. I don't want you. Now go to bed and remember my warning."

The bathroom door creaks open and my eyes meet the surprised ones of Stephanie. Her nose isn't in the air. No, her nostrils flare with anger. Tears well in my eyes as I fear a lashing from her too. But she shocks me when she pushes inside and digs her claws into Phil's bicep.

"What are you doing?" she demands. "Why are you half naked in here with a little girl?"

I'm not a little girl.

"You don't know what you're talking about," he replies with a grumble. "She had a bad dream and I was comforting her."

Stephanie shoots him a scathing glare. "Out. I'll comfort her."

His shoulders hunch as he goes to leave, but not before sending me another look of warning. Once he's gone, she wraps me up in a hug. I need a hug after the rejection I just suffered.

"Did he...oh my God..." She trails off. "Did your coach, um, touch you?"

He touched my thigh. I touched his penis.

"No."

"Oh sweetie, thank goodness. It looked much worse, I suppose, from my end," she says, her voice coming out in a relieved rush.

"I still feel terrible," I admit. "My, uh, dream was a nightmare. In my dream, someone hurt me." But my dream was re-

ality. Phil hurt me in reality.

"Listen, honey," *she whispers and hugs me again.* "You're awake now. And if you ever need anything, you come to me. Not Phil. The way he was in here with you in nothing but his underwear and touching you, that was inappropriate. I hate to think of what it could have escalated to had I not come inside."

I could tell her the truth. Bask in her comfort. Revel in the way she soothes my heart that still stings. But I don't.

Because I'm selfish.

If I tell what happened, not only will Phil try and kick me off the team, but he may also get in serious trouble. Then, they'll take him to jail or make him stop coaching. I wouldn't be able to see him again. I wouldn't know if we could have ever had another chance like tonight in the bathroom.

Because I'm selfish, I lie.

"Coach is a good man," *I tell her firmly.* "He would never take advantage of a little girl." *The words taste like venom on my tongue, but I say them anyway.* "Plus he's an old man. Ew."

She laughs, and I let out a crazed giggle of my own.

"I like you, Hannah."

"I like you too, Stephanie."

My thoughts vanish into the air the moment I hear a slam from inside the house. Gabe's form paces around the kitchen as he searches for something. Gabe would have liked Stephanie I think. She was a bad girl too. I still remember the scandal of her ending up pregnant by Phil's younger brother. It put our coach in such a pissy mood for an entire season. Wasn't until he held his "nephew" for the first time that he began to thaw. He never made eye contact with me again, though. And the only time he remotely smiled at me was when Mrs. Collins came onto the field and slapped me.

It was a smug grin.

A smile that said, *I fucking knew you were trouble*.

If only he knew how much trouble I was now…

I climb out of the pool and dry off. Once I make it inside the chilly house, I find Gabe leaned against the counter with a bottle of Jack in his grip.

"You should go to bed," he says, his voice low and gravelly.

I shiver at his words. "I'm not tired."

He tilts his head back and parts open his lips to swallow back a swig of the amber liquid. His Adam's apple bobs with the motion. My mouth waters to lick him there. Once he swallows, he turns his hard gaze on me, snuffing out the heat that was kindling inside me. "Fine. But I'm not in the mood to babysit. Go find something to do. Without me." His words flay me. Cut me right open and make me bleed.

"You're an asshole."

He smirks. It reminds me of the smirk Phil gave me that day. "And?"

With a huff, I storm over to him and steal his bottle. I take a swallow of the nasty stuff. His eyes flicker with irritation when I take another swig. He yanks the bottle from my hands so he can drink.

And so begins the next half hour of our evening.

Angry glares.

One bottle of Jack, quickly emptying.

Two hurt people.

A fire that seems to be building again with every second that passes.

"You look so much like your mother, it's fucking disturbing," he blurts out, his eyes narrowing and falling to my breasts still hidden in my towel. "Your tits are nicer, though. You…not so much."

I flip him off. "I bet you wish she was here, so you could make love to her. Is that why she's so special? You made love to her and told her she was perfect and shit?"

His laugh is more like a loud bark. "She was special because I fucked her just like I fuck you. Hard and without apology. Your mother, unlike you, denied how much she loved it, though. Unfortunately for Baylee, her weepy cunt couldn't lie."

Snarling my lip at him, I shake my head in disgust. "You're a pig."

"And you're a psycho."

When I haul off and kick him, he pounces on me, tearing my towel from my body in one fluid movement before backing me up against the counter.

"Apple doesn't fall far from the tree. I bet your pussy's dripping for me right now, even as I talk to you like you're a piece of shit."

"Maybe my pussy is wet because I'm thinking about stabbing you and burying you with your whore girlfriend, Maria," I seethe.

He chuckles and his eyes light up with amusement. "You're feisty as fuck."

His palm cups my breast. When he dips down to suck my nipple into his mouth, I let my head fall back, enjoying the sensation of his tongue on the sensitive flesh. I latch my fingers into his hair while his kisses my breasts.

"What did you do to my mother that made her hate you so much?" The question always lingers in my mind.

Hot breath tickles my flesh. "It was either the time I fucked her ass with a cucumber shoved up her tight cunt or the time I shot your precious daddy in the chest. I'm really not sure."

His words should disturb me. But you can't disturb the disturbed. A giggle starts in my throat and soon I'm full-bellied laughing with tears rolling down my cheeks. He pulls away with an arched eyebrow and a half-smile on his lips.

"Do I entertain you?" he muses.

I nod and guide his hand between my legs. "You're crazy like me."

"You just now figured this out?"

He slightly sways and I giggle again.

"It explains why she's *'allergic'* to cucumbers," I tell him, a wicked grin on my face.

"I could make *you* develop that '*allergy*' too," he threatens, but it falls flat since he's smiling.

Running my fingertip over his lips, I murmur my naughty words. "You could try."

I officially know what it would feel like to have two men at once. Gabe wasn't gentle or kind or loving as he fucked my ass with a frozen vegetable up my twat. He didn't assure me everything would be okay. He didn't make any sort of empty promise.

He just fucked me until I came so hard I collapsed.

The entire time, I imagined it was Phil's frozen prick inside of me while Gabe drove into my ass. It made for a fantasy that would only ever happen in my dreams. And, oh what beautiful dreams they were.

After we finished and cleaned up, he wouldn't stop laughing at me. I was annoyed, but I couldn't help but be tickled by his boyish amusement.

He said I was too good to be true.

Nothing but his own fantasy come to life.

It was then, in our perfect post sexual haze, that I gave him what he wanted.

"I want you to be happy. When the summer is over, let's go get your girl and bring her home to us."

Once I uttered those words, Gabe flipped me over and made love to me so sweet, it made me cry. With our fingers intertwined while he thrust into me and our eyes connected, he whispered promises I hope he can keep.

About forever.

About family.

Love.

Us.

"This isn't over, baby," he assured me. "It's only just begun."

XVII | Gabe

Three and a half weeks later...

WE'RE OUT.

Been out for five days.

I'm going to kill her.

Stroking her blonde hair while she lies with her head in my lap, I contemplate my next move. There's always online Mexican drug companies. Or, I could get her a fake ID so we could see a doctor. But the testing could take more time than we can afford. I don't need them to waste precious fucking time trying to diagnose my girl. I already know what she needs. She needs the goddamned Clozapine and Celexa or I'm going to choke her to death.

When she's high and happy and in love, the girl fucks like a goddess and we can't get enough of each other. But when she hits her lows, I worry she'll cut my throat in my sleep. She's unpredictable. She's unstable. She's motherfucking insane.

I'm going to have to do something that could really be dangerous to us both.

I'm going to have to go to War.

Sure, the fucker probably wants to put a bullet through my skull—even though I doubt the pansy could stomach it. Hannah's worth whatever shit I have to go through because I need her well and whole again. I was an idiot to ever think she could exist free of medication. I'd had no idea the depth of her mental illness.

"I love this movie," she says softly, her finger drawing hearts on my kneecap. "It's so romantic."

I chuckle and raise an eyebrow. "Dracula is romantic? Or is Luke Evans just sexy? You're kind of hot for villains."

"Villains need love too," she retorts.

That they do.

And in our story, we're both the motherfucking villains.

"Sweet girl?"

"Mmm?"

"I want to take you on a trip. We can go swim at that secluded beach. This time I'll let you fuck me," I say with a smile.

She sits up and flashes me a worried look. Her brows are furled together as she bites on her bottom lip for a hair before speaking. "Why? That's awfully close to home. What if someone recognizes us?"

I run my thumb along her bottom lip. "We'll be fine. San Diego's a big city. Plus, I need to get something for you while we're there."

Her pupils dilate for a moment, anger flickering in her eyes. "What?"

"Your fucking meds."

She scrunches her nose and snarls her lip. "I don't need them. I'm fine, see?" Her slender fingers motion at her face. And today, she is fine. So fucking fine. I wish I had her like this all of the time. It's when she's not fine that's the problem. Her ups and downs are too high and too low. We need to coast in the motherfucking middle.

"I love you," I assure her. "You know this. And that is why I am doing this for you. Trust me, baby."

She straddles my hips and wraps her arms over my shoulders. Her lips are pouting, but her eyes tell me she'll concede. "How do you plan on getting my medication?"

I close my eyes and let out a sigh. "I'm going to have to contact your dad."

"No."

Popping my eyes open, I glare at her. "What do you mean no?"

"You're not going to hurt him."

I cup her cheek and drag my thumb along her full bottom lip. "I swear to you, beautiful, I'm not going to fucking hurt him. He might try and hurt me, but I'm not going to touch a hair on his goddamned head. He can refill your prescription, though, and get it to me until I can secure your new identification and doctor. We have to do this."

She frowns. "Dad might involve the police. What happens if he sets you up? They'll tear us apart. I can't live without you. I'm happy for the first time ever."

"I'll be careful."

"You don't know my dad. He's smart and can hack into any computer network out there. If we weren't out in the middle of nowhere, I have no doubt he would've found me already."

Once upon a time, he evaded me and holed away my Baylee. But I found them. I always do. And they never found me again. I've got this.

"We'll make it work. I promise you."

"Hello?" the deep voice answers.

I lean against the shitty pay phone with my eyes on Hannah. She'd wanted a cherry Icee at the convenience store. Instead of blending in, she's drawing motherfucking attention from every male who walks past her. Her blonde hair blows in the wind while she sucks on the red straw as if it's the most delicious fucking thing she's ever wrapped her lips around. The short dress she's wearing keeps flapping up, and I swear to God, if some asshole approaches my girl, I'll beat the shit out of him in the parking lot.

"War?"

A growl in response. "Gabe?"

"We need to talk," I tell him bluntly. "About Hannah."

"Jesus Christ," he hisses into the phone. "She better be all right."

I can hear tapping on his computer. The motherfucker is probably trying to triangulate my location or some shit. "Stop trying to find us," I tell him. "We're coming to you."

"You're bringing her home?" The surprise is evident in his voice.

"Fuck that. She doesn't want to come home. But we do need something that belongs to her."

He remains silent.

"I need you to refill her prescriptions. Today."

"She's been off them for a few days now," he clips out. "Is she okay? Has she tried to hurt herself?"

I think about Maria's bloody bloated corpse. And that was when she actually was on meds. I don't even want to think about Hannah at her worst.

"She hasn't tried to hurt herself. She's safe and happy. But I'm afraid I can't keep her that way all of the time without them."

He lets out a breath of frustration. "What am I supposed to do? Just hand over my daughter's meds and pray you don't shoot me in the chest again?"

I smirk. "Don't be a pussy. That was nearly two decades ago. You lived. And yes, that's exactly what I want."

"We want to see her. To talk to her."

"Not going to happen."

"Why the hell not?" he demands.

"Because I'm not fucking stupid. You'll try and convince her to come home."

The line goes silent again. "She can't come home."

At this I laugh. "Wow, man, she really was too much for you to handle like she said. Poor girl. I can fucking handle her."

He growls again. "I can handle her just fine. I love my daughter. Problem is," he says lowly. "She's wanted in connection of the murder of Alejandra Cruz-Diaz. Alejandra's husband is wanted as well. Her fingerprints were all over the house and the murder weapon. This is really bad for her."

My eyes flit over to Hannah. She's sitting on the hood of the car, looking like the finest damn hood ornament a man has ever seen. The girl sticks out like a sore thumb. If she's wanted, I need to hide her.

"Okay, so we meet in private. How do I know you're not going to set us up?"

"Because I'll come alone. I can't tell Baylee. She'll flip out and want to bring an army against you. They'll take Hannah away from us," he spits. "Put her in a prison cell where she cannot survive. Or, she'll want to commit her to an institution. We've gone 'round and 'round about it. Hannah needs love. That's what my daughter needs. And I'm supposed to believe you of all people have found a way to reach her? That you have some sort of fucked-up love for her?"

I smile. I do have a fucked-up love for her. "Sounds like you don't have much of a choice in the matter," I tell him, my tone smug. "What about Coronado Beach?"

He curses, and I half expect him to hang up on me.

"Fine," he snaps. "I can get the medications filled this morning and meet this afternoon. I'm going to see her, though. You only get the meds if I can hug my daughter."

Annoyance flits through me, but I concede. He's her father after all. I'd do anything right about now to hug my own daughter. "Deal."

"How do I know you won't grow tired of her? Just like everyone else? Swear to me you'll bring her home before you do anything stupid." His plea is meant to be threatening, but it's filled with devastation.

"I'm not bringing her home and I'm not going to hurt her. But I can give you something in return. For insurance."

"I'm listening."

"Find my daughter. Gabriella Cruz-Diaz. They took her somewhere, and I need to find her. She belongs home with me and Hannah."

He huffs. "And how is this insurance for me?"

"Because if you find her, then I'll let you see your daughter again. And if we need more medication, I'll let you see her again. And if you're a real good boy, War, I may let you see her from time to time. Don't fuck this up."

"I can work with that. See you in a few hours."

The fucker said he'd be alone.

I should have known better.

"Is that Ren with Dad?" Hannah asks, shielding her eyes from the sun.

When we'd gotten to the beach earlier, we'd decided to make a day of it while we waited. I fucked her in the ocean with people swimming around. It was hot and wicked. And my sweet girl didn't care that we had spectators. She just moaned and begged for an orgasm until I silenced her with kisses.

So much for not drawing attention to ourselves.

"I told him to come alone," I mutter with a growl as I stalk over to our bags where my 9 mm hides inside. I towel off and pull my T-shirt back on, never keeping my eyes off the pair.

War is cautious, his eyes searching the crowded beach, and he wanders along hesitantly. His boy Ren wears an angry but determined scowl on his face, clearly the more badass of the two as he follows behind. It isn't until War's gaze finds Hannah, toweling off beside me, that he visibly relaxes.

As soon as he sees her, his eyes dart over to mine. The

unease is wiped right from his face as his brows furl together angrily. He looks like an overprotective bear ready to maul me for even breathing the same air as his daughter. His little cub behind him already has his claws out.

Too bad for the little bears…

Their Goldilocks is the motherfucking dragon.

A fire-breathing, full on psycho, unpredictable beast.

And she just happens to look like a fucking swimsuit model in the process.

"Hannah," War calls out, his eyes back on his daughter.

She lets out a gasp, and much to my dismay, runs for her daddy. Her cute ass jiggles in her tiny swimsuit. My cock jerks in my trunks at the sight.

Her arms sling around her father's neck the moment she nears him, and he pulls her to him in a tight embrace. The boy stands behind them, his menacing glare gone, and I swear the little pussy looks like he might cry.

Trudging through the sand up to them, I lift my chin to acknowledge them. War's gaze flies to mine and his nostrils flare with fury.

"You just don't die, do you?" he snarls, his entire body stiffening. "A damn cockroach."

Hannah jerks away from him. "Dad, be nice."

War's jaw clenches and the boy fists his hands beside him.

"Where are the meds?" I demand, crossing my arms over my still-wet chest. "You aren't reneging are you?"

He snaps his gaze over to his son and shakes his head. "No," he huffs. "They're in the car."

"Han, come home with us," Ren urges, almost inaudibly to her. "It's not too late."

War's features crumple in devastation. "Ren, we talked

about this. She can't come home."

Smirking at them, I grab hold of Hannah's wrist and haul her to me so her back is flush with my chest. Both War and Ren glare at me as I wrap my arms around her bare middle.

"Did you hear that, sweet girl?" I whisper on a hot breath into her ear. "You can't go home. Did you want to go home?"

She shakes her head and turns to look up at me. I plant a wet kiss on her fat lips, just to piss them off.

"Can you please not rub this in our face?" War snaps.

"I love him," Hannah proclaims. "We're not trying to make you mad."

War runs his fingers through his hair and casts a wary glance farther down the beach. "Was it you? Did you kill that woman?"

She freezes in my arms. "What woman?"

"Alejandra Cruz-Diaz."

I watch War as he studies her. His eyes dart all over her face, assessing her well being. He pulls his lips into a disappointed frown. I can see that he doesn't need for her to answer to know the truth. He knows, beyond the shadow of a doubt, his daughter killed my wife. As much as that thought crushes him, he is still protective over her. I hate to admit it, but he's a good father. She deserves a good father.

And now she deserves a man who can carry the torch in his stead.

I'm a good father too.

But I'm a very bad man.

Good thing she's a bad girl too.

"It just…" She trails off, her slight body tensing in my arms. "I don't know what happened, Dad. She would have tried to stop us."

War closes his eyes, and Ren stalks off back to the car. I keep my eyes on the boy, in case he tries to do anything funny.

"Listen to me," War says, his voice deep and broken, as he reaches for her hand. "What you did was horrible. And they want to arrest you as soon as they can find you. But I can't stand to think what would happen to you if you went to prison. They'd hurt you."

He pulls her from my grip, back into his arms.

"I'm sorry, Daddy," she says with a sob, her slender arms tight around his waist. "I didn't mean to."

We all know she meant to. Little lying girl.

"I know," he coos as he strokes her wet hair. "I'm going to do everything to keep you safe. Is he good to you? Now is the time to tell me the truth. People are everywhere. If he hurts you, I'll find a safe place to keep you. I'm dying to send him away to prison where he belongs."

She lifts her head to look up at him. "He understands me. Like you do sometimes. But he understands me all of the time. Plus, he protects me. When you and Mom were in Italy…"

Her body quakes with sadness. I'm tempted to rip her right out of his arms so I can hold her. Instead, I let him have his fucking moment with his daughter.

"Did Mom tell you what those men did to me?"

War lets out a garbled choke and he grips her shoulders to look at her. "She said they assaulted you."

"Sexually," she hisses. "And Gabe saved me. He killed them for hurting me. He's been protecting me ever since. Sometimes even from myself."

At the last bit, War's shoulder's hunch. "I'm so sorry, baby."

With the backs of her hands, she swipes away her tears and slips under my arm, pressing her hot cheek to my chest. "I'm happy now, Dad."

War's gaze meets mine, and he shoves his hand into his pocket. When he pulls out a phone and offers it to me, I shake my head.

"I'm not stupid. You're not going to track us." I laugh at him.

He scowls and thrusts it at me again. "This is so I can warn you if the authorities are onto where she's at. I've hacked into the San Diego PD's network and am following the progress on her case. It's also to inform you of when I locate *your* daughter. And, yes, it's also so I know where the fuck my daughter is in case I need to see her. So take the phone and don't destroy it. You'll get the meds, and we'll both have our insurance."

I snatch the phone from his grip and glare at him. "Find Brie. And so help me, if you screw me over, you'll pay dearly." Baring my teeth at him, I let the threat of my thinly veiled words sink in. For effect, I slip my hand around Hannah's throat and stroke her flesh gently. His eyes flit down for a brief moment before they're back on me.

"I'll find her. And I'm not going to screw you over."

Grinning wolfishly at him, I nod. "You just made yourself a deal with the devil."

XVIII | Hannah

One week later...

"TELL ME A STORY," I MURMUR AS I WIPE THE SLOBBER and leftover cum from my bottom lip. His eyes hold a certain twinkle for the rest of the day when I wake him up with a blow job.

"What kind of story?" he questions.

I crawl my nearly naked body back up the bed and curl against his chest. His fingers thread through my hair, working out the tangles from sleeping.

"A story about my grandparents."

He chuckles. "More about the Viking and his angel?"

"Yeah."

"Tony and I didn't get along too well at first. It was your mother and grandma who took to me in the beginning. I tried with the fucker. Man, how I tried. But every time I thought we were cool, he'd bark out some warning or snide comment. I'd damn near given up on a friendship with the asshole when…"

I lift up to look at his face. The smile falls, and his eyes darken. His features become hard as he remembers.

"What happened?"

"My dad's friends showed up." He sighs and scrubs his face with his palm. "Lance, Gordon, and Jack. They wanted to include me in on a new business venture they were working on."

"That's nice, though, right? You said you'd nearly run out of your money."

A growl rumbles in his chest. "There was still a matter of some assets—a fuckton to be quite frank—that I'd inherited from my father. Accounts that were set up in such a way that I'd only become a trustee upon my producing a child. Bullshit money that I knew I'd never see a dime of. It was money that they knew of nonetheless."

"You have Brie now," I offer.

He laughs. "I also have millions from your father. I don't need that money."

"But you did, Gabe. You needed it back then."

His body tenses beneath me. "That I did."

"So what happened?"

"We were sitting in my living room and I told them I'd have to pass on their offer. They wanted to take their sex trafficking shit to a whole new level. Online forums hidden in the dark web. Places where men could shop for pretty much any type of sex they were into. Old bitches. Fat ladies. Pregnant mothers. Little girls."

I curl up my lip in disgust. "Gross."

"At one time, I might have gone along with their 'gross'

business venture. But I was too damn enthralled by Lynn and her daughter to even care about that shit at the time. I told them as much. They'd probably have left if it weren't for Baylee letting herself in, per usual, and prancing right over to me like she owned the place in her little purple swimsuit begging for me to take her to the pool. I'd seen their hungry gazes all over her. She was a fucking kid, and they licked their old lips like she was on the goddamned menu."

His hand fists my hair but he doesn't pull on it. My panties, the only thing I'm wearing, become wet at his possessive grip on me.

"I told them to leave. I'd made plans with my neighbors and that it was time to go. Gordon just wouldn't stop looking at her with his beady eyes. Asked her if she wanted to come sit on his lap. I wanted to bash his fucking face in."

"Did she?"

"Fuck no!" he roars, a possessive growl rumbling through him. "I kept her in my lap where she belonged. Jack went on and on about how little blondes were a favorite. Could bring in a hefty sum. To reconsider their offer. When I refused and threatened to haul each of their old asses out to their car by the damn throat, the situation escalated."

"Did they hurt her?"

"They fucking tried. Gordon pulled a gun out of his briefcase and pointed it at me. Baylee was too wrapped up in trying to braid my hair with her back to them. She had no fucking clue. Those pricks told me to put her in their car. Like they were going to fucking take her from me."

"Were you scared?"

"I was fucking petrified!"

"Did they get her? Did they take my mom from you?"

He laughs, and the dark, sinful tone cloaks me. "I gave her a little kiss on the head and told her to go play Mario in my bedroom. That I'd be in there shortly—after I dealt with some business with the men. As soon as the bedroom door slammed shut, I rose to my feet. If I had to, I was going to take all three of them out."

The room goes silent. His body visibly shakes with rage.

"The dumbass still had his gun trained on me when the Viking bursts through the front door, a murderous glare on his face. He didn't like his little girl playing alone with me. All it took was one meaningful look at Tony and then flicking my gaze back at Gordon for him to understand the situation. Your grandpa was perceptive. As if on cue, he lunged for Jack while I charged for Gordon. The old fuck never squeezed off a shot. My fist broke his nose upon impact and I wrestled that gun out of his hands. I was beating the fuck out of him when someone got me in a chokehold from behind. Fucking Lance. I'd always sort of looked up to him as a fill-in father figure. Hell, his boy and I even used to be friends for a while there. These friends of my father's were the only fucked-up family I had, and they turned on me. For money. Lance was the trustee on all of those accounts. If something were to happen to me, he'd handle the appropriation of funds at that point. And since I wouldn't let them use my money, they planned to take matters into their own hands."

"Did they overtake you and Grandpa?"

His laugh, this time, is humorous. "A Viking and a monster? Three old men never had a chance. Your father pulled Lance off me and proceeded to beat the fuck out of him. When they were all three moaning and groaning but incapacitated, he helped me load them into their trunk. Stuffed all three fuckers inside."

"My grandpa helped you? Why did he do that? What happened to the men?" I question.

"We retrieved your mother from the bedroom and sent her back next door with her mother. Then, he followed me in his car. I drove and drove upstate until I found a piece of my dad's old property Lance had 'bought' from me. I'm still not sure if I sold it to him for a fair price or not—my guess is the latter. The assholes were screaming and begging from the trunk."

"What did Grandpa say?"

"When we got out, he asked what those men wanted. I told him about the sex trafficking business venture they wanted to start. I also told him how they looked at little Baylee. How they wanted to take and hurt her. His face was bright red with fury, and he nodded. That nod was the beginning of our friendship. He climbed into his car and waited for me. I set a rock on the gas pedal of their car and sent them careening into the secluded lake to drown. We never spoke of it again, but Tony had my back from that day forward. I watched over his daughter and wife, and he looked out for me. He became my best friend. My motherfucking brother."

I slide a leg across his waist and cage in his head with my arms. My long, messy hair hangs down, tickling his face. "I'm glad you killed them."

"Why? Because they were bad men? I'm a bad man too, sweet girl."

I laugh and peck him on his nose. "No, because it made you and my grandpa grow closer. Because it gave you a best friend. My grandpa knew you would take care of his girls."

He becomes quiet and his eyes close. "I still miss that

fucking Viking. And the angel." He lets out a sigh. "And your mother."

I stiffen at his words. "I thought you loved *me*."

"I *do* love you."

"What would you do if you ever saw her again? Would you want her?" I probe, tendrils of jealousy threading their way through me.

"I have you. I don't need Baylee anymore."

"But what if she wanted you. What if she showed up naked right now? Would you fuck her?" My voice quakes and tears well in my eyes.

"Hannah," he growls in warning.

A tear slips out and lands on his forehead. Our eyes meet. His dark gaze penetrates me.

"Would you tie her up and take her ass, like old times?" My voice is cold. "Would you want to hear her scream and beg?"

His cock twitches beneath me.

"No."

Rage surges through me.

"LIAR!" I fist my hands and start hitting his face. "Your cock still wants her!"

Before I can land another punch, his strong fingers are around my throat squeezing. I hiss out, clawing at his fingers for him to release me. He flips me over onto my stomach, pressing my face down into the mattress. I squirm and scream and claw at the bedding.

"My cock wants you, you fucking psycho," he seethes. His other hand rips my panties down my thighs and yanks them away. He shoves his knee between my legs to part me open for him. I let out a furious scream when he slams his hard cock—hard for my mother—into my still wet pussy.

"Stop it! I hate you!"

He grunts and fists my hair, yanking me back. "You love me, you lying bitch!"

A traitorous moan rips from my throat as he pounds into me. "Fuck you!"

His full-bellied laugh sends ripples of pleasure coursing through me. He pounds into me roughly, like the savage he is, until I come around his cock with a wail. No sooner do I drench him with my juices, does he pull out and then slam into my ass.

"Ahhh!" I screech. The sudden intrusion there leaves me breathless, tears pouring down my cheeks. "You're hurting me!"

He groans as he fucks me without slowing. "Good!" he snarls. "You deserve it for being a jealous cunt. You know it's you. It's always fucking you. So get the fuck over it already."

You know it's you.

It's always fucking you.

His words have their intended effect, and I relax. With every thrust that his huge cock fills my ass, I grow closer and closer to another orgasm. This one is an orgasm of the soul. My entire body spasms with pleasure. My only thought on him.

You know it's you.

It's always fucking you.

I moan in relief when his hot seed bursts inside of me. His cock seems to double in size, threatening to rip me in two. "Gabe!"

He hisses out my name as he comes. When his cock stops throbbing, he slips it out of me and crushes me with his body.

I let out a whimper when his mouth finds my neck.

"I love you, sweet girl. Don't you ever fucking forget it. But keep this jealous shit up, and I'll punish you until you can't walk. Is that what you want?"

Shaking my head, I give him the answer he desires. "No."

"Good girl."

You know it's you.

It's always fucking you.

"I just worry someone will take you away from me. I worry I'm not as good as my mother. That you miss her." My honest words cause him to take pause.

"Nobody is ever taking my girl away from me, understand?"

"Okay."

"And I do miss your mother. But that doesn't change how I feel about you. You're my world," he murmurs.

You know it's you.

It's always fucking you.

You're my world.

"Gabe!" I shriek.

He storms into the kitchen, worry painted over his features. "What?"

"The phone is buzzing. It's Dad."

A groan escapes him as he answers. "War."

All irritation leaves his face as he listens. He gives me a quick glance before stalking out the back door. I watch from the window as he paces along the pool. His hand waves in the air as he seems to yell at my dad through the phone.

Are the police coming?

Will they take me away from him?

I'm still frozen in fear of what's to come when Gabe bursts back through the door with the phone outstretched to me. "Here."

Confused, I take the phone and put it to my ear. "Are they coming for me, Daddy?"

A rush of breath comes out on the other end. "No, baby. They're not coming for you."

"I was scared."

"Don't be scared. I was giving Gabe information about his daughter. But I want to see you. I'm coming to Arizona."

A flutter of butterflies takes flight in my belly. "Are you bringing Ren or Calder?" The hope in my voice is evident. Then, my voice drops. "You're not bringing Mom are you?"

He sighs, clearly frustrated. "Your mother still doesn't know I've made contact with you. Neither does Calder. I'll bring Ren again, though."

I smile at knowing my dad is keeping our contact a secret from her. She would only try to ruin it all by making Gabe go to prison. Mom would destroy me by attempting to destroy him.

"I love you, Daddy."

"I love you too," he assures me, adoration flooding his voice. "I'll see you tomorrow."

When I hang up, I turn to see Gabe leaned against the counter. His palms scrub his face in frustration.

"What's wrong?"

His dark gaze lifts to mine and his brows furrow. "Everything."

Bouncing over to him, I throw myself into his arms. "Tell me. Dad seemed fine on the phone. Was he lying?"

His body is tense and his heart is pounding in his chest. "It's not about us. It's about Brie."

Irritation courses through me. "What *about* her?" I attempt to keep the scathing tone down, but I know he senses the harshness in my voice.

"War's found a lead. And," he hisses against my hair, "it's fucked up. So fucked up, sweet girl."

Lifting my head, I search his warm brown eyes. With his brows pinched together in frustration, he seems every bit his age. Lines crinkle the corners of his eyes, and larger lines mar his forehead. Giving him an encouraging smile, I run my fingertips through his hair on the side of his head. Strands of grey streak at his temples.

He's a silver fox.

My sexy old man.

Delicious.

"Hannah."

Blinking away my daze, I frown. "What?"

"Did you take your medicine today?"

Rolling my eyes, I push away from him, but he grabs my elbows hard enough to bruise me. "Yes, *Daddy*," I smart off.

Annoyance flickers in his eyes, and I immediately hate that I choose all of the wrong moments to let my crazy shine through.

"I'm sorry. What's happening with Brie?" I smile sweetly at him and bat my eyelashes.

He hauls me to him for a bear hug. "Some rich fucking family is taking necessary steps to adopt her. This is wrong." The despair in his voice makes my chest ache. "She's fifteen.

Who the fuck wants to adopt a fifteen-year-old girl?"

"But you're her father. They can't just do that anyway."

"Johan Cruz-Diaz is listed as her father on her birth certificate. Johan Cruz-Diaz was wanted in connection with the murder of his wife. That is," he lets out a huff, "until they found his death certificate from before Brie was ever conceived. The State of California has no legal documentation of her *real* father."

A small current of excitement courses through me. "What does that mean?"

"It means the only way I can claim her is to submit to a paternity test. But as soon as I do that, since the police are heavily involved, they'll nail my ass and haul me off to prison. They found those fuck face's bodies who raped you. It won't be long before they tie that shit to me too. Thankfully, your parents have kept silent on how they know 'Johan' and have feigned innocence because they know the moment they say anything about what happened with Baylee and I all those years ago, this shit will go national. If it goes national, we're fucking screwed. They're trying to protect you, but that means protecting me too."

Just me and Gabe...

"I'm sorry," I tell him, my bottom lip trembling. But I'm not sorry. I'm happy. "What are you going to do?"

"I don't fucking know. War's getting me names and shit. He's coming to see you tomorrow. I don't think this is a setup or anything. His concern for Brie was surprising. I'm curious why he was so fucking concerned come to think of it."

While he broods and his mind races with worry over Brie, I silently thank the heavens for letting her find a family who wants her. She can be their daughter and have a normal life. Her teen years can be spent doing traditional things. If she came with us, she'd be locked away. He'd have to homeschool her.

He would spend all of his time doting over her.

Apologizing about her dead mother.

Choosing her over me.

And I would become angry.

I know how I am.

I would be jealous just as he always accuses me of being.

Then, I would hurt her too.

A single tear rolls down my cheek. Gabe's attention returns to me—where it should be—and he swipes away the wetness with his thumb.

"We'll get her back," he promises, as if that's the reason why I'm upset.

I nod and another tear rolls out. If we get her back, she'll be cooking under the Arizona sun in another homemade grave with that whore, Maria, who Gabe brought home. Brie, although I only saw her once, was pretty and looked sweet. She looked like a daddy's girl…like me.

She would have easily stolen him from me.

My body begins to shake as the gravity of reality sets in. If he finds her and brings her home, it will be the end of us. A choked sob escapes me. The man I love blurs in front of me. He shuffles and soon I'm scooped into his arms. I clutch desperately to him as he carries me into our bedroom.

"Shhh," he coos as he sets me to my feet. His deft fingers tear at my clothes until I'm naked and shivering. Once he's naked too, he slips an arm around me and guides us onto the bed. In the next breath, he's inside me. "You're perfect, sweet girl. So perfect."

I cry as he makes love to me. His full lips suckle on my neck and his teeth nip at the flesh. My fingers thread into his hair as I guide him to my mouth.

"Kiss me," I beg.

"Always."

And this is why it needs to be just us.

Gabe, my furious and raging storm, brings me calm. He pulls the real Hannah from the darkness to wrap his arms around her so she won't be lonely. Together, we fulfill a need nobody else ever can.

His fingers skim over my flesh, worshipping me with his touch as he thrusts into me. He rubs against me in such a way that has my body jolting with pleasure. It's him. It's not his touch or his expertise or his taste or his words.

It's.

Just.

Him.

"Oh, Gabe," I cry out, ripping at his hair as I climax.

He kisses me deeply as I feel him release inside of me. His heat warms me. I wish we could stay joined like this forever. No worries of Brie or my mom or anybody.

Just us.

When he pulls out of me and lies beside me, I let out a disappointed sigh at the loss of him. His seed trickles out of me, soaking the bed below. Watching me with a peaceful look, he circles his fingertip around my nipple.

He gives me the most breathtaking smile I've ever seen.

My heart thumps to life in my chest.

"Sweet girl…"

"Mmm?"

"I swear," he says and presses a kiss to my nose. "I'll get

her back. Then we'll be a family. I promise."

The blood in my veins turns to ice.

"A family." My voice is a whisper.

"*My* family." His voice is a growled proclamation.

I nod in agreement because he looks so happy. I even try to smile back. It doesn't reach my eyes, though. The moment he has her in his clutches, all of this will be destroyed. *She'll* be his favorite. I bet she doesn't have to take medications. I bet she behaves and follows rules. I bet she's never hurt a soul. The pretty teenage girl with the wide brown eyes will obliterate my whole world.

I'm going to have to ask my dad tomorrow for a favor.

A huge favor.

And he'll say yes because I'm *his* little girl.

XIX | Gabe

A S THE SUN RISES, I SIP MY COFFEE AND WATCH THE LONG driveway, my 9 mm tucked safely in the front of my jeans. War may not have anything planned, but I'd be a dumbass not to prepare anyway.

Nobody is taking her away from me.

Over my dead fucking body.

If I were a smart man, I'd pack my sweet girl up and drive her ass halfway across the country to a new location. Someplace safe. Someplace hidden. Texas, maybe.

But, apparently, I'm stupid.

I'm stupid because love makes you that way.

Crazy fucking stupid.

I let out a sigh as I think of my baby—the baby War is going to help me get back whether he wants to or not. A smile tugs at my lips as I lose myself to a memory of her.

Gabriella Alejandra Cruz-Diaz.

Not legally a Sharpe, but still mine.

So fucking perfect.

We've been home for over six weeks, and Alejandra is finally back at work. Her tight body bounced back only leaving a little more meat on her ass than usual. No complaints here. She let me fuck her long before she was cleared to have sex. But she said she was a doctor and she was fine. Again, no complaints.

"My Brie," I murmur, running my thumb along my baby girl's soft cheek. So fucking soft. "Such a good baby."

Her dark lashes blink open revealing her pretty brown eyes. Alejandra claims she looks just like me. I don't see it. To me, she looks like herself. A tiny, perfect baby. Mine. I hope one day she'll look like Alejandra though. The woman's a knockout. If Brie even looks half as good as Alejandra, I'll be cutting some throats, no doubt, by the time my daughter hits puberty. Boys wouldn't fucking dare touch my girl.

She starts to whimper so I stand with her swaddled in my arms and step out onto the back patio. After one colicky night where she screamed nonstop for fucking hours, I took her outside. I was so frustrated, and Alejandra was beat. I'd contemplated tossing her in the ocean. Not really, but I was over the screaming. Over it.

Thankfully, though, her screaming stopped the moment the warm, salty wind touched her skin. The crashing of the waves seemed to soothe my upset baby. And now, every time she cries, I take her outside. It calms her. Always.

"There we go," I murmur as I sit in the lounge chair on the patio. "You like this, Brie baby?"

Her chunky legs kick inside the blanket like she's trying to go somewhere. I chuckle and press a kiss to her forehead.

"Not yet, pretty girl. When you get older, I'll take you swimming."

I tear my gaze from my child and let my eyes wander down the beach toward the familiar house I'm always stalking.

My other daughter.

She's three now.

I know this because I saw the big hot pink balloon tied to the mailbox the other day. It was in the shape of a three.

It took some stalking on my part, but I also learned her name was Hannah. Such a pretty name for a pretty blonde little girl. Mine.

"You have a sister," I tell Brie. Her eyes are heavy but she fights to remain awake. "One day, you two will be friends. We'll do everything together. As a family."

Brie's mouth quirks up on one side with a smile. Alejandra says she isn't really smiling—that it's gas—but to me, she's fucking smiling. Who the fuck smiles when they have gas?

"I knew that you'd like that," I say with a laugh. "Don't worry. You'll always be my little baby."

Her tiny hand swats at me. When I hold my finger up, she clutches onto it. Those wide brown eyes find mine and they fucking twinkle. This little girl has a grip on my heart so tight, I fear one day she'll suffocate me with her love.

What a way to go…

My mind is brought back to the present, and I think about Alejandra. We mostly had good times. When she became pregnant with Brie, we grew closer. I miss her and hate that she's gone. But it was always going to be this way for us. The moment I had my Hannah in my clutches, Alejandra would be gone. I hadn't planned on killing her, but it's probably easier that she died. She'd have done everything in her power to keep the three of us together as a family.

But she didn't fit in the equation.

Hannah fits.

And Brie.

I try to imagine a world where they are friends. Would Hannah take my daughter under her wing and be kind to her? Would she fill the void Alejandra left?

Blinking away my stupid fantasy, I let out a low grumble.

Of course, she wouldn't be fucking kind.

I'd have to watch her every second of every day.

Brie could become a target.

Fuck.

With a hiss of frustration, I rake my fingers through my hair. I'll figure out a way to have them both. There has to be a way. Brie will have to toughen up. There's no changing Hannah.

But can my little girl be who she needs to be around my wild woman?

I think of Brie's innocent giggles when she gets tickled about a show she's watching.

I think of the way her wide brown eyes become watery when someone hurts her feelings.

I think about how she, even at fifteen, is a daddy's girl—always wanting to curl up on the couch with me to watch movies.

Hannah, her mother's killer, would smash her sweet world.

Hannah, the unstable wild woman, would smash her.

My chest aches as I ponder how to fix this. I love Hannah with all my heart. She's beautiful and sexy as fuck. I've never had a lover be able to keep up with my insatiable need and extreme fetishes. But hell, Hannah helps me pick out the fattest fucking vegetables at the store and provokes me to do the most depraved shit to her. She's perfect.

A click of the door behind me jerks me from my thoughts. Hannah saunters out wearing nothing but my white T-shirt. I can see her dark nipples through the material, and five bucks says she's not wearing panties. Dirty girl. Her hair is messy and tangled. Those bright blue eyes are tired and bloodshot. She chews thoughtfully on her fat bottom lip. I want to fucking chew on it too.

"Good morning, beautiful."

She flashes me a brilliant smile before climbing onto my lap to straddle me. Her palms run up my bare chest and I'm instantly hard beneath my jeans.

"Morning, handsome." She leans in and presses a sweet kiss to my lips. I watch her every movement as she slips the gun from my jeans, hesitates for a brief moment, and then sets it down on the table beside me. "You look sad today."

I palm her ass and am satisfied to know I was right. No panties. "Just thinking."

Her brows scrunch together. "About what? Are you tired of me yet?"

And this is why my head is a fucking mess. Brie has a chance. Brie's sweet and smart and compliant. Maybe this rich family could give her the love and guidance and safe environment she needs. My daughter could thrive like she always has.

Yet, out here in the Arizona desert?

Brie would be a captive.

She'd be trapped with two monsters: the one she loves but doesn't fully know and the one she doesn't know at all, who also killed her mother.

Gabriella would be miserable.

She may grow to resent me. Hate me even.

Unfuckingacceptable.

Hannah wins this war. Nobody but me understands her. Nobody but me can control her. Nobody but me can keep her safe from everyone in the godforsaken world...but especially from herself.

The choice has been made.

"I could never grow tired of you," I vow, earning a grin from her. "Just you and me, baby, until the end."

I've barely spoken the words before she's tearing at the button of my jeans. She tugs the zipper down to free my eager cock. Without any hesitation, she sinks her wet pussy down along my length, gasping in pleasure once she's completely seated on me.

I grab the hem of the T-shirt she's wearing and yank it over her head so she'll be bare for me. Her hips buck in a slow, teasing manner. Leaning forward, I suck her pink nipple into my mouth and bite down hard enough to make her whimper. She spears her fingers into my hair to latch on. When her hips rock against me harder, I suck and nibble at her tits until she's making obscene noises that I've never heard before.

"So fucking perfect," I praise as she bounces on my cock like I'm her favorite riding toy.

Her mouth parts open in pleasure, so I shove my finger into it, coating it with her saliva. She makes a sexy show of sucking on my finger like she does my cock and I nearly come right then. Jerking my finger back out, I then use my other palm to pull on her butt cheek. A small whimper, fear laced with excitement, escapes her as I tease the tight hole of her ass with the tip of my wet finger.

"I'm going to shove my finger up your ass," I say with a growl as I nip at her tit, "and you're going to love it."

She nods and leans closer to me, giving me what I want. I push my finger deep inside her and relish the way my cock squeezes with the extra pressure.

"You like that, sweet girl?"

"Mmm."

"Tell me."

"I like when you fill me up with…you. All you."

I fuck her ass slowly with my finger while she bounces in a quick rhythm on my dick. Her pussy keeps clenching and her ass as well, so I know my girl will be coming like a hurricane soon. Wild, uncaring, intense.

"You like it when I control and punish you. You're not a sweet girl at all, are you?"

She shakes her head, but then abruptly tilts her head back. "Oh God!"

Using my free hand, I pinch at her clit. She screeches and clenches down around me harder than before. So I do it again and again and again, each time more brutally. This not-so-sweet girl rakes her claws down the front of my chest, no doubt drawing blood, making me hiss in pain.

"Fucking bad girl," I chide as I bite on her breast. My thumb and finger twist her clit, just enough to have her raising off of me to escape the pain. But just when I think she's trying to get away, she drops back down on my cock and shudders so hard I think she'll collapse. Her pussy clamps down around my throbbing dick as she goes wild with her orgasm.

"Gabe," she moans, her body still quaking.

I yank my finger from her so I can grab onto her hips. She's tiny and fucking perfect and doesn't argue when I lift her up off my cock only to impale her ass in the very next movement. Once again, those wicked claws rip at my flesh as she cries out. Her body falls forward against me, shivering and trembling. When her teeth scrape against my neck, and she bites me like a rabid goddamned dog, I explode inside of her hot, tight ass. My dick pumps until the girl bleeds me fucking dry.

"You're going to kill me."

She giggles—a sound too pure for the act we just committed—and sits up to look at me. Her eyes are no longer bloodshot and tired. They twinkle with love and happiness. I make this girl happy. Me. She's the right decision. The only decision.

Brie will be okay.

Brie is strong and capable.

I'll make sure the fuckers who want her are good people.

And then I'll let my baby girl go, so she can be safe.

So I can take care of this girl.

The girl who I have loved, in some capacity or another, for her entire eighteen years of life.

"Come on," I say and slap Hannah's ass with both hands. "Let's get you cleaned up so your daddy doesn't see how dirty you really are."

Her lips quirk up on one side wickedly. "Only you know how truly dirty I am. Only you."

She climbs off of me and jiggles her sexy ass back into the house.

I look down at my softening cock and smile.

Hannah is the right decision.

"That's Dad's car," she breathes and bounces on her toes.

My eyes are drawn to the back of her tanned thighs. After we had showered, she made us a gigantic breakfast and ended up putting on a cute little yellow dress. She braided her blonde hair down her back making her look a thousand times more innocent than she really is. I'm aching to take her in that dress, but know I won't get the chance until they leave.

A cloud of red dust billows behind War's car as he travels up the road. Another five minutes and I'll have to share my girl with him. Storming over to her, I lift the back of her dress and palm her ass.

"Bend over. Right now," I order.

She laughs but bends to touch her toes. Hastily, I yank my cock out and stroke it while I push her panties to the side. A second later, I'm inside her. Fucking her in that innocent little dress.

"Touch your clit. You don't have much time to come, sweet girl."

With my grip on her hips, I pound into her ruthlessly. She moans and groans, but her finger feverishly rubs at her clit. As the car nears, I wonder if they can see what I'm doing to her. Just the thought of War or her little brother watching me fuck her has me coming deep inside her hot cunt.

"Are you close?" I demand, my dick still throbbing and leaking my seed into her.

"Yes!"

I yank at her braid and she screams in pleasure. I know she's climaxing the moment her pussy squeezes the fucking life out of my cock. She's mid-orgasm when I yank back out of her, letting her panties slide back into place. Her dress falls over her ass. Nobody would ever be able to tell.

As I tuck my dick back into my jeans and shove my gun into the front of them under my shirt, I watch as she straightens back up. She glances at me over her shoulder and grins at me. Her cheeks are rosy after having just come.

With satisfaction, I watch a trail of my cum race down the inside of her thigh toward her knee. If the goddamned car weren't pulling into park right as we speak, I'd clean her sexy legs up with my tongue.

"Dad!" she chirps and takes off running to the car.

Her dress bounces up, revealing her panties with each long stride she takes. My dick starts to harden again until War climbs out. All serious and Debbie Fucking Downer.

"Han," he chokes out in relief, wrapping his arms around her for a tight embrace.

The boy climbs out of the passenger seat and glares at me. Still a little prick, I see.

"What's up, kid?" I greet, just to fuck with him, and acknowledge him with a lift of my chin.

He waves a middle finger up toward the sky. Smartass. Dragging my gaze back over to my girl, I wait for them to approach.

"Well, come in," I say. "It's hot as hell out here. Might as well talk about this shit where there's air conditioning."

I usher them into the house, careful to take up the rear. I'm not turning my back on either one of those motherfuckers.

War's gaze darts all around as he inspects the space. Hannah's a messy girl, but I make her clean up her shit. Germ boy should be fine.

"Looks like you're being treated nice," he says tersely. His eyes cut over to mine. I expect disgust or hate, not fucking gratitude.

"Good girls get nice things," I say with a smirk.

His face reddens and his jaw clenches. The boy beside him fists his hands.

"You're an angry little shit, aren't you?" I ask Ren.

He laughs sardonically. It comes out as a cruel bark. "You don't even know."

Rolling my eyes, I slap Hannah on the ass. "Why don't you get them some of that lemonade you made this morning? Your brother certainly needs cooling off."

When she runs off to pour them a drink, I gesture for the couches. War and Ren take a seat, side by side, on the couch. I plop down in the middle of the love seat and arch a questioning brow at War.

"Tell me what you know about this family."

He lets out a rush of breath, releasing some of the hostility he brought in with him. "They look great on paper. Wealthy. Philanthropic. Always volunteering. It appears they have one child already. A girl about Gabriella's age. I'm wondering if they maybe couldn't have any more children? Maybe they wanted her to have a friend? The girl, despite their wealth, remains homeschooled. Again, it could be due to social issues or perhaps a health problem. Their finances are clean.

No criminal record. And they live about an hour north of San Diego. From all outside perspective, they seem legit."

My heart clenches at having her live with another family, but this family doesn't sound like the foster fucks I've heard about on the news who hurt children. They seem normal.

"Anything bad?"

"Not bad, per se," he says with hesitation.

I level a *don't-fuck-with-me* look his way. "Out with it."

He scrubs his face with his palm. "They hold a lot of social events at their house. Looks like parties for political people, a few celebrities, and even local authorities."

"Are these like ragers or some shit?"

Ren snorts, and I give him a glare.

"What?"

"Ragers? You really are old," he bites out.

Ignoring him, I frown at War. "Are these wild parties? Is Brie in danger being around them?"

He shakes his head. "Not from what I can tell. It just seems like the wrong people could slip in…" His eyes narrow at me and his brow crinkles with worry. It actually fucking moves me once I realize what he's so goddamned concerned about.

He's concerned for her.

My Gabriella.

"You mean, people like *me* could get in and see her?" A smile tugs at my lips.

He nods. "Yeah."

"Why do you seem to care about her, man? You fucking hate me."

War glances over his shoulder into the kitchen. Hannah is flitting around making the drinks, a serene smile on her pretty face. She enjoys this shit—being the center of attention.

"I do. But she's just"—he turns to look at me—"an innocent. I hope she gets the life she deserves."

I clench my teeth knowing Hannah stole what little normal and deserving life my Brie did have when she murdered Alejandra.

"I'm glad for your concern. If these people are good to her, then I'm cool with them. But I like that I can slip in and check on her whenever I want."

His eyes are blue steel as he fixes me with his hardened gaze. "Don't hurt them, Gabe. I gave you this information so you could see your daughter, not do something stupid like slaughter their entire family one day on a whim."

"It's not me you have to worry about," I assure him, flicking my gaze to Hannah, who waltzes into the living room carrying the tray of lemonade. She even cut lemon wedges to put on the rim of the glass. Suzy fucking homemaker.

Understanding washes over War, and his features fall. He knows what his daughter is capable of. He knows that, unlike me, she can't be reasoned with. Her moods and emotions dictate her actions. Warren McPherson knows the safest place for his daughter is with me. And only I can prevent her from hurting people like the ones who want to adopt my daughter.

"Here, Dad," Hannah says sweetly as she hands him a lemonade. "Made with bottled water and fresh lemons. I made sure to wash well beforehand too." She winks at him and then hands one to her brother. When she makes her way over to me, she boldly sits in my lap. We share her lemonade, much to the horror of War and Ren judging by their disgusted gazes.

"What's the name and the address?"

War lets out a sigh and pulls out an envelope from his pocket. Hannah snatches it and hands it to me.

"What now? We all best friends?" I taunt, pulling Hannah back against my chest.

Both the man and the boy glare at me, their gazes turning murderous when I let my palm slide up her bare thigh. I stop just before where her dress hits her upper thigh.

"Oooh, Ren," Hannah says with excitement, "we could go swimming."

My girl would prefer her world this way: the three men she seems to care about most under one roof doting over her. If that makes her fucking happy, and her family doesn't try any shit, I'll indulge her. Anything to see that beautiful smile on her face.

"Go swim, sweet girl. Your dad and I still have business to discuss."

XX | Hannah

"**W**HAT'S WRONG, REN?" I ASK, SHIELDING MY EYES from the sun.

He's sitting at the edge of the pool in nothing but his plaid shorts with his legs dangling in the water. I already tried to get him to swim with me, but he refused. His eyes never leave our dad, who now sits at the patio table with Gabe talking in hushed voices.

"He's not going to hurt Dad," I tell him firmly.

Ren drags his gaze to me and frowns. "You really fucked up, didn't you, Han?"

"I didn't fuck up."

"You killed that woman. Gabe's wife."

I stiffen at his words. Legally, they were never married. She was not his wife. But I will be one day. "It was an accident."

He scoffs and begins emptying his pockets. Ren looks bigger—broader. Like maybe he grew since I saw him last.

"It was on purpose, and you know it," he snaps, calling

me out like usual. "Own what you've done."

He slips into the water and dunks under the surface. When he reemerges, he gives a shake of his head to knock off the water and then runs his fingers through his unruly hair, slicking it back. His dark eyelashes are thicker looking now that they're wet.

"Own it," he hisses, splashing me with the water.

"She was going to try and break us apart," I tell him with a huff. "He's the only person who gets me."

Ren's jaw clenches and he regards me with a dejected look. "I got you, Han. I always got you."

My bottom lip wobbles. He and Dad were the only ones who I truly could connect with.

"I'm sorry," I whisper, hot tears welling in my eyes.

He lets out a sigh and opens his arms to me. I throw my arms around my brother's neck to hug him tight. We're not ones to be openly affectionate, but I've missed him and apparently he's missed me.

"Come home with us," he begs against my ear, in a voice low enough for only me to hear.

"I can't."

"Please."

Sniffling, I look over at Gabe who's watching me like a hawk. The aviators in front of his eyes can't hide his scowl. It thrills me to know he's jealous of my little brother.

I've seen Ren's cock before.

Many times as he's fisted himself to orgasm through the crack of his door late at night.

Ren, while well endowed, has nothing on Gabe.

Hell, the cucumbers have nothing on Gabe.

With a smile, I turn back to regard Ren, who's still holding onto me like I might vanish from his life forever. I can feel Gabe's possessive gaze on me which has me wanting to taunt him.

"Do you have a girlfriend?" I question.

Ren's hard gaze softens and his lips quirk up on one side. "No, but I like this girl."

Curling up my lip in disgust, I scoff. "Who is she? Is she prettier than me?"

Ren rolls his eyes and tries to push me away, but I lock on tighter. "You're such a fucking weirdo, Hannah. You're my sister, you perv. I'm guessing you're pretty by the way that motherfucker stares at you, like he wants to eat you, but to me you're just my sister."

"But this girl?"

He sighs but smiles. "She's just cute. I want to get to know her."

"Is she nice?"

"Seems that way."

I glance over my shoulder and Gabe has repositioned himself to where he's leaning forward with his elbows on his knees. His hands are fisted and his lips are pressed firmly together as Dad talks. Ren was right, Gabe does look like he wants to eat me. And he eats so well...

"Earth to Han."

Blinking away thoughts of Gabe's scruff scratching the inside of my thighs as he tongues my clit, I shiver and look back at Ren.

"As long as she's good to you, I'm happy," I relent with a huff.

Ren is all smiles at that. I know that wicked smile. Before I have a chance to jerk away, he clutches onto me and drags me under the surface with him. I squeal and squirm under the surface. Bubbles of laughter leave my brother as he terrorizes me like usual.

Finally, I kick him in the balls, leaving him sputtering and surging to the surface. I swim away from him and when I resurface, I yell at him. "Brat!"

The next hour becomes a war between my brother and I. Who can kill who first. Who will beg for mercy by the end. Eventually, Dad stands and whistles for us.

"You two kids get out. Your mother still doesn't know about this…" He sighs, shooting Gabe a frustrated glance. "Situation. Ren and I need to head back, so I can call her. She's not answering my texts."

Ren dunks me one more time before he swims over to the side. I watch my brother's back muscles flex as he climbs out. His shorts mold to his ass. The girl he likes will be lucky to get a boy like Ren. He's a catch. She better be good to him… or else.

Gabe's eyes are on my body as I get out of the pool. I wore his favorite bathing suit on me—a skimpy black thing that my mother would hate—and he's been licking his lips in appreciation ever since.

He wraps a towel around my shoulders and pulls me to him. "You know how difficult it is to listen to him talk when I've got an hour long hard-on for his daughter? Fucking impossible," he whispers against the shell of my ear.

I shiver and let out a giggle as I rub my ass against his impressive need behind me. "Thank you," I say, my voice growing serious. "Thank you for putting everything else from the past behind you to let me see them."

He kisses my neck before pulling away, flashing me a

wide smile. "Anything for you, sweet girl."

I can hear the crunch of gravel out front and I wonder who could be visiting. Gabe tenses, unease in his gaze.

"You brought the cops here?" he snaps at my father.

Dad growls. "Hell no. I wouldn't jeopardize seeing my daughter."

"Stay here," Gabe orders and stalks off into the house.

I take my opportunity and pounce. "Dad," I hiss, "you can't let him take her. Do whatever you have to do but don't let him take Brie."

Dad frowns and glances over at Ren. "Why? Are you afraid for her safety? Will he hurt her?"

No, I will.

"This is just no life for her. She belongs with those people. I'm afraid Gabe will take her and then she'll be unhappy. Plus," I say lowly, "I don't want her here."

Dad's jaw clenches. "Hannah…"

"We won't let him take her. That's a promise," Ren barks. "You're right. She belongs to those people. I'll make sure he doesn't do anything stupid."

I beam at my brother. "Thank you."

Dad's gaze is worried as he skims it over me. "If things get weird or you become unhappy, call me. I will come for you."

Leaning forward, I kiss Dad on the forehead. "This is the happiest I've ever been. Tell me you see that."

He sighs and Ren grumbles, but they both nod in agreement.

"Like you said," I remind Dad, "I don't belong in prison or some institution. I belong with him. He can protect me and keep me safe."

Dad goes to say something when we hear a screech.

A familiar screech.

"WAR!"

Mom.

XXI | Gabe

BAYLEE.

My angel.

Bright blue eyes. Pretty blonde hair.

Exactly the fucking same as the day she stabbed me in the fucking chest and left me to die.

And furious.

I've never seen her so mad in my entire life.

"You psycho motherfucker! What have you done to my family?!" she screeches. Her body trembles as she looks past me into the house. "Where is she? What have you done to my daughter?"

I grin at her. "Hey there, sweetheart. Miss me?" When I take a step forward, she pulls a gun from her purse and points it at me.

"Don't move!"

I do as the woman—and God is she all woman with her soft curves and long legs—says and stay still. Footsteps thunder from behind me. She lowers the gun slightly just as War shoves past me.

"Babe, put the gun down," he urges, his tone calm and comforting.

Baylee doesn't drop the gun, though. Her face crumples as she starts to cry upon seeing Hannah and Ren walk past me out of the house. "You let my babies into the same house as him? You came to see him and didn't tell me?"

Smirking, I shoot War a look that says *Pussywhipped fucker is in trouble.*

He groans and slips the gun from her grip. "She didn't want you to come. She thought you would institutionalize her. The only reason Ren and I are here is because he let us see her in exchange for her medications. And I'm helping him find his daught—"

"DOES IT LOOK LIKE I GIVE A FUCK ABOUT HIM?" Baylee's entire chest heaves as she sobs so hard she nearly fucking chokes.

Hannah glares at her mother with more hate than a daughter should ever have. "You should leave, *Mother*. You aren't welcome, *Mother*." My sweet girl storms over to me and throws herself into my arms. She makes a great show of kissing me on the mouth.

"Oh my God," Baylee hisses. "I'm going to throw up."

And she does. The poor woman wretches and wretches. Despite being the doting husband, War takes a few steps away. His throat works up and down as he gags. The boy—maybe he does have balls—pulls Baylee's hair back while she vomits and he attempts to soothe her.

"I'm going to call the police. You're going to prison, you sick fuck!" Baylee threatens. "You'll never see my daughter again. You'll pay for touching her!"

"I LOVE HIM!"

Baylee's bloodshot eyes find Hannah, and her bottom lip trembles. "No, you don't. Believe me, baby girl. He's gotten into your head, but you don't love him." Baylee reaches into her purse and pulls out her cell phone. "Get your sister, Ren. We're going home. War, shoot him if he moves."

"Mom, please don't call them," Hannah begs. "I'm happy. You're ruining everything!"

Baylee snaps her gaze to mine as she speaks. "Detective Price," she says coldly into the phone, "I'm at his property, and he *does* have my missing daughter. Yes, the sick bastard I told you about." An angry pause and her nostrils flare. "No, I will not leave until you all arrive. I'm staying here until that man is in cuffs and doesn't have his dirty hands on my daughter!"

Hannah sobs. "Why is she doing this?"

"Because she loves you. Because she doesn't understand us."

"I can't live without you," she cries and presses her mouth to mine for a sloppy, wet kiss. "Don't let her take me."

"Shh," I say, hugging her to me. "We'll figure something out."

She jerks from me and screams at Baylee. "I killed Alejandra! I cut her throat with a knife. And then I killed Maria while Gabe was tied up. I cut her throat, too!"

Baylee's flesh pales and she drops the phone into the dirt. "No…no, baby. No…"

Hannah's entire body shudders with rage. "I killed them, and it made me happy! I killed them because they tried to come between Gabe and I. I'll kill you too if you do the same!"

"Hannah!" Ren shouts.

War pulls Baylee to him a moment before she collapses.

His face is crumpled in devastation. His boy is seething mad.

The cops will be here soon.

And that detective is still on the line. The phone is still lit up in the dirt.

Pulling my gun from the front of my jeans, I aim it right at the back of Hannah's head. "Well, it's been real fucking exciting, but I'm over this shit. Hannah didn't kill anyone. You all hear that? Nobody. I, Gabriel Motherfucking Sharpe, killed Alejandra Cruz-Diaz, two rapist motherfuckers, some dumb bitch from a Tucson grocery store, and a shitload more."

Three sets of eyes are wide and worried as they stare at us. Hannah remains completely still. I grab on to the back of her swimsuit bottoms and pull her to me. Sliding the end of the barrel against her temple, I hiss at them. "Get in your goddamned cars and leave before I splatter her brains all over the stucco of this house."

Baylee shakes her head. "No. Not without my daughter."

"She's not yours anymore, sweetheart. I've staked my fucking claim on her. Now leave already, dammit!" I roar, shoving the gun hard enough into Hannah's temple to make her cry out in pain.

But I know better.

My girl is fearless and tough.

Her ass rubs against my cock like she'd love nothing more than for me to fuck her right here in front of her family.

"Gabe," War snaps, his body trembling with anger. "You promised not to hurt her."

"And you fucking promised not to bring your wife!"

"I didn't bring her," he growls. "She must have found out on her own. Just don't hurt my daughter." His head snaps over to his son. "Take your mother to the car. Drive far away from

231

here. I'll take care of this."

"But Dad—"

"DO IT!"

Baylee screams as her son drags her away. I'm fixated on how her ass jiggles as she fights him that I don't see War take a few steps forward. The gun he'd taken from her is now pointed at me.

"Just let her go, man. You're too far gone now. The police are on the way. I can still look out for Gabriella, even when you're in prison. But you have to let Hannah go. Please." He must have grown some balls in the last two decades because his hand doesn't shake or waiver. His steely blue eyes are fixated on me with the promise of death if I don't comply.

"Gabe, don't listen to him. He won't hurt you if I'm with you. Just get the keys and we'll go. Just the two of us," Hannah begs tearfully.

I inhale her wet chlorine-smelling hair and murmur against her ear. "No matter what, you know I love you. We'll be together forever in some shape or another. Souls as powerful as ours don't let prison or death or *any-fucking-thing* tear them apart. You hear me?"

She sobs and shakes her head. "No! Stop it!"

"Say it back, sweet girl. Tell me you love me back."

Baylee climbs out of the passenger side of the car and runs for War.

"Say it," I hiss and nip at Hannah's ear.

"I love you so much." She cries so hard she doubles over, as if I've caused her great pain.

Everything that happens next is a blur of commotion. Baylee rips the gun from War's grip, like the crazy protective mama bear she is, and raises it at me. With a grunt, I shove

Hannah as hard as I can away from me to protect her from the inevitable.

A second later.

Pop! Pop! Pop!

Turning on my heel, I charge back into the house and— *pop!* A motherfucking burst of pain hits me in the back, and I nearly stumble on my way to the back door. I can hear screaming and crying and fucking feet pounding behind me.

But as soon as I reach the back door, I fly through it and charge away from the house. Away from the woman hell-bent on killing me. Away from her family. Away from my Hannah.

Pop!

Another fiery blast of heat explodes on my ass cheek. She shot me in the fucking ass!

Pop!

I run like the damn devil and don't look back, despite the excruciating pain rippling through me. I run until I can't hear Baylee's screeches of hate. I run until I can't hear Hannah's sobs as her heart breaks. I run until the pain from my gunshot wound radiates through my chest and constricts my lungs.

A mile.

Maybe ten.

I don't know how far I run, but that's all I do until my vision grows black and cloudy.

It's daylight out but everything is black.

Black.

Blink.

Black.

Blink.

I suck in a breath, only to find I can't get it to enter my

lungs.

That bitch shot me, and I'm going to actually fucking die this time.

Unbelievable.

Despite being blind and suffocating, I keep charging forward until my legs cease to work. I tumble into some thick brush. Cactuses or bushes—I don't know fucking what—scratch and pierce me as I crash.

I try to stand again.

I try to breathe.

I can't.

Baylee finally fucking did it.

But it isn't Baylee's perfect face I see in the darkness.

No, it's my sweet girl, Hannah.

My perfect, psycho, unstable girl.

I love you, Persephone.

See you in hell.

XXII | Hannah

Six months later...

THE WALLPAPER IS DANCING AGAIN. FLOWERS THAT MOVE and talk. One flower named Fred tries to council me often.

You'll have to forgive her one day.

I snarl. *Never.*

But she's your mother, Fred argues.

My mother killed the man I love. She killed him and then committed me to a fucking institution.

Fred the flower laughs. *Your mom is a bitch it would seem.*

At his words, I laugh too.

I go to claw at my head to try and rip the confusing drugs from my head, but then I remember. I'm wearing these stupid little mitts since I kept trying to claw at my chest earlier. When your heart is dead, you don't want it in your chest anymore. They make sure I'm in a constant state of euphoria to

K WEBSTER

keep me from talking about him.

Obsessing.

Obsessing.

Obsessing.

And also, so I don't hurt myself.

Or anyone else.

Dr. Feelgood is coming, Fred warns.

I cackle as I remember not long after I first was institutionalized. I'd attempted to seduce the doctor. Surely an old, fat fuck like him would want some young pussy. I would do anything to get the hell out of here—even sleep with that loser. Gabe's soul would probably haunt him until the end of time, but he'd forgive me. He'd want me to do whatever it took to get out of here. But Dr. Feelgood rejected my advances. And he didn't like it when I tried to stab him in the throat with his pen either.

He's gay, I tell Fred.

We both laugh.

You should get some sleep, Fred says seriously. *The nurse said you'd require more sleep nowadays and—*

Fred's words are cut off as the heavy thud of the bolt lock to my room disengages. I try to focus my blurry gaze on the nurse. A man. It's never a man. But they say I'm strong. Perhaps they need someone strong to hold me down these days.

"Hey, baby," I slur, attempting to focus on the man wearing blue scrubs. "Let me loose and you can do whatever you want."

He stalks forward, and I writhe in my bed, unable to make my body function like I want it to because of the mind-altering drugs surging through my veins. "Shhh."

His palm finds my breast, and I jolt with shock. So warm.

236

So powerful. Possessive. Maybe I can seduce him. He definitely doesn't seem gay, unlike Dr. Feelgood.

I whimper when the nurse's hand slides up over my belly. He lets out a hiss of pleasure. Then, he slides back down my belly toward my pussy. His fingers lift my gown and push past my panties. Even through my confusing haze, I buck against his touch as he pushes inside me.

I haven't been touched like this since…

Tears well in my eyes, only further blurring the world around me.

"Come for me, sweet girl."

I'm hallucinating again.

Always the fucking same.

Always him.

Always Gabe.

"Yes," I moan.

"Shhh…"

His fingers expertly touch me until I'm exploding with pleasure. Fred the flower winks at me.

"Time to go home," the nurse says.

Home?

"Not with her. I'm not going anywhere with her," I seethe and rage. My mother is responsible for all this. My fate is all her fault. That I'll die in this wretched place. Alone. Sure, Dad comes to visit on occasion, but it upsets him too much. In his eyes, I'm gone. Unreachable. Lost. Vacant.

The nurse's finger—a finger that smells like me—shushes me against my lips. "Not with your mother. With me. Where you belong."

He pulls a shiny, big knife from the back of his scrubs and saws through my ID bracelet with ease. When he frees me of it, he slips a white doctor's jacket over my gown. I blink through my haze to read the tag.

Dr. Stephchinski.

Dr. Feelgood's *other* name.

I'm then scooped up like I'm a sack of potatoes.

"I can see they're feeding you well, sweet girl."

I squint and try to focus on his face.

Brown eyes.

Handsome smile.

"Gabe?"

"Shhh."

He carries me out the door, swiping his security access card through the reader. I don't even get to say goodbye to Fred. That flower was my only friend. I squint, looking for Dr. Feelgood or his other nurses, but nobody comes. The hallway floor is painted in a radiant shade of red. One of the crazy patients must have gotten into the art closet. Had a heyday spattering red paint all over the place.

So pretty.

Like blood.

Brilliant.

Door after door, he swipes his magical card and I become entranced by the musical sound it makes each time as we make it through the maze of the facility. It's heavenly and freeing.

"Are you an angel?" I ask.

His lips press a kiss to mine and soon a frigid gust of air chills my exposed skin. It's black outside and cold. "Your dark, avenging angel."

I smile.

Just like the angel who saved me once before...

"Am I dying?"

"You're not dying," he says with a chuckle as he loads me into his car.

The car door slams. Then, he climbs into the driver's seat beside me. A moment of clarity hits, and I focus on him.

Gabe.

Mine.

He's alive and he came for me.

His palm finds my belly and he strokes the very swollen flesh. "Sweet girl…"

"She's yours," I assure him.

It's certainly not Dr. Feelgood's or Fred the flower's.

"I know."

"How?"

"Because everything about you is mine. Even that clearly very big baby girl kicking inside you. Mine. Every single part of you belongs to me."

I sigh when he kisses me quickly on the lips before peeling out of the parking lot.

"I love you, Hades."

He stretches his arm out and strokes my cheek in a reverent way. "I love you too, Persephone."

"Are we going to hell?" I question, yawning big.

He laughs. "Not today, baby. Not today."

"Where then?"

"A place almost as hot…"

I reach for him and he takes my hand. "Where?"

"Texas."

"Texas…" I echo. "Should we name her Dallas? Is that where we're going?"

We sail along the dark highway, and he leans in to steal

a kiss.

"We're going to Corpus Christi."

"The beach," I say with a happy sigh. "Christi. Let's name her Christi."

I fight to keep my eyes open, but fatigue drags me under.

"Get some sleep, sweet girl."

Jolting upright, I shake my head in vehemence. "No! If I fall asleep, this will all be a dream. I don't want this to be a dream."

He squeezes my hand and gazes at me in the darkness. The red glow from the dash lights make him look like some sort of evil villain. A monster. *Beautiful.* Villains need love too, though. "This isn't a dream," he assures me. "Besides…" His lips quirk up into a wolfish grin. "Even a dream couldn't keep me away from you. Some nightmares simply won't die. Some nightmares will haunt you until your last breath."

Leaning back against the seat, I relax and run my fingers over my belly. "I trust you. Don't ever leave me. Please."

"I'll follow you anywhere," he says with a low, possessive growl. "Even into the darkness. Especially, into the darkness."

I'll follow you anywhere.

Even into the darkness.

Especially, into the darkness.

EPILOGUE
Gabriella

One year later...

I STARE INTO THE VANITY MIRROR IN MY ROOM.

My room.

What a joke.

Nothing belongs to me here...not even me.

I belong to *him*.

To be paraded around and groomed.

I'm to join two powerful families by marriage.

All in due time. It's what *he* tells me every chance *he* gets. Due time really means the moment I turn eighteen. In eighteen months, that is, I'll be wed to one of the Rojas brothers. Esteban, second in command to his father, who has a terrible scar running down his cheek. Duvan, the hot but scary college kid, who likes to taunt Esteban for fun. And finally, Oscar, the youngest brother who is still in high school, like me. He seems the better choice of them all and is sweet to me...

but it's not like I'll have a say in the matter.

He will choose for me.

He always chooses for me.

I look down at the black dress *he* bought for me to wear tonight. It had been hanging on my closet door when I awoke this morning. He'd purchased it and brought it to me. His decision. My *real* father always let me make my own choices. My real father loved me...

Until he didn't.

Until he chose that girl over me. The murderer.

Tears well in my eyes as I think about finding my mother that day. Tied to my parents' bed. Eyes wide and glazed over. Blood soaking her throat and the bed below.

She was stolen from me.

By that crazy bitch.

And then he was stolen from me too.

I was left for others to decide my fate.

And Heath Berkley was more than happy to take the rein over my life.

Heath is the man who makes all of my choices now.

A shudder ripples through me as I try to block out his scent, which always lingers in my room. I block out the way he touches me when his wife Izzie isn't looking. The quick hugs. The stolen kisses. The way his hand caresses my thigh when he's had too much to drink...

I swallow down the bile rising in my throat and stand quickly. Rushing over to the window, I pull it open to suck in some fresh air.

Vienna says *father* would get angry if he saw me open the window.

Vienna worries too much.

I feel sorry for my *sister*, Vee. She's my age. Pretty with bright red hair and a smattering of freckles on her cheeks. Her green eyes are the color of grass…

Heat floods me, and I shake away the feeling.

My *sister* was the reason *he* adopted me.

The Rojas brothers didn't want a redhead. Those Colombian boys weren't interested in a ginger. Their words, not mine. They wanted someone like them. My exotic Venezuelan features I inherited from my mother make them salivate every time they see me.

Like tonight.

They'll be drooling like a bunch of starved dogs.

Sometimes I wonder if I can run away from it all… Would *he* find me? Of course, *he* would. Heath is successful in everything he does. I know this because he tells me so.

The sound of bass thumping from a vehicle starting has me jolting out of my thoughts and practically hanging out the window. This is the real reason I open the window. The real reason Vee worries.

The boy comes twice a week like clockwork to mow.

It's the highlight of my crappy life—watching him pull his T-shirt off and toss it into his suped-up black truck. Watching the way his shoulder muscles flex when he weed-eats. The way his shorts hang low on his narrowed hips, showing a delicious V that leads straight down.

But mostly, the way his eyes always lift to find me staring down at him and twinkle to see me.

Always.

Each and every time, he flashes me a handsome grin that makes me weak in the knees and gives me a wink.

I live for that moment.

I'm boldly staring at his sculpted chest when he lets out a whistle. My eyes dart to his and my cheeks flame at having been so blatantly caught.

"What's your name, Princess?"

I laugh. "Princess?"

He puts his hands on his hips and gives me a crooked grin. "You look like a sad little princess locked away in a tower."

At this, my laughter dies. His words are spot on. "Gabriella. You can call me Brie."

"Pretty name for a pretty girl."

The heat from my cheeks spreads to my neck, revealing my embarrassment. "What's your name?" I question, avoiding his compliment.

Before he can answer, Heath's black SUV turns into the driveway. The boy pretends to fool with the mower until the garage door closes behind Heath. I know I only have a matter of minutes to get the window closed and wait dutifully for Heath to fetch me.

"The name's Ren," the boy calls out. His features harden and his chest flexes. A muscle in his neck ticks and a sheen of sweat forming on his throat glistens in the sun. It has me wondering if he tastes salty. I've always preferred savory over sweet. "One day I'm going to save you from that tower, Princess Brie."

Our eyes stay locked for a long moment until I hear footsteps thundering for me down the hallway. I wave quickly and slam the window down. I've just turned around and smoothed out my black dress when the door nearly flies off the hinges.

I force a pleasant smile on my face and greet the wicked

dragon in my story. With fluttering lashes, I sashay over to him and give him his expected kiss on the cheek.

When I pull away, his icy blue eyes skim over my dress and he frowns. "This isn't you, baby," he motions at me. "Too long. Put on the green fitted one you wore a few months ago. We want you to be pretty tonight. Business is business, sugar."

I hate the green dress. Low-cut. Short as can be. Molds to my every curve. The last time I wore it, I thought Esteban and Duval would shed blood in our living room over me in the dang thing. Those two dogs hate each other enough as it is without dangling a teenage steak with a nice rack wrapped up in a tiny green bow in front of them. They literally growled at each other.

Looks like tonight, I'll be teasing the dogs again…

"Sure," I tell him with a wobbly smile as I head for my closet.

His strong hand snags my bicep and he pulls me to him. I suck in a sharp breath, suppressing an all-body-consuming shudder, when his arms wrap around my middle and he hugs me to his large frame. "I missed you, Gabriella," he tells me, his nose nuzzling my hair. "I always miss you."

This time, though, instead of noticing how he inhales me or how his palms drift to my hips, his fingertips sprawled out over my lower stomach, or how he grows hard behind me, I think of *him*.

Ren.

The lawn boy.

My dragon-slaying prince.

Time's a tickin,' Ren. There are more dragons waiting to swoop in—three in fact. Eighteen more months and I'll belong to one of them.

But quite frankly, the one with the sharpest teeth behind me may not be able to wait that long. It takes everything in him not to devour me as it is. Time is of the essence.

I'll be the princess in the green dress surrounded by salivating dogs.

Tick tock.

The End.

Coming soon…*This Isn't You, Baby*

PLAYLIST

Listen on Spotify

Disturbia – Rihanna
Bloodstream – Stateless
Angry Johnny – Poe
Obsession – Golden State
Soothe My Soul – Depeche Mode
Violet – Hole
The Devil Within – Digital Daggers
Bad Intentions – Digital Daggers
Bad Romance – Lady Gaga
The Monster – Eminem
Monster – Meg Myers
Animals – Maroon 5
The More You Ignore Me, The Closer I Get – Morrissey
Creep – Radiohead
Baby Did a Bad, Bad Thing – Chris Isaak
You've Haunted Me All My Life – Death Cab for Cutie
I Will Possess Your Heart – Death Cab for Cutie
Six Underground – Sneaker Pimps
So Happy Together – Juice Music
Love the Way You Lie – Eminem
Stubborn Love – The Lumineers
Hey Ya! – OutKast
We're In This Together – Nine Inch Nails
To Be Alone – Hozier
Heart Heart Head – Meg Myers

ACKNOWLEDGEMENTS

Thank you to my husband, Matt. You are always give me a kiss of inspiration to start the day and a kiss of pride at the end. Each hour in between you make me feel loved and worthy and special. You'll always be my favorite.

A huge thanks to Sunny Borek for loving Gabe when nobody else really did. You saved his life in book one and for that he will always belong to you. Hear that? GABRIEL SHARPE BELONGS TO SUNNY BOREK FROM HERE UNTIL THE END OF TIME AND THEN INTO THE AFTERLIFE.

I want to thank the people who read this beta book early and gave me incredible support. Elizabeth Clinton, Ella Stewart, Amanda Soderlund, Amy Bosica, Shannon Martin, Brooklyn Miller, Robin Martin, Amy Simms, and Sunny Borek. (I hope I didn't forget anyone.) You guys always provide AMAZING feedback. You all give me helpful ideas to make my stories better and give me incredible encouragement. I appreciate all of your comments and suggestions.

A big thank you to my author friends who have given me your friendship and your support. You have no idea how much that means to me. Thanks to Jessica Hollyfield and Ella Fox for reading it early and giving me your encouragement.

Thank you to all of my blogger friends both big and small that go above and beyond to always share my stuff. You all rock! #AllBlogsMatter

I'm especially thankful for my Krazy for K reader group. You ladies are wonderful with your support and friendship. Each and every single one of you is amazingly supportive and caring. #Cucumbers4Life

I am totally thankful for my author group, the COPA gals, for being there when I need to take a load off and whine. Y'all rock!

Thank you, Nikki, for helping me run my author page!

Vanessa Bridges, you're a super star! Without you, I'd have crummy books for sure haha. And, Manda Lee, you rock for being there to make sure my story is awesome. Love you ladies! Also, a big thank you to Bex LovesBooks and Vanessa Renee Place for proofreading my story.

Thank you Stacey Blake for being amazing as usual. You make my books gorgeous and I always get giddy when you send them back to me. Love you!

A big thanks to my PR gal, Nicole Blanchard. You are fabulous at what you do and keep me on track!

Lastly but certainly not least of all, thank you to all of the wonderful readers out there that are willing to hear my story and enjoy my characters like I do. It means the world to me!

ABOUT THE AUTHOR

K Webster is the author of dozens of romance books in many different genres including contemporary romance, historical romance, paranormal romance, dark romance, romantic suspense, and erotic romance. When not spending time with her husband of nearly thirteen years and two adorable children, she's active on social media connecting with her readers.

Her other passions besides writing include reading and graphic design. K can always be found in front of her computer chasing her next idea and taking action. She looks forward to the day when she will see one of her titles on the big screen.

Join K Webster's newsletter to receive a couple of updates a month on new releases and exclusive content. To join, all you need to do is go here (http://authorkwebster.us10.list-manage.com/subscribfe?u=36473e274a1bf-9597b508ea72&id=96366bb08e).

Facebook: www.facebook.com/authorkwebster

Blog: authorkwebster.wordpress.com/

Twitter:twitter.com/KristiWebster

Email: kristi@authorkwebster.com

Goodreads: www.goodreads.com/user/show/10439773-k-webster

Instagram: instagram.com/kristiwebster

A special sneak peek at the prologue for:

PRETTY stolen DOLLS
by Ker dukey and K webster

PROLOGUE

Jade

Eighteen years old…

Daddy always told us to be careful. Not to talk to strangers, no matter how friendly they appeared. To question everyone. With two naïve little girls growing up in a wicked world, he wanted to educate us and explain the evil that ran rampant on the news channels. He forced us to watch the happenings of the world far from what seemed like our own, educating us on the beasts walking the earth with faces just like ours, just like his—even in middle America. We lived on a quiet street in a quiet neighborhood in a quiet town, but that didn't mean the monsters of the world weren't always lurking.

They're everywhere, he said, *not just in the shadows.*

He wanted us to perceive the world with narrowed eyes and closed hearts.

And so I did. I'm my daddy's girl, through and through—a

skeptic by nature. Suspicious. Standoffish. Untrusting. I heeded his instructions to the letter and kept my sister and I both safe.

Until I didn't.

Until the one day my world spun, turned on its axis, and everything was stolen from *us.*

Or should I say, until *we* were stolen from the world.

Four years ago, I let my guard down for one man. I allowed the curious girl within me to forget the most important message our dad taught us: *not all monsters hunt in the dark.* Dropping my constant guard for the attention of soft, golden brown eyes and a crooked smile, the walls I held strong, weakened, stealing my equilibrium and sending my hormones into chaos. At fourteen years old, I was weak in the knees for a man much older than me.

Benny.

At least, that's the name he told me. He lied about that...
he lied about everything

Benny's Pretty Dolls.

I relive that day over and over, fantasizing a different outcome, but I always end up here. My heart still stammers at the memory of first seeing him, I'll never forget that day.

* * *

My feet are sore. I should have worn my other sandals like Macy. She skips ahead through the narrow, crowded aisles of the flea market, stopping to gush over anything remotely shiny along the way. How she can be so energetic in this heat astounds me, but that's our Macy—full of life and openly sharing it with the world. Sweat trickles down over my lip and the burst of salt stirs over my tongue, reminding me how thirsty I am. My dress sticks to my damp flesh like an extra layer of skin. It's somehow hotter under the shelter of the tents versus the blazing, unforgiving sun. I swipe away the sweat on my upper lip with the back of my hand and send a nasty glare to one of the grown men with an overhanging tummy, flicking his hungry gaze over my younger sister while licking his fat lips and adjusting his slacks. Pig.

We need to leave.

I'm worried like Daddy taught me. My heart thunders in my chest with the need to drag my sister back home where Momma is expecting us for supper in the next half hour.

Of course, Macy won't be deterred easily.

Always curious, smiling, and eager to know the world.

The flea market is the highlight of her week and the only freedom outside the perimeters of our street Daddy allows us to have. Every Saturday she clutches the dollar she earned from helping with random chores around the house and pines over the items she can't afford before settling on a simple toy within her price range, which she will later break or lose and I will have to replace with something of my own to stop the tears she will shed.

As for me, I'm the saver.

Each and every dollar.

Just like Daddy taught me to.

One day, I want to go to one of those big cities we always see on the TV shows Momma watches and find those lurking monsters. I'm going to be a policewoman and protect more than just my sister.

I'm not impulsive or rash.

I can wait.

Unfortunately, my sister can't.

"Oh my goodness, Jade," she says with a squeal, sending a bright smile in my direction, which reflexes my own at her excitement. "Look how beautiful they are."

I bare my teeth at the man with the potbelly and salacious grin who happened to be walking in the same direction as us for the last ten minutes. He watches my sister as she bends over to pick up a doll from the table. When he notices my death glare, he has the sense to look ashamed and turns away.

"Twenty-eight dollars," she murmurs, a twinge of sadness in her voice.

Jerking my attention to my sister, I smile when I see the doll. It's a twelve-inch porcelain doll with silky chin-length hair and wide green eyes—an exact replica of Macy.

"Oh," I gush, "she's beautiful, but too expensive. Pick something else, Macy."

Macy frowns and nods before setting the doll back down on the table. We're just about to walk away when a voice halts us.

"Pretty doll for a pretty doll," a man states in a smooth tone.

Macy and I lift our gazes to the booth owner. The dolls are a thing of the past as we both drink in the handsome guy regarding us with a mischievous crooked grin.

A mop of overgrown brown curls hang down over his eyebrows into his amber-colored eyes. With just the smallest dusting of facial hair, I can tell he's older—maybe early twenties— but he carries an innocence about him that makes him appear younger.

"She can't afford the doll," I tell him, a slight quiver in my voice. He's cute like the guys from the teen magazines Momma sometimes lets us buy from the grocery store when funds aren't too tight.

His gaze darts between us and he grins. "Maybe we can strike a deal. I don't think I quite like it when girls as pretty as you two are sad. I prefer them…" he pauses, his top teeth piercing into his thick bottom lip as he gazes at me in thought. I hold my breath, almost hypnotized as I await his answer. "Smiling." He grins and motions toward me. "How much you got?"

I try not to focus on the fact that he has muscles, unlike Bo from next door. He's a senior in high school and still doesn't have muscles—not like this. This guy is better than Bo, better than those guys in the magazine. He is dreamy. My stomach clenches into knots.

Momma calls these knots hormones. Says I'll be a woman soon. Ack.

"I have a dollar," Macy tells him proudly, lifting her chin, gaining his attention back, and I mourn the loss of it. Her cheeks turn rosy and I suspect she's just as embarrassed to have this cute guy's attention. I want it back on me…

At this, he chuckles. It doesn't seem rude or like he's making fun of her, more like he's entertained by her words—like he thinks she's cute, too.

A pang of jealousy spikes through me. I quickly squash it down and remember I'm supposed to be looking after my sister. Protecting her from getting into trouble and leering men. The air begins to feel a little cooler and the crowd starts to thin, alerting me to how much time has passed.

"Come on, Macy," I hiss, snatching her elbow. "We need to get home. These dolls are too expensive. And you know Daddy doesn't want us talking to strangers."

"Benny." He smirks at me. One dark eyebrow disappears under his curls and a small dimple forms in one cheek. "I'm strange, but I'm not a stranger. My name's Benny."

My cheeks heat and I swallow. "We can't afford the doll."

He shrugs, his eyes moving like he's watching a ping pong match between my sister and I. "Suit yourself." His shoulders lift in an uncaring shrug and he rearranges the doll so she's back in place.

Macy swivels around to glare at me. My sister is sweet and carefree, not once have I seen the way her green eyes seem to glimmer with anger. "You have some money saved. Maybe I could borrow a few dollars. I've never had a dolly like this before." Her eyebrows crash together and her bottom lip protrudes.

Guilt trickles through me the way the sweat dribbles down my back: slow and torturous.

"I don't have twenty-eight dollars," I tell him, my voice hoarse.

His smile is warm and does nothing to cool my heated skin or nerves. Time is ticking and it's a long walk home. "I could sell the doll to you for twenty." He tilts his head, studying me. I squirm under his gaze.

Macy gives me a hopeful look. Her anger is gone and her eyes twinkle with delight.

"Fifteen. All I have is fifteen dollars," I say in defeat, my breath coming out in a huff.

Benny scratches at the scruff on his jaw as he contemplates the deal. There's a glimmer of victory on his up-tilted lips. "Fifteen it is."

Macy lets out a squeal and scoops the porcelain doll into her arms. She spins in a circle as she hugs it to her chest. Brat.

"Thank you! I swear I'll pay it back soon!" she gushes.

Swallowing, I break the bad news to them both. "The money is at home. I'm not sure I have enough time to get there and back before the flea market closes." Or if Daddy will allow me *to come back once I'm home.*

He frowns, his eyes dragging between us both. "I suppose I can wait."

Macy's hands tremble as she sets the doll back down on the table, clearly defeated.

"Or," he says with an easy grin, "you two could help me pack up here. I'll knock off another five bucks for your services and then I can run you by your house on my way out of here. I can even meet your folks. Who knows, maybe we can talk your dad into buying one for you too." His eyes flit over to mine and my flesh heats again.

"I don't play with dolls anymore," I tell him in a clipped tone. For some reason, I want him to think of me as a girl closer to his age rather than one who plays with dolls like my sister.

Disappointment mars his features and his brows knit together as if I've personally wounded him. I instantly feel horrible and fear he will take back his deal, leaving Macy angry and upset.

"I mean, uh…Daddy doesn't want us taking rides from anyone."

His eyes widen with understanding. "I'm not anyone. I'm Benny."

"Little girl wants a doll?" a deep voice sings behind me. A chill, despite the August heat, creeps up my spine. The scent of alcohol and chewing tobacco suffocates me. "Maybe I should buy one for them both. But what would I get in return?" The man from before has returned, and this time, there's no shame on his face or in his suggestion.

Benny snaps his attention to the man behind me and glares. I'm momentarily stunned by his sudden fierceness and step closer to Macy. "Back the hell away, prick, before I call the police on your pedophile ass."

"Yeah, fuck off, faggot," the man grunts before stomping off.

Moments earlier, I worried Benny was a threat. Now, I realize he's simply a nice guy, wanting a girl to have her doll and warning off predators. Daddy would want to meet the man who scared away a monster.

"Actually," I tell him, my voice brave, "we'll help you. Maybe Daddy will buy me that one." I point to a boy porcelain doll with honey-colored eyes like Benny and messy brown hair.

Benny grins. "You've got yourself a deal, little doll."

* * *

"Last box," Benny says with a grunt as he heaves it into the back of his tan aging van. This must be where all those muscles tensing in his arms came from. These boxes are heavy. Macy and I couldn't even lift one together, but we were good help packing them up.

"Now we can meet your pops and I can try to talk him into two dolls. Does your momma like dolls?"

Macy giggles as he closes the back doors of the van. "She plays Barbies with me sometimes."

Benny flashes her a smile before opening the side door. It rattles on its hinges. "I like your momma already." His hand motions inside the vehicle.

"I can sit up front," I tell him.

A flicker of emotion passes over his features before he hardens his gaze. "Actually, the hinges on the passenger side door are rusted shut. Damn door might fall off if we open it. You said you live close by. I'll crank up the AC. You'll be fine in the back and we wouldn't want this little doll to be back here on her *own." He ruffles Macy's hair and she beams up at him.*

I glance nervously at my sister, but she's already climbing into the back of the van.

"I don't know. Maybe we should just call our parents from the pay phone. I really don't think Daddy would like us riding with you."

When he starts laughing at me, I turn beet red. "Y-You think I would do something? Like that man earlier? What are you? Eleven?" At this, he snorts. "I'm not into little kids. Trust me."

Anger wells inside me. "I'm fourteen, and I'm not a little kid!" I exclaim, folding my arms in defiance.

He tampers down his laughter, but holds his palms up in defense. "Okay, okay. I get it. You're not a little kid. Little kid or not, I'm not interested in you, short stuff. I typically go for girls with boobs."

Now I'm just annoyed and humiliated. I've been ogling him this entire time and he just sees me as a child. Not that I wanted anything else, but it still pains me a little. With a huff, I climb in to the backseat and cross my arms over my flat chest. "Just take us home."

By the time he climbs in and gets out onto the main road, his humor is gone. He messes with an ice chest in the front seat beside him and retrieves a bottle of water.

"Thirsty?"

God yes.

Macy snatches it out of his hand and greedily gulps down over half the bottle before I steal it from her. The cold moisture seeping down the bottle feels incredible in my hot palm. I polish the rest off within seconds and rub the cold plastic over my neck to steal the remaining frost from the bottle.

"Aren't you going to ask us where we live?" I question after several minutes of driving. He hasn't spoken much at all and that easy smile that once graced his lips is now stoic. His eyes keep tracking me in the overhead mirror. It's hot and stuffy in the back of the van, despite his promise of AC, and I feel light-headed. My eyes swimming and mind woozy, I reach toward the door handle for stability and grab air...where's the handle? When I glance over at Macy, her head lolls to the side and she curls into the upholstery to get comfortable.

"You already told me," he says, his voice distant.

My eyelids feel heavy and I struggle to keep them open. This heat is really starting to affect me. "I didn't tell you..." Every muscle in my body seems to weaken. My heart thunders in my chest, but I feel powerless to do anything about it. "Take us home," I demand with a slur.

His tone is dark. Not friendly like the Benny who sweet-talked me into forgetting all our Daddy's lessons. "You will be home."

The world spins around me and a wave of nausea passes over me. "What's wrong with me?" My voice is a mere whisper.

"Nothing. You're perfect. You're both perfect. Exactly what I was looking for. Two precious little dolls."

I barely have the strength to lift the water bottle up. It's then I notice the chalky residue in the bottom of the plastic.

He drugged us. He's a monster—the monster lurking in plain view, just like Daddy warned.

"Help." The soft murmur of my plea can't be heard over Benny's humming. I soon recognize it when he starts singing a nursery rhyme Momma used to sing to us when we were ill.

Miss Polly had a dolly who was sick, sick, sick.
So she phoned for the doctor to be quick, quick, quick.

The doctor came with his bag and his hat,
And he knocked at the door with a rat-a-tat-tat.
He looked at the dolly and he shook his head,
And he said, "Miss Polly, put her straight to bed!"
He wrote on a paper for a pill, pill, pill,
"I'll be back in the morning, yes I will, will, will."

"Stop," I choke out, but he ignores that I've said anything at all. After he finishes the final verse, he does stop singing, though, and turns on his stereo. Heavy rock music works its way into my head as everything goes blissfully black.

Help.

* * *

A soft moan from the cell beside me jerks me back to the present. Bloody dents in my skin from my grip sting as I release the hold I have on my arms. For four years, we've been imprisoned by Benny. *His Dolls.* Except I now know his name isn't Benny—or at least, that's not what we're allowed to call him.

Benjamin.

He makes us call him Benjamin.

Benny with the golden brown eyes and easy smile never climbed into the van that day. *There never was a Benny.*

Instead, we willingly got into the vehicle with a monster. A monster who has spent four agonizing years making us his personal dolls, which he likes to play with often—and he's not gentle with his toys.

I'm long past tears; they went with my innocence.

Occasionally, Macy cries when he's being especially brutal, or when he leaves her cell and she pleads with him she can be better. She knows if she doesn't try to be the best dolly she can be, she won't be fed for a day or two.

I'd rather starve than be his good dolly.

Because of this monster and his warped mind, I'm desensitized. Instead of begging and pleading for him to let us go—which always falls on deaf ears and gains us the manic pacing Benjamin, who sings his nursery rhyme and then sits there painting the faces on his dolls—I plot our escape. I plan his death. I make sure to go on breathing so my sister and I have a future.

The metal door slams shut on the cell beside me with a screech. Whatever he was doing with Macy, he's done now, and her whimpering notches another dent in my heart.

My turn.

I'm always forced to listen to him with her. It's his special way of torture. Forces me to hear her cries so by the time he comes for me, I'm rabid. He loves it when I fight and tear at his flesh any chance I get. The sicko gets off when I go on the offensive. He always takes dresses and makeup into her cell. I hear him decorating her into the perfect doll, but not me. He leaves me bare and untamed.

One of these days, he'll slip up and I'll be ready.

His muscled frame comes into view under the single halogen bulb in front of my cell. He's only wearing a pair of jeans that hang low on his hips. Sweat rolls down his solid chest and his hair is soaked from exertion. Smelling the coppery scent of my little sister's blood on this man is something that will forever be burned into my senses. Erasing that will never be possible unless it's with the scent of his own blood as he gurgles his last breath.

The man who crafts dolls outside our cells on a work station during the hours that could be night or day is a man beyond crazy. He's more monster than man—one more brutal and deranged than Daddy could have ever imagined lurking out there, waiting.

A full-on mentally deranged sicko, and when he wasn't out there working, waiting, taunting, Macy would constantly ask when he was coming back, *if* he was coming back. He always came back and I couldn't save her from it.

When he's in his sick rage, his normally honey-colored eyes darken to more of a milky chocolate. I've watched his every move, listened to his every word, studied his every mannerism.

I know him better than he knows himself.

I know his patterns.

His tells.

His weakness.

And one day, I'll pounce. I'll end this and save us—save *her*—like I was supposed to.

"There's my dirty little dolly. So wild and scared, but still so fucking pretty." His eyes narrow as his gaze travels down my body. It's a hundred degrees easily, but I can't help but defy him. I'm not naked and cowering. I've instead ripped the sheet from the mattress and tied it around my body like a dress. He will take the sheet with him when he leaves and when night falls and the walls to my cell cool, I'll be exposed and wishing for the sheet. But defying him is just too appealing—it's the only ounce of control I possess.

I'm about to smart off to him when I notice the sway. It's slight and almost unnoticeable, but I see it. He's drunk. He's *never drunk*. Drunk is good. Drunk means weak.

Fisting my hands at my sides, I wait. An opportunity like

this is too big not to act on. When he comes inside, I'll attack him. Surely I can overtake him. There's a swagger to his movements and all I need is for him to let down his guard once.

"Your master wants to play. What game are you going to play with me today, dirty little dolly?" he questions, a smile on his lips as he fumbles with the keys.

"We could play Eye Spy, but your dick is so small, no one can really spy it," I snap, goading him.

A low growl rumbles in his throat. "Or I could play with your insides when I gut you for being a bad little dolly."

I was used to his threats. They were always deadly and vicious, but he never followed through with actually killing me. I think he liked my insolence; it made his games more fun for him.

The click of the lock unengaging causes my sweaty skin to erupt with goose bumps. Soon, he'll be inside this cell taking what he wants—just like every night.

Not tonight.

The thought—so sudden and fierce—charges me with adrenaline. And when he drops the keys, the sound chinking around my cell like a starting pistol urging me to go, I make my move. Slinging the door hard to the right, I wrench it open with a rage-filled scream. He barely has a chance to register I've come out of my cell before I slam my fists into his chest and push him hard. His unstable body hits the floor with a *thud*.

"STOP!" he roars as he clambers to his feet.

But I don't stop.

I run for my life. I run for both our lives. If I can get the heck out of this hellhole, I can find us help. I can save my sister. I take the stairs, which shockingly lead down two at a time.

His home is a blur as I rush toward a door to the right of a kitchen. I was in an attic turned dolly-dungeon. As if my world weren't screwed up enough, of course it would be straight from a horror movie. I don't stop to inspect the kitchen along the way, to look for a phone, or even look over my shoulder to see if he's coming the moment I shove through the front door.

I.

Don't.

Stop.

Cold air hits me in the face, coating my entire body like a cloak. We're surrounded by woods. Trees, green and vibrant, whizz past my face as I run as fast as my legs will carry me. I ignore the bite of sticks and pinecones with each step I take. I ignore the scratching of branches as they whip and hiss at my body. Nothing matters but finding help. Behind me, I hear the crunching of leaves and grunting. He's hot on my tail, but not close enough.

He's weak.

Drunk.

An unworthy match.

With each long leap through the thick woods, I distance myself farther from him. Numbing the pain humming throughout my body, I run until my chest aches from my lungs burning for air. I'm dizzy, hungry, and not used to such bursts of exercise, but I don't stop or slow until I'm pretty sure I haven't heard him in ages. Death will take me before I allow him to take me again.

I got away.

I freaking got away. My mind screams at me in hysterics, but no sound leaves my lips.

And I'm going to get her back.

Willing myself to keep going, I take off again, faster this time.

A loud sob escapes me as realization courses through me. We're finally free. As soon as I find help, they'll take that psycho to prison and we'll go back home to Momma and Daddy. I'm still holding on to darkened, fading images of my parents in my mind when I bolt from the edge of the woods. A hundred yards ahead is a road. Headlights from about a half-mile away are heading right in my direction. Elation echoes through my bones as I stretch them wide to signal the car coming.

"HELP!" I screech and power forward.

The vehicle seems to be going slow enough, surely I can wave it down and be rescued.

"HELP!" My voice is hoarse, but my legs keep moving.

When the vehicle starts to slow, I start crying so hard, I'm blinded. It doesn't stop my journey, though. I run, waving my arms wildly, until my bloody, cut-up feet slap the warm pavement.

"HELP!"

The screeching of tires signifies the driver saw me. They'll stop for me and save me. They'll help me—

THUD.

Metal slams into me from the side with the force of a speeding train. Bones crack and pop in my body like a symphony of hollow drums. I don't know which way is up until my head slams painfully against the pavement with a crack that resonates inside my skull.

Then, I'm staring up.

Bright stars glitter in the sky as something warm pulsates from the side of my head, soaking the pavement beneath me. I haven't seen the sky in four years. It's bewitching, beautiful, and sparse.

I try to speak when an older woman with greying hair shouts for me to hold on.

But I can't hold on.

The stars dim, the sky darkening and filling the void around me.

Her features fade.

And darkness steals me this time.

Hang in there, Macy. I'm coming back for you.

63187831R00152

Made in the USA
Charleston, SC
30 October 2016